The Trail

By

Nathan Wright

Nathan Wright

This is a work of fiction. All of the characters, organizations, and events portrayed in this novel are either products of the author's imagination or are used factiously.

The Trail

The year was 1886, the month November, a cold November. This late in the year, and this far north, meant the town of Clear Creek Colorado was already experiencing snow. Today was just the light stuff, flurries with little accumulation but that wouldn't last. Storms would soon march through the town one after the other.

"You recognize that feller across the street, Amos?" a man standing by the front window asked.

The man named Amos was an underpaid, and underappreciated, small town deputy and at the moment he was trying to scrub out the coffee pot, something the pot badly needed. Amos said he cleaned the pot four times a year, once at the beginning of each season.

Amos put the pot down and walked to the front window. He peered in the same direction as the man who had asked the question. The frost on the outside of the glass made him strain to make out what it was he was supposed to be looking at.

Across the street stood a man dressed in unconventional garb. He seemed to be covered from head to toe in homemade hand-me-downs. He was acting about as strangely as he was dressed, a small step forward and then a pause. It seemed he was either lost or just couldn't figure out how to make his feet work. "You talking about that man over there on the boardwalk with the limp?" Amos asked.

"Yep, looks new in town wouldn't you say? Something about that man just doesn't seem right." Both men stood shoulder to shoulder at the window as they tried to make sense of what they saw.

Amos at first didn't answer the question that was asked of him as he continued to look across the street. After the longest time he finally said, "I don't believe I recognize him. Now that you mention it, he does seem to be a little out of the ordinary. Can't say as I've seen that much homespun on a man in years, he's even wearing moccasins. Last time I saw a man dressed that poorly was... well, I can't say for sure, but it's been years.

Amos continued to look, something about the stranger might have been familiar but he really couldn't say what it was. "You think we should go have a talk with him Sheriff? I think he's drunk by the way he walks, and at this time of day a man has no reason to be drunk. Hell, a man should never have a reason to be drunk but who am I to judge?" Amos had once been a drunk, many years back, but now he couldn't remember why he had ever let himself fall so far so fast. Now he was respectable, and proud of it.

The man that first noticed the stranger was Sheriff Parness Bevins. He liked to stand by the big front window each morning as he sipped his coffee, bad coffee, and look out over the town's main street. It gave him time to think, and time to reflect. Parness had been sheriff in the town of Clear Creek for the better part of five years and he was starting to feel this was what he would be doing for the next five years as well. He had fallen into a monotonous rut of being a small town sheriff and it was starting to bore him. A week from now he would relish a little boredom.

There was a sudden racket from the back of the jail as the sheriff and his deputy peered out the front window. It didn't take the two long to figure out who was making all the noise, there were only two men back there and one in particular was loud and obnoxious. His name was Stank Collins. Now on any other day, and in any other town, a name like Stank might get some notice, but not in Clear Creek. Stank had been a fixture for the better part of two months now and the town had grown accustomed to his ways, but not the smell.

"You better go back there and see what Stank is hollering about Amos," Bevins said. It wasn't even seven o'clock in the morning and the man was already causing a ruckus.

Amos headed back to see what all the hollering was about; he could probably guess what it was though, breakfast.

"Stop raising a racket Stank, and stop that cussing. We run a respectable jail here, you damned nuisance; the way you talk might give folks the wrong impression."

"Cussing is all you listen to, Amos, now where is my biscuits?"

"It ain't been daylight more than ten minutes, you know when breakfast gets here. As much time as you've spent in jail lately I ought to charge you room and board. We ain't running no charity."

"You know I ain't got no money, Amos. Why are you talking such talk anyway? If I had even a dime to my name then I would pull out of this one horse pig pen and head to warmer climes."

"We go through this every morning, Stank. I for one will be glad when your sentence is up. We won't have to listen to you, or smell you for that matter."

Stank shook his head in disbelief. "Did I hear you say something about the way I smell Amos?"

"You did, and I ain't the only one. The whole town thinks you stink. When's the last time you got acquainted with a cake of soap anyway. The way you look, and smell, I'd bet I could chase you all over town with nothing more than a bucket of water and a scrub brush."

Stank scratched his head as he tried to remember his last bath. "Oh now let me think, it'll come to me in a minute. Oh yeah, it was last spring. I do a good scrubbing every spring. Now top that, Deputy, I'll bet you don't scrub that often."

Amos just shook his head in disbelief as he headed back out front where the air was warmer and the smell was better. "Sheriff, when did the judge say Stank could leave?"

Bevins was still looking out the front window at the stranger across the street. "When the judge was here three weeks ago I asked him, he said drunk and disorderly was a two week sentence. In Stank's case I convinced him that a week was about all we could stand. He agreed. I told him the jail smelled like a hog lot so he told me to release him as I saw fit any time he was in here for that particular crime. I figured as soon as he gets his breakfast I'll let him go. You can give him the good news."

"Doubt if he'll consider it good news, Sheriff. I think he likes it here," Amos said.

"You're probably right. Hot meal twice a day and a roof over his head. For a man like Stank this place is a palace."

The Trail

Amos looked back across the street at the stranger, he wasn't walking anymore, he was lying on the boardwalk. "Sheriff, we better head over and check that man out, either he's passed out drunk or hurt."

Sheriff Bevins looked back toward the street and saw what Amos was referring to; the man was lying on the boardwalk and didn't appear to be moving. The two hoped it was the former, rather than the latter.

Bevins grabbed his coat off a wooden peg and headed out the front door, followed by Amos. As they got closer the scene became clearer, there appeared to be a few drops of blood on the boardwalk where the man had walked just before he fell. This was hurt, rather than drunk.

Bevins knelt beside the man and eased him onto his side, he was out cold. There was a bullet hole in the front of the man's coat, a coat that looked to be made of deerskin. It was a heavy coat and worn shiny from what looked to be years of use.

"He appears to be shot," Bevins said.

"Is he dead, Sheriff?"

"Not yet, he's still breathing. Better wake Ramey and get him over here. See if he has something we can carry this feller on to get him out of the cold and over to the doc's place."

Joe Ramey was the doctor for the town of Clear Creek. He worked on both man and beast. In a small town like Clear Creek anyone trying to practice the art of doctoring might find himself short on patients, and money, if he only looked after those that walked on two legs. Ramey always said he made more off horses and cattle than he did off anything else. Said folks would let their broken bones heal on their own but now you let a horse or cow get to feeling poorly and he was sent for and told not to dally. He even worked on a few dogs and cats from time to time. The doc really liked dogs, hated cats though. He claimed, for a fact, that it was a cat's intent to take over the world if they could only get themselves organized.

Amos took off at a trot as the sheriff stayed to make sure the wounded man didn't get worse; although if he did there was little Bevins could do, other than watch. As he waited for Amos to get back with the doctor he heard the sound of footsteps behind him coming down the boardwalk.

"Why hello Pedro, what are you doing out and about this early on such a cold morning?" the sheriff asked. All he got in reply was a puzzled look.

Pedro was the town's common law dog. He arrived in Clear Creek the previous spring and was promptly adopted by nearly everyone in town. Pedro had a schedule he stuck to each day. He knew which houses had breakfast first and which had supper last. He traveled to each house at a time when the morning scraps were placed outside just for him. Pedro had managed to put on a few pounds during his stay in Clear Creek. He was well liked and for this reason he was also well fed.

The big dog walked over and sniffed the wounded man lying on the boardwalk. After a quick sniff he looked up at the sheriff. Pedro had first suspected the man was drunk but the sniff didn't indicate the nasty smelling drink he first suspected was the problem. He then stepped away from the fallen man and sniffed the air. Bevins watched as the dog started off in the direction the man had come from. Wasn't more than a couple of minutes and the big dog was out of sight.

Ten minutes later Amos was back with the doctor. "What on earth happened here, Sheriff?" Ramey asked as he knelt beside the man.

"Don't know, Doc, appears he's been shot."

Ramey eased the man's coat open and then untied the rough looking hide he wore as a shirt. "He ain't been shot Sheriff, this looks to be the work of a knife," Ramey said as he looked at the man's hands. "Looks like he might have seen it coming, his left hand is stabbed clean through. Let's pick him up by his feet and shoulders and get him to my place." Ramey didn't have anything that might resemble a stretcher, although it was something he knew he needed.

By the time Amos and Bevins got the man to the house where Ramey lived, and worked, both men were winded. The cold air made each man's lungs hurt, not to mention the rawness to their throats.

"Put him on the table in the back," Ramey said as the two entered the front door.

By the time Amos and Bevins had the man where the doc wanted him both felt as if they had put in a good day's work, the injured man was heavy. Not heavy from body weight but from all the clothes he wore.

Ramey went to work cutting the man's ratty buckskin shirt off to see what he was up against. The coat had already been removed as soon as the man had been carried through the front door.

"Take that nasty shirt, along with the coat, out of here," Ramey said as he looked over the man that lay on his table. A quick check revealed the man had nothing in his pockets, not even a match. In this kind of weather a box of matches was something you always kept in a pocket.

"Amos, stay here and help the doc. I'm going back to where this man fell and see how far the blood trail leads me," Bevins said.

Bevins walked back to the sheriff's office and stepped inside to warm his hands by the big potbellied stove. A taste of coffee might warm his hide a little too, so he filled a cup and walked back to the window. As he stood there looking at the spot where the man had fallen he heard another ruckus from the back, it was Stank again.

"Is that you, Amos, I still ain't got no breakfast."

Bevins walked to the back, as he did he pulled a big key from his coat pocket. As he unlocked the cell Stank occupied he said, "You're free to go." After that he put the key back in his coat pocket and walked out front.

Stank protested, "I ain't had no breakfast yet, Sheriff."

"Can't do nothing about that, Stank. You are not a prisoner of the jail so I can't be feeding you anymore. As I said, you're free to go," Bevins told Stank, more out of spite than anything else.

Stank looked out the window onto the street as a stiff breeze blew flakes of snow along the boardwalk. He now wished he had kept his mouth shut. "I reckon I can hang around for a while, Sheriff. When them biscuits get here I would still like to eat, if that's alright with you?"

Bevins knew he would let the man eat, he wasn't without feelings. "I reckon you can stay and eat, Stank, if you answer me one thing. Where do you go when you leave here?" The sheriff wanted to know if the man had a home or at least a place where he wouldn't freeze to death.

"Got me a shack up in the hills. Found it a couple of months back before the weather turned bad. It looks like a place where maybe an old homesteader might have stayed but I ain't sure."

"I know that shack, Stank. If I ain't mistaken it collapsed a few years ago."

The Trail

"Yep, Sheriff, that's the one. For a man like me it's a mansion. The roof leaks a little and the wind is hardly slowed by the walls but I call it home. You're right, Sheriff, about the roof caving in but it was only one side. I managed to prop it up a little and just between me and you I think I did a fair to middling job of it," Stank told the man as he looked out the front window.

Bevins knew he needed to be investigating the circumstances of the injured man over at the doc's but first he had to make sure Stank wasn't going to freeze to death. "What are you going to do about heating that place in a time like this? I doubt anyone can survive in this kind of weather without a means of heat."

"You know, Sheriff, I've been giving that some thought. I got me a couple pieces of stove pipe spotted just outside of town. Someone tossed a wagon load of scrap out there and wouldn't you know it, right on top is some stove pipe. Now all I need is a stove and I'm set."

Bevins knew there wasn't a stove lying around because something like that just wasn't anything someone tossed out unless it was beyond repair. "Well it sounds like you've been giving the stove problem some thought Stank. What are you going to do about food?"

"Well Sheriff, I ain't got that far yet. All my attention has been concentrated on a stove. I reckon after I get some heat I'll start working on the food problem. Say, what got you and Amos heading out of here so fast a little while ago?"

"Got an injured man over at Ramey's, he come walking down the boardwalk over there a little while ago and collapsed on the other side of the street. I'm heading over to have a closer look right now," the sheriff said as he pulled up the collar of his coat and grabbed the door knob.

Stank looked out the window, it didn't look like any biscuits were on the way so he figured to follow the sheriff. "Hang on there, Bevins; I think I'll tag along."

The sheriff walked to where the injured man had fallen not more than thirty minutes earlier. The slight blood trail was more evident now that there wasn't a body lying around to soak up all the attention. There was a small amount of blood where the man had fallen and from there it led back up the street toward the far end of town. It was the same direction that Pedro had headed after stopping by to check out the man lying on the boardwalk. Bevins wondered if the dog might have some bloodhound in him.

"Is this blood from that feller you said you took to the doc's earlier, Sheriff?"

Bevins didn't answer as he looked at the red markings on the boardwalk. The trail was faint but still noticeable in broad daylight. As the sheriff worked his sight up the street toward the edge of town he wondered if he should go back and get a shotgun but decided he wouldn't need it unless he found himself farther from civilization than he felt comfortable with.

"Looks like this man was knifed, Sheriff, by the amount of blood and the way it dripped on the boardwalk," Stank said.

Bevins looked up at Stank. There was no way the man could have known that; the doc had only told him and Amos after they got the man's coat off.

"How would you know what kind of injury the man had?"

Stank was still looking at the slight blood trail. "Bullet wound will do one of two things, bleed out or stop. A knife wound won't act as such. The blade leaves such a clean cut that the wound won't stop bleedin unless it's bandaged. Was this man bandaged, Sheriff?"

Bevins stood and faced Stank, "No, he wasn't. How is it you know that?"

"I just know it, Sheriff. And something else, this man traveled a ways before he got to where he fell. Maybe a couple miles, might even have been three is my guess."

Bevins looked at the man and then back at the blood trail. If Stank knew what he was talking about then it might be wise to take along a shotgun. "Tell you what, Stank, let me grab a Greener and then we'll head on a ways. Maybe see if we can figure out what happened to that man."

"Might be a good idea, Sheriff. I don't fancy facing a knife this early in the morning. If I had me some breakfast then maybe, but as it is let's go prepared."

The sheriff was impressed with what he had just heard. Apparently Stank was a man that knew a little about something after all. If he knew how to use a bar of soap was anybody's guess, probably not.

After retrieving a shotgun, and ten shells, the sheriff and Stank headed out of town following the blood trail. The going was easy this close to town. About a mile out of town Stank stopped and looked the situation over.

"Looks like he fell over there, Sheriff, then dragged himself over here beside this cottonwood tree. He spent the night here, or at least four or five hours. Probably just resting is my guess. A man knifed and losing a little blood will get weaker and weaker. He probably had just enough spunk after staying here all night to make it into town where he passed out," Stank said. "The wound must have stopped seeping while he sat here but once he was up and moving around it began to bleed out again. Knife tracks in a man will do such things."

Bevins looked on up the trail as he thought about the injured man spending a cold night propped up against a tree. Seven wonders he didn't freeze to death. The heavy dear skin coat must have been what saved him. The shoes he wore were indeed some sort of high topped moccasins, heavy and lined with some sort of fur. Bevins remembered them as the doc took them off at the door and tossed them on the floor. If it hadn't have been for the heavy homespun clothes the man wore then he would have surely froze to death the night before.

"We better head on and see if we can find out where he was attacked," Bevins said.

Stank continued to look things over as he considered what the sheriff had just suggested. "Might be a bad idea Sheriff. You're the only one armed, if we run into whoever did this then that injured feller might have some company. Don't get me wrong, I want to see this through but not without a gun."

"You even know how to use a gun, Stank?"

The man rubbed his chin as he continued to look the situation over. "I know how to use a gun, Sheriff. In a younger life I was a peace officer, just like you, sworn to uphold the law."

Now this caught the sheriff off guard. "You used to be a lawman, Stank?" he asked.

"I did, been a few years but I was a lawman. Back east I was a server of warrants and in the process killed a few men, wounded a few more. Not proud of it but what I did was necessary," Stank said as he continued to look at the trail.

The Trail

Bevins considered what Stank said. He was impressed with what the man knew about a gun or knife wound; he would probably need to also consider his observations about this trail and what trouble might be waiting if they continued.

"Alright, Stank, me and you are gonna head back and see how that feller at the doc's is doing. After I arm you up we'll head back this way and see what we can find."

"Sounds good, Sheriff, I want to walk out a ways after I get me a shooter. We'll just see what this trail has to offer in the way of clues to what happened to that man."

Thirty minutes later both men walked back in the sheriff's office. Bevins unlocked the gun rack and took down a Sharps, he also grabbed a Peacemaker from his desk drawer and then reached both to Stank. "Here you go. I don't have an extra belt and holster handy so you'll just have to carry that Colt in your waistband."

Stank looked over the old Sharps, it had a busted stock that had been repaired, poorly repaired. Someone had wrapped wet buckskin around the wood and then sewn the ends together. When the hide dried it shrank doing an adequate job in repairing the stock.

Stank ratcheted a round into the breech as he checked the action, it worked as smooth as if it were new. He looked over the Colt, it was old but functional. "These have seen better days Sheriff but both seem to be well kept, at least the workings are anyway. We got time for a cup of coffee before we head back out?"

"We do, them biscuits might be showing up pretty soon too," Bevins said. It brought a smile to Stank's face.

"Sheriff, I got a favor to ask," Stank said.

"What's on your mind?"

"Well, it's about what you and the rest of the town have been calling me. I figure I've endured that name long enough."

Bevins put another lump of coal in the potbellied stove before he turned to face the man. He realized the name might have been a bit harsh, but it also seemed appropriate.

"Go on," was all the sheriff said.

"Well my name ain't really Collins and it surely ain't Stank."

"We thought your name was Collins because that's what you told everyone. The name Stank, well you know where that comes from," Bevins said.

"My name's Clarence Walker."

Bevins looked at the man in disbelief. "You can't be serious?"

"I am serious Sheriff. Ain't no way to prove it but that's who I am."

Bevins topped off his coffee and went to his desk. "Are you telling me you're really Marshal Clarence Walker from out Tennessee way?"

Stank, or now Walker, looked at the sheriff, "That would be me Sheriff, the one and only."

"Last I heard you were dead, killed in a gunfight in St. Louis. If I remember the story correctly you went up against three men who had done some terrible things in that town."

"That story has some truth to it, Sheriff, but there is some myth in it as well. I did go up against three men, all three are now dead but I ain't."

Just then the door pushed opened and a man came in carrying two paper sacks. Bevins knew what the sacks contained, biscuits.

"Just put them on my desk if you don't mind. Tell the cook there's only one prisoner for the time being," Bevins said. The man placed the food on the edge of the desk and headed back out the door without saying a word.

"Grab one of these pokes, Stank, I mean Walker, while I head this other one back to the prisoner. We'll head over toward Ramey's and check on the wounded man he's got after you finish your breakfast. Be nice to know the name of that feller, maybe he'll be awake when we get there and I can ask him." Bevins said this but realized there was just as much chance the man might be dead.

Walker grabbed a sack of food as he sat down by the fire. In it were two big cathead biscuits and two sausage patties. He tore both biscuits in half and crammed the sausage inside each. He had one finished and was starting on the second when the sheriff came back in.

"Walker, I might have another problem this morning to add to the one that collapsed out there on the street earlier," Bevins said.

Walker looked up from his biscuit, "What kind of other problem, Sheriff?"

"That other prisoner back there, the one that was your cellmate up until a couple of hours ago. He was acting real squirrelly just now when I took him his breakfast. If I didn't know any better I would say he knows something about that man that collapsed across the street a while ago."

Walker wadded up the paper sack and tossed it in the potbellied stove. "Did he ever give up his name Sheriff?"

"Never did, I arrested him on a drunk and disorderly two days ago; he wouldn't tell me his name when I brought him in. I figured he was just too drunk but the next morning, after he sobered up, he still wouldn't say what his name was. I told him I couldn't release him until I knew who he was so I could make sure he wasn't wanted anywhere else in the territory. Even after telling him that he still wouldn't talk."

Walker stood, "I was back there when you brought him in, he was knee walking drunk that night. He never mentioned his name to me, as a matter of fact he really wouldn't say much of nothing other than to check on how many times a day the jail provided food. Say, Sheriff, what did he have on him when you brought him in?"

Bevins swirled the coffee he had in his cup as he thought. "Usual stuff I guess, gun, knife, tobacco and such."

"Did he mention a horse and saddle?"

Bevins really didn't know, the deputy, Amos, had actually done the arresting and the sheriff had only walked along as the deputy brought the man in. "I can't say if the mention of a horse and saddle came up, Walker. I probably should have checked into that but didn't. As soon as you're finished with your breakfast I say we pay a visit to the doc's and then the livery."

Walker wiped his mouth on the back of a filthy sleeve, he wondered how smart Bevins and Amos were considering they had locked a man up and didn't bother to check on whether he had a horse or not.

"You and your deputy might have locked him up for drunk and disorderly but I got a feeling that man back there is way more than that, he's a killer, Sheriff, plain and simple," Walker said.

Bevins looked toward the back where the cells were located, "What makes you say that?"

"I don't really know, Sheriff, but I know. I've been around men like that, men I intended to kill by the power of a warrant signed by a judge. Dead or alive was the only way I liked to chase the outlaws. You might say it gave me the opportunity to put them out of their misery before they got a chance to put me out of mine. I've seen the look, he's a bad man times two if you ask me."

"Well, I can't argue with what you think he is or isn't. We best be heading over to the doc's and then the livery. I need answers to what's going on around here."

Both men headed out the front door, minutes later they were at Doc Ramey's house and glad of it, the wind and cold didn't seem to be letting up in the least. Bevins pushed the front door open and hurried inside out of the cold. The doctor was standing in the kitchen looking in a thick book. "How's he doing, Doc?" Bevins asked.

"I think he'll survive, Sheriff," Ramey said as he looked at the filthy Walker standing beside him.

"That's good news; did he happen to say what his name was?"

"Nope, hasn't said a word. Amos was here when he came to and tried to get him to talk but didn't have any luck."

"Say, Sheriff, you mind if I head over to the barber while you and Amos check on things at the livery?" Walker asked.

Bevins looked at the man; he was overgrown in hair and whiskers. "Why don't you do that, Walker. By the time you're finished me and the deputy should be back over at the jail. If you plan on getting a cut and shave how do you plan on paying?"

"I got means, Sheriff, my scruffy ways have done me good but I figure it's time to straighten up." Walker pulled up the collar of his worn out jacket as he headed back outside. Ramey and Bevins watched him go.

"That is the smelliest feller I believe I've had the bad luck to be around," Bevins said.

"No wonder they call him Stank, the name sure fits," Ramey said.

"Me and Amos are heading over to the livery unless you think he needs to stay here with your patient?"

Ramey looked at the sheriff suspiciously, "Should I be worried about that man back there?"

"I don't really know, he did show up in town with a knife wound. If he comes to, do you think you can handle him on your own, Doc?"

"The wound he's got will slow him down a bit, I should be alright," Ramey said. "He's lost some blood and it don't look like he's had much in the way of food in a spell. It'll take a few days for him to get his strength back. When he comes to again I suppose I can handle him if he thinks about getting rowdy. I doubt that notion will show up though, he'll probably just want to rest."

With that Bevins and Amos headed out the door. The livery was a good ten minute walk owing to the fact that livery barns were kept away from the main streets of any respectable town. You would think it really wouldn't matter, a horse did its business in a livery or on Main Street, horses didn't care about such things.

By the time the two men made it to the big barn both were nearly frozen to death. The weather had turned the previous day and neither man had thought to dress for the occasion. Most men tend to think a heavy coat isn't necessary unless it's zero outside and knee deep in snow. Most men can be real dumbasses when it comes to the temperature.

The Trail

Buster Adams ran the only livery in the town of Clear Creek. Buster was a young man in spirit although the years tallied up to sixty-four. He had operated his livery for thirty-five years and would probably run it till his dying day, which hopefully was still a number of years off. Buster Adams loved working with horses and also appreciated the fact that he could make a living doing what he loved.

The barn was a large affair having been expanded and improved over the years. Buster had grown cold natured as of late and for this reason he had installed a logwood stove near the front door. A partition kept most of the draft from the back of the barn away from where Buster spent the bulk of his time. He had a hand pump for water with pipes that ran underground to keep them from freezing solid during the cold winters. The water buckets for the livestock, and the coffee pot, were easily kept filled with fresh well water without the need to go out into the frigid weather.

Buster had just refilled the coffee pot and was putting it back on the stove when the walk door opened and two nearly frozen men walked in, it was Amos and Bevins.

"What can I do for you on such a fine day as this, Sheriff?" Buster asked as he tended his fire.

"Some hot coffee would be nice if you got any. I can't remember it being this cold this time of year. We don't usually have this kind of weather for at least another month."

Buster looked through the window, the wind was blowing and a dusting of snow could be seen swirling around on the street. "I just put a fresh pot on the stove; it'll be hot in a few minutes. You two look like you might need to find some heavier coats if you intend on tramping around town in this kind of weather."

"I was thinking the same thing, right up until my brain froze," Amos said.

"Say, Buster, you got a horse here that might have been left a couple of nights ago?" the sheriff asked.

"I do at that, Sheriff, had a feller stable one here a couple days back. He wouldn't give me a name and he wouldn't pay up front either. I told him when he came back he would either pay then or I would keep his horse, damn if he didn't agree. The man was half drunk by the way he acted and anyway, why would anyone agree to leave a horse at a livery if he didn't have the money to pay for its keep."

Amos suddenly yelped, he had eased backward to the stove trying to thaw himself out and by the time he realized what was happening his trousers were smoking. Both Bevins and Buster got a laugh out of the deputy's misfortune.

"Is there anything else you can tell us about him? I've had him locked up in jail for a day or two and would like to know something about the man before I let him loose," the sheriff said.

Buster thought for a minute before saying, "You might check his saddlebags Sheriff. When I stripped the gear off his horse I noticed them bags were a mite heavy."

"You didn't have a look inside, Buster?" Amos asked.

The livery man looked offended. "In all my years of working this livery I have yet to peek inside another man's saddlebags. If you want to have a look then go ahead. It's the dark brown pair against the wall over there by that busted up old saddle, the pair that looks like they are nearer the end of the trail than the beginning."

The Trail

The sheriff filled a tin cup with coffee and sat it on top of the stove so it wouldn't get cold. "I believe I'll do just that, Buster."

Bevins walked to where the leather bags lay and looked over the two. They looked to be old and nearly worn out. When he picked the pair up he was surprised at how heavy they were. "Damn if this rig wouldn't wear the hide off a horse."

"They would at that, Sheriff, but he had an extra horse blanket doubled up underneath. They were so heavy I couldn't lift them off; I had to slide the pair back over the horse's rump. Throw them on the table over there and let's have us a look inside, you might say I'm a bit curious myself," Buster said.

Buster had a table near the fire with two ladder-back chairs close by where he took his meals. The sheriff carried the saddlebags over and gently placed the pair on the table. After he had them where he wanted them he reached for his coffee. He pulled out one of the ladder-back chairs and took a seat.

After a sip of coffee he untied the first of the bags. The first thing he pulled out was a Remington double Derringer .41 caliber, otherwise known as a hideout gun. There was a box of ammunition to fit the little gun, .41 rim fire rounds were effective at close range but not the man-stopper some might think.

Next out of the bag was a pouch of chewing tobacco and a small piece of cake tobacco of the same variety, apparently this man liked a choice when it came to his chew. There was some rolling paper and matches and other trail junk. In the bottom of the bag were Twenty-five gold coins, each of the hundred dollar variety. This last find got the attention of all three men.

"That was the lighter of the two bags. This other one is nearly twice as heavy. What kind of fool would weight his saddlebags uneven like that? He was lucky the heavier one didn't drag both off the side of the horse," Bevins said as he opened the second bag.

Again the first thing out was a gun, a Mighty Colt Walker made in 1846. The gun might have been old but that could be deceiving, it was the heaviest, most powerful handgun, made at the time. There was half a box of ammunition to go along with the gun. There was a heavy burlap sack in the bottom of the second saddlebag and after pulling it out it was apparent this was the last of it. Bevins sat the sack on the table as he tossed the worn out saddlebags to the floor.

"Amos, how about you finishing up with that sack? I need to warm my hide by the fire for a spell before we head back over to the jail," the sheriff said as he refilled his tin cup with coffee.

Amos untied the seagrass string that held the burlap sack closed and peered inside, what he saw nearly made him lose his breakfast. He dropped the bag on the table and turned away. "I'll let one of you empty that bag," he said as he tried to calm his nerves.

Bevins looked at Buster as he stepped from the stove. Something in the sack had made the deputy turn pale as if someone had walked across his grave. The sheriff eased open the sack and peered inside, he now knew what had made Amos turn away.

In the sack there appeared to be teeth, human teeth. Bevins eased the sack onto its side and gently poured the contents onto the table. Besides teeth there was eight or ten pairs of spectacles and lots of jewelry in the form of rings and necklaces. There were six fine looking pocket watches, the type someone might carry if they were well-to-do, not the type a working man could afford. If the teeth weren't startling enough, the last of the contents to fall from the bag was. Badges, five in all, four deputy badges and one sheriff's badge. Amos and Bevins looked in disbelief.

Upon closer inspection it was found that each of the teeth contained gold, again something that any working man, or woman for that matter, couldn't afford. At least not anyone from around Clear Creek.

Buster looked at the pile lying on his table, "This looks like the work of witches, or demons, Sheriff."

"Amos, you feeling alright?" Bevins asked his deputy.

"I might still be a bit queasy, Sheriff. I've never seen teeth before unless they were smiling at me. Would you look at that, some still have blood on them."

It was true, all contained gold and some were even more gold than tooth. More than one was tinted with blood. It was truly a gruesome sight. All three men looked at the pile lying on the table in disbelief.

"You reckon that man you got locked up over there is a grave robber, Sheriff?" Buster asked.

After some thought the sheriff said, "I don't think this came from any grave, Buster, at least not from anyone that's been buried around here. I don't know of a family ever burying pocket watches and jewelry with their loved ones. Most would consider this stuff as heirlooms, keepsakes not to be put in a grave."

"What about the teeth, Sheriff?" Amos asked.

"I suspect they came from someone alive or recently so. If the man we got locked up in jail is a grave robber then how would you explain away the blood?" Bevins asked.

"I can't figure out what this represents but it's a fair guess a crime has been committed, maybe several crimes, Sheriff," Amos said. He was starting to get over the shock of what had been found but still looked a little pale.

"Let's get this stuff packed back in the saddlebags. I want to get back to the jail and ask our prisoner over there a few questions. Buster, I'll see that you get paid for the keep of that horse. Twenty-five gold coins of that denomination would stable a horse for two–hundred years I reckon. I'll need to count this up and then store it at the bank. That man has some answering to do," Bevins said.

None of the men wanted to touch the teeth so it was decided to hold the burlap sack at the edge of the table and then rake the gruesome contents into the sack using a small shovel. After the sack was tied and back in the saddlebags Buster grabbed a horse brush and a pail of soapy water and began scrubbing the table.

"I may never be able to eat off this again," the liveryman said as he scrubbed. "Might just throw it out and build a new one." Both the deputy and the sheriff thought it might be a good idea.

The two lawmen left the livery man scrubbing his table and headed back toward the jail. Both men were quiet, each trying to come to terms with what they carried in the saddlebags. Not every day a man comes across such a gruesome find, at least not in the town of Clear Creek.

When the two entered the jail there was a tall stranger sitting at the sheriff's desk, he was going through wanted posters and sipping coffee from a tin cup.

"You mind telling me what you're doing at my desk, Mister?" Bevins asked.

The Trail

When the man looked up he seemed vaguely familiar. When he spoke both Amos and Bevins knew who he was, the transformation was remarkable. The man who had once been known as Stank was now clean shaven and sporting a close cropped haircut. Not only that, but he appeared to also be clean from his head to his toes. The clothes he wore were different, clean but still raggedy.

"Evening, Sheriff, looks like I refilled the coffee pot just in time. Grab a cup before the both of you freeze to death. I also cleaned out the ash dump and stoked up the fire while you were out. This is one drafty old building," the clean shaven man said.

Amos slowly walked over to the desk and looked the stranger in the eye; it was Stank alright, although without the dirt and smell. Amos stepped back and grinned, "Is that really you, Stank?"

Before he could answer Bevins said, "His name is Clarence Walker."

If Amos was surprised at the transformation a little soap and a razor could do it was nothing compared to the shock he got from hearing the man's real name.

"Now I don't believe that for one minute, Sheriff. This can't be the Marshal Walker from back east, it just can't be. That man is dead I reckon, killed in a gunfight with three no-goods."

Walker stood and went to the stove to check on the pot of coffee. "That's my name, Amos, I'd swear it on this pot of coffee," he said with a chuckle.

Bevins walked around the startled deputy and sat at his desk. "Walker, how about you looking in those saddlebags and give me an idea or two about what the contents say about the man I got locked up in the back."

Walker looked at the sheriff suspiciously. "There something in those bags I should be aware of before I open em'?" Walker only asked this because he didn't want to be the butt end of a joke.

"Just look in the bag and then tell me what you think," Bevins said.

Walker sat the coffee pot back on the stove and grabbed the saddlebags. He slowly took everything out and lined the items up on the sheriff's desk. When he had it all placed the way he wanted it he tossed the ratty saddlebags back on the floor.

"Looks like a waylay bag, Sheriff. I believe these items were taken from folks against their will, maybe stage robberies or the like." Walker was basing this on the glasses, jewelry, and pocket watches. These items hadn't been placed back in the burlap bag before the men left the livery.

"That might explain away the glasses and pocket watches but I doubt it will explain what that burlap bag contains, or those badges," Bevins said.

Without hesitation Walker started untying the burlap sack. Amos already knew what the bag contained and wasn't looking forward to seeing its contents again, he turned away.

As the teeth rolled onto the top of the desk it didn't seem to bother Walker in the least, he reached over and picked one up. After he examined the tooth he sat it down and then picked up another. He did this to at least five or six before he stopped and went back to the stove.

"Well, what do you think?" Bevins asked.

Walker, without hesitation said, "They are all teeth pulled from men, my guess is they are early to middle aged men. None of the teeth appear to be worn or decayed very much other than the gold fillings," Walker said.

"How many different men are we talking about?" Bevins asked.

"I can't say with any level of certainty but my best guess is at least a dozen, maybe as many as fifteen."

Amos was curious as to how Walker had come to such a number by only looking at a few teeth. "You say a dozen, maybe more. How on earth would you know that?"

Walker went back to the table and picked up another tooth. "Nearly all these teeth are molars, teeth near the back. Most teeth that are repaired are the rear teeth or molars. By the looks of this I would say these teeth each came from a different man. Maybe a couple might have come from a single person but still that adds up to more than a dozen."

Amos and the sheriff considered what Walker said. If what Walker said was true, and there was no reason to believe otherwise, then the prisoner in back had some explaining to do.

"You say those saddlebags belong to the man you got locked up, Sheriff?" Walker asked.

"They do, me and Amos just came from the livery. Buster said the man that left them there, along with his horse and saddle, was real unfriendly like. Said he might have been a little drunk. When Amos arrested him he was real drunk."

Walker looked toward the door that led to the cells in the back. "You plan on talking to him about this Sheriff?"

"Damn right I do."

"Well good luck with that. The day or so I spent back there he didn't say much of nothing. When he did speak it was only to ask when he was going to get fed. I can tell you right now

Sheriff; you got you one ornery prisoner back there. He's the type that slinks around in the shadows, not one for bright light and blunt straightforward questions."

Bevins thought about what Walker had just said, the words seemed accurate. He had been impressed by the way he pulled bits of information out of the objects lying on the desk.

"How would you go about finding out something from a man that refuses to talk?" Amos asked.

Walker went to the front window. As he peered out he said, "Maybe show some kindness, most men tend to reciprocate whatever they are presented with."

Both the sheriff and the deputy only looked at each other. Walker turned from the window when he never got a response; the look on the two men's faces told him they were confused.

"Reciprocate means he might respond to you by the way he is treated by you."

Both lawmen shook their heads now that they understood what Walker had said. Sheriff Bevins thought the man once known as Stank might be an educated man.

"Amos, how about me and you bringing him out here in the front office, maybe offer him a little coffee and a chair by the stove, see if that might get him in a more talkative mood. If we get him out of that cold cell for a few minutes maybe he might be more inclined to cooperate," Bevins said as he pulled the keys from a peg attached to the wall.

Walker continued to look out the front window, the weather outside didn't look to improve anytime soon. The temperature was cold and looked to get colder, especially this time of year. He had never known a November to be pleasant this far north. He also couldn't remember a November being this unpleasant this time of year.

After a minute or two Bevins and Amos came out of the back with their prisoner, he had a sullen expression. It was a look that at first glance meant the man was a long ways from being anything resembling cooperative.

Amos took a somewhat clean tin cup from a shelf near the stove and filled it with hot coffee. As he reached it to the prisoner he asked if black would be alright, the man spoke as he eyed the cup suspiciously, he said black would be fine.

The prisoner looked at the three men in the room; he had seen Amos and Bevins several times over the last two days but couldn't place the clean-shaven man standing by the window, although there was something familiar about the man.

Bevins waited for the prisoner to sample his coffee before asking any questions. He also wanted the man to understand that he was brought out for a reason other than coffee.

"I never did get your name when we locked you up. Being as this town is too small for a full time judge, they leave it up to me to administer justice as I see fit. I gave you two days in jail and the two days are up today, but I can't let you go just yet," Bevins said.

The man looked at the sheriff with nothing but hate. "If my time in your little jail is up then why are you going to keep me locked up?"

"Because I always check dodgers on a man that's locked up just in case he might be wanted in another town for another crime. I looked at the dodgers and didn't recognize your face on any but without a name how can I be sure. If you want to be released today then I need a name. Now you can sit there with that sour look on your face but if I don't get the information I need then you will be sitting back there in your little cell wearing that sour face for a long time. Makes no never mind to me."

The man took a slow sip of his coffee before saying, "I don't remember being locked up in any town before and being forced to give my name." The man didn't know it but he had just given up a bit of information, he was a troublemaker who had seen more than one jail cell in his day.

Bevins didn't like this man; he also didn't like the tone he just used. "I don't give a damn what happened in any of the other towns you say you've been locked up in, I only care about this town. Now you either give me your name or I'm prepared to keep you locked up until hell freezes over."

"Tell you what, Mister Sheriff, I believe I like your warm little jail. As a matter of fact I like it so much you can just keep me locked up for the entire winter if you like," the man said with a smile.

Suddenly the sheriff realized this wasn't working out the way he intended. He had managed to alienate his prisoner and still hadn't gotten any closer to finding out a name. What he wanted to do was beat the living hell out of the smartass but decided for the moment to hold off on that little plan.

Walker turned from the window. "Sheriff, I was wondering if you might allow me to talk to the prisoner?"

"I know that voice stranger, but damn if I can't remember the face. What did you say your name was?" the prisoner asked.

Bevins started laughing. "You won't tell us your name but you want to ask this feller his, why you son of a bitch."

Walker knew the prisoner was trying to provoke the sheriff; he was doing a pretty good job of it too.

The Trail

"Again sheriff, would you allow me?" Walker asked.

"Be my guest," the sheriff replied.

Walker walked over and sat on the long bench by the wall. He sat there and looked at the man, didn't speak, just looked at him.

The prisoner was starting to get a little nervous now, he couldn't put his finger on it but somehow he knew the clean-shaven man sitting across from him. The longer Walker silently sat the more nervous the prisoner became.

Bevins had calmed considerably by now and was actually starting to enjoy this standoff; Walker was silently intimidating the man. The sheriff refilled his cup and took a seat back at his desk.

Amos too was enjoying what he was seeing. The prisoner was starting to get nervous, real nervous. His hand, the one that held the coffee, was starting to shake. It shook to the point that he was beginning to slosh coffee onto the floor.

"I think I would like to go back to my cell now, Sheriff," the man with no name said.

No way was Bevins going to end this little party now; he was enjoying it too much. "That's alright, mister, you stay out here with us a little while longer and enjoy your coffee."

The relaxed tone the sheriff used did little to calm the prisoner's nerves, it actually made them worse.

Walker continued to study the man. He watched him with such intensity that he didn't even blink his eyes, or at least it seemed that way to the prisoner. Finally, when he felt he had kept the man over the fire long enough he said, "Alright, Sheriff, you can put him away if you like. I suppose we'll get to use your idea after all."

"What idea? What have you got planned, Sheriff?" the prisoner asked. His look had gone from placid to worried.

Bevins motioned for Amos and with that the deputy led the prisoner back to his cell. Once Amos was back and the door between the front office and the cells was closed Bevins asked Walker what he thought.

"As I said earlier, Sheriff, you got yourself a bad one back there. He's guilty of something bad and knows if he gives his name then he's caught."

"If that's true then all he has to do is give us an alias. Why hasn't he done that you reckon?" Amos asked.

"My guess is he likes it here. He's safely locked up in jail, no one knows his name and no one here recognizes him. If he was an innocent man then all he needs to do is tell us who he is and then ride out. He also thinks we don't know about the saddlebags. He believes they are safe over at the livery," Walker said.

"Sounds about right, he could hide out in this jail as long as he likes if he don't tell us who he is. What we need is a witness, someone that knows this feller and knows what he's done. I figure something like that might take weeks, maybe even months," Bevins guessed.

"Sheriff, I figure we got a couple more hours of light left if you still intend on tracking that blood trail," Walker said as he placed his cup back on the shelf.

This was something the sheriff had nearly forgotten about; he had a wounded man over at Joe Ramey's and needed to find out how it happened. "We better get to it. How about we use horses, we can cover more ground that way and then get back here before dark?"

The Trail

"Sounds good, Sheriff but I seem to be without a horse," Walker said.

"You can use that horse over at the livery, the one that belongs to the bastard we got locked up in back."

"Alright then, let's get to it," Walker said.

Thirty minutes later and both men were on the blood trail. It didn't take long to get to the spot where they had turned back earlier; the two went another mile or so before they decided to give up, at least for today. Bevins didn't like leaving Amos alone in town. With a mysterious prisoner in jail, and a wounded man at Ramey's, he wasn't going to take any chances. If those worries weren't enough to turn the two men back then the weather surely was. The wind had picked up and the light snow from earlier was back.

The two were silent as they rode back toward town. Both were deep in thought, with all that had happened today they had plenty to ponder over. They made it back to the jail about thirty minutes after dark and both were glad of it. The warmth from the old logwood stove was more than welcome.

"What do you plan to do about tracking that trail again Sheriff? By morning the snow will have covered up anything obvious," Walker asked.

Bevins knew he was unlikely to find anything but he still had to try. "I think you got it figured about right. We still need to follow the trail we've already scouted and see if it might shed a little light on that feller over at Ramey's. An hour or so after first light I'm heading back out there, I'd like you to accompany me, that is if you don't mind."

"I don't mind a bit, might be a good idea though if I'm more adequately armed. I don't like traipsing around without a sturdy weapon. I appreciate the use of them two old shooters you loaned me this morning, but if trouble is about I would like something a little more dependable."

"Tell you what, since you're riding that man's horse, I don't think he would mind allowing you to use his gun belt and pistol. It's an old 1873 Colt Peacemaker, shoots a .45 cartridge. You ever fire an old Peacemaker?"

"Peacemaker was the gun I used back in my lawman days, but if I had my druthers, I would rather have that Walker he had stashed in those saddlebags. It's heavy enough not to buck, and powerful enough to do the job in one shot, assuming you hit what you're aiming at. That rig will do just fine if you allow the trade," Walker told the sheriff.

Bevins noticed the cartridge loops on the belt contained two or three shells of the .44 caliber to fit the old peacemaker. He opened his desk drawer and pulled out a box of .45 cartridges and tossed it to Walker. "Might be ten or twelve bullets in that box, it's all I got. You might check over at the general store before they close and see if they have anymore. That caliber ain't the most popular around here, if they got any I doubt if it's more than a box. His saddlebags had a few shells too; you got enough to maybe fill half the loops on that belt. There's also an old Derringer in them bags. Either he stole it or bought it, either way he was one well-armed hombre."

Walker was filling the bullet loops on the belt as he said, "If I'm buying bullets then I suppose you ain't giving this back to the prisoner?"

"I might need to think on that a spell. If he's planning on not giving us his name then I might just confiscate his horse, his saddle, and his three guns. Let's call it room and board fees. You know something funny, your name is Walker and that gun

I just loaned you is a Walker. Quite the coincidence don't you think?"

Walker strapped on the belt and then slid the gun into the holster. It brought back memories of his lawman days, some good, some not so good.

"I count twenty-seven rounds counting the six in the gun, doubt I'll need to go looking for another box at the general store, Sheriff," Walker said.

Bevins just realized Walker didn't have any money, or at least that's what he assumed. "Tell you what, if you use any of that ammunition while helping me then I promise to buy the next box. How does that sound?"

"You got yourself a deal, Sheriff. I still think you should consider giving me this old Walker, and the belt, that is if you still plan on keeping it as compensation to cover room and board for the prisoner back there."

"I might just do that," Bevins said. "One or two of those gold coins might just get confiscated too. This jail needs more coffee and sugar. As a matter of fact about everything around here is running low, especially ammunition, that stuff doesn't come cheap. Maybe when the judge gets here he will assess a fine on that bastard in the back, a fine that will help the jail a little."

Trevor Bostwick and Mathew Brooks walked beside their big freight wagon as it rumbled its way north. The two men were four days into an eleven day run.

Bostwick and Brooks had been driving this same trail for the last five years and hoped to continue until they were either too old to work or found some energetic soul to sell the freighting company to.

The two men made this trip once each month, eleven days in either direction with four left over days at each end. The extra days were used to either unload or re-load, and to also rest the eight animal string of mules. Their little freight company was the life-blood for the small town of Clear Creek.

The journey would start from the rail depot at Bristle Buck and eleven days later end up at Clear Creek. During the drive in either direction the men would always have two half-day stops to work on the rough and tumble road. Some of the work was to improve rough stretches where the team struggled to pull the heavy wagon. On more than one occasion they had to stop to repair a washed out section or remove a fallen tree that blocked the trail.

Bostwick and Brooks had been teamsters practically all their lives. The only time the two weren't pulling freight was when they both fought during the Civil War, Bostwick for the North and Brooks for the South. Prior to the war the two had separate, but more professional careers. Neither had shared that story to anyone other than themselves.

Most folks wondered what kept the two from killing one another due to their differing opinions about the war; it never seemed to be a problem though. They might throw a snide remark at each other from time to time but it was all in good natured fun. Both men respected the other man's service.

"Trevor, how about we pull into Clear Creek a day late? We can use the extra day to do a little excavating on Dead Mule Curve," Mathew asked.

Dead Mule Curve was given its name when one of the team a year or so earlier slipped while trying to navigate a protruding rock. The animal injured its left front leg and couldn't continue the journey. Neither Mathew nor Brooks had the heart to put the poor animal out of its misery so it was decided to abandon the mule and let it fend for itself. The leg wasn't broken but it was giving the animal so much trouble they knew it couldn't continue on. It was summertime and the grazing and water was good so the mule was left behind in hopes it could mend on its own. Although injured, the animal could still hobble about and forage for food. It was the last the two teamsters saw of the mule, maybe it wandered off, or worse, got killed by one of the cougars or bears that frequented the area. A lean mule that was unable to run would make a tempting meal for any number of predators that inhabited the region.

It was agreed that the two men would stop at Dead Mule Curve and do a little excavating. The weather had turned bitter and both men knew the eight mule hitch could use the rest. One good day might do a world of good for that little stretch of road.

The two walked that evening until about an hour before dark. Walking was something the two teamsters were used to, freight wagons didn't have a seat for the driver. The two took turns walking alongside the mule hitch and directing the lead animal, a contrary old cuss they called Satan.

Satan was considered stubborn, as most mules are, but in actuality he was just cautious. Mules are intelligent animals, aren't skittish unless they sense danger, and generally affectionate. If handled with care and not overworked they tend to be good work animals. If mistreated or underfed they tend to be stubborn. This is simply a characteristic of self-preservation.

Both Trevor and Mathew were good mule handlers. They treated their string almost as good as family, which wasn't saying a lot considering both men rarely made it home for anything more than a couple of days each month. It was assumed the two had mean wives and spent as little time with them as possible. A mean wife can do that to a man. Many a man has attributed his success to long hours on the job. Long hours because they would rather work than go home. You ask any hardworking man and see if it ain't true.

"I say we pull up here and make camp. Got water and sage for the mules and a couple of knocked down spruce for firewood," Trevor said.

Mathew stepped to the front of the hitch and looked the spot over. It was within a hundred yards of Dead Mule Curve and near enough to water to make the spot ideal. As Mathew looked over the terrain Satan reached around and grabbed the hat from his head.

"Damn you, Satan, give me back that hat."

Trevor started laughing as old long ears began chomping on the brim of the other man's hat. By the time Mathew retrieved it the brim was chewed clean through, a mule has a tendency to chew on anything that might look tasty. Satan had been eyeing that hat ever since Mathew bought it.

"Would you look at that, damn thing is nearly ruined," Mathew said as he tried to bend it back into shape.

"Crooked and bent all out of shape suits you," Trevor said.

Mathew gave his trail partner a sour look as he put the broken hat back on his head. Satan had gone back to looking over the terrain; he knew it was nearing the time when he and the other seven mules would be staked out for water and rest.

The Trail

He also knew he and the others would be getting a scoop of grain, the highlight of the day as far as he was concerned.

Satan was six years old, the oldest of the eight by a full three years. He had pulled this freight wagon for the better part of five years. Being six made him nearer the end of his working life than the beginning. Freight mules usually lasted until they were five and then were sold to some farmer where they would spend their remaining days pulling a plow, but not Satan.

What endeared him to the two teamsters the most was the fact that he was not only the oldest of the hitch but he was the smartest as well. Trevor and Mathew trusted him to maintain the pace and keep the others pulling steady. Once, a couple of years back when a mountain lion stepped from cover, no doubt thinking about having a mule for supper. Satan brayed harshly and loudly, cutting such a shine that the startled cat turned around and headed back the way he came. After the threat was gone Satan continued as if nothing had happened. During times of stress the old mule seemed to have a calming effect on the rest of the hitch.

"Let's get these animals unhitched and taken care of. For some reason I'm craving supper," Mathew said.

This didn't surprise Trevor; Mathew seemed to always be hungry. It took the two men the better part of thirty minutes to get the eight mule hitch situated for the night. After the mules drank and fed on some of the buffalo grass and brush that abounded in this area the two men would give each a scoop of grain. Satan knew the routine; he had been pulling long enough to know that the days never really changed and always ended with a little grain.

Satan pulled and tugged on some tough leafy brush as he looked over the rest of the hitch, and also the surrounding area. He was uneasy, uneasy for Satan usually meant there was a predator around. As he tugged and chewed he kept his eye on a spot on the other side of the stream near a stand of spruce and cottonwood. He hadn't yet spotted anything that might add up to trouble but he sensed it was there. He had a good nose for trouble and was rarely wrong.

"What do you suppose has old Satan so fidgety this evening Trevor?" Mathew asked as he peered into the growing darkness.

Trevor had been trying to start a fire using some damp wood and was having a bad time of it. "I can't rightly say; he's got a whiff of something he don't like though. You think we ought to bring them in a ways after they get their water?"

After finally getting a small flame started Mathew walked over and was digging around in the side bin of the freight wagon. He was trying to get the coffee pot and skillet out from under the shovel and the pickaxe the men had used earlier. When he finally managed to free the two he found the skillet to be covered in dirt and grime from the shovel. As he rubbed the skillet against the seat of his pants to clean it he said, "Might be a good idea. If it's a mountain lion then it could sneak in and kill one of the mules before we knew it. I ain't worried about a bear, them critters don't know the first thing about sneaking up quiet like."

Trevor gave the hitch another look, he was confident Satan would warn them if a predator was about. "I say we do it after we boil some coffee and burn some beans. After we eat it might be a good idea to dig that old Navy out of the side bin. I don't fancy facing a big cat with just my skinning knife." The skinning knife Trevor was referring to was a bit more formidable than he let on. Handle and blade together measured more than a foot and not only that, he was good with a knife. More than one rebel sentry had met a silent death at the end of his blade.

As the two men prepared their supper Satan continued to watch the stand of trees, he knew something was there. Whether it was man or beast he couldn't tell but he was certain danger was about on this cold night.

Just when the beans began to sizzle and the smell of coffee began to fill the camp Trevor stood and looked toward the freight wagon. As he did he noticed Satan standing still as a statue looking into the darkness on the other side of the stream from where the men had the hitch picketed.

"Maybe I'll dig out that old Navy before we have our beans," Trevor said.

Mathew poked the fire one more time before he stood and looked around. "That might be a good idea; I just had a cold chill run up my spine. I feel a mite spooked and I don't usually feel that way unless my old woman is around."

"I've seen your old woman, Mathew; I'd be a bit spooked too if I had to share a tent with her."

Mathew looked at his trail partner, "Did you really just say that Yankee? You're one to talk, that female you answer to is meaner than my old woman by at least double." Whenever either of the two men used the name Reb or Yankee it was a sign that the conversation might devolve into a wrestling match at any moment.

"Well, we ain't got neither one of them two here so unless you plan on confronting a cat or bear with just your looks then I suggest we get that old Navy," Trevor said with a growl.

Just then Satan looked at the two and brayed, he heard the two arguing and knew neither was paying attention to the danger that had just stepped from the trees.

"Howdy boys, how about the two of you standing real still like so we can have us a little talk," a man said as he stepped across the stream that ran near where the mules were tied.

Trevor and Mathew looked in the direction of the voice they just heard, both men knew they had let their guard down and were now in a bad way.

Facing the two were three men, one held a rifle as the other two pulled Colts from their holsters. Neither Trevor nor Mathew were armed other than the skinning knife stuck in the sheath behind Trevor's belt. The knife wasn't visible from the front and this was by design, Trevor liked to keep his options open when it came to the knife.

"What are you doing coming into our camp brandishing weapons?" Mathew asked. He might have been a rough and tumble teamster but he did know a word or two.

"Just you shut up, old man, me and the boys here noticed the fire, and also the smell of beans and coffee and decided to come in and share your supper," the man holding the rifle said.

"Alright, mister, you come on in and grab a bite to eat. Just keep them shooters pointed in another direction. By the way, do any of you men have a name?" Mathew asked.

"You can call me Rifle and these two go by the name of Pistol," the man holding the long gun said with a laugh. He looked at one of the two pistol toting men and said, "Why don't one of you introduce yourself."

One of the two men holding the Colts raised his gun and shot Mathew; the teamster went down in a heap. Trevor was both shocked and startled at the sudden violence. He looked at

Mathew and saw the shot had grazed his right thigh; either by luck, or design, the bullet didn't appear to have caused much damage.

"You got anything to add?" the man with the pistol asked Trevor.

"Nothing I reckon. Will you allow me to tend to my friend here?"

"Your friend can tend to himself. You on the other hand can finish up with them beans and coffee," the man with the rifle said.

Mathew nodded at Trevor as he pulled a dirty neckerchief from his pocket and tried to tie up his leg. Once he had the bleeding stopped he climbed back to his feet and stood there figuring out if his leg could support him, it could.

It didn't take more than a few minutes for the food and drink to burn and this suited the three outlaws just fine. Anything hot in this kind of weather was suitable.

"What have you two got in the wagon old man?" Rifle asked.

"Freight for the town of Clear Creek, we just tote the stuff and don't really know what the crates contain," Trevor said, he lied. He and Mathew knew what every crate and sack contained; both men had been hauling nearly the same type of merchandise to that town for years.

Rifle looked at the two men holding the Colts. "I reckon after we get through with this fine supper here we'll just have us a little look see." He looked back at Trevor and Mathew, "After that we'll need the two of you to hitch up them mules so as this freight wagon can move. In the mean time you two sit down by that wagon of yours until we tell you to hitch up them animals."

Trevor and Mathew both eased down by one of the big wheels, just as they were told. As the three gunmen ate and drank coffee Trevor whispered under his breath, "I think them three plan on stealing the wagon."

Mathew was still trying to get the bleeding stopped where he had been shot as he said, "After that I figure they plan on shooting the two of us. I doubt they intend on letting us go, we done seen their faces."

"I agree, if we get the chance, any chance at all, we need to put up a fight. I doubt we'll be successful but we have to try just the same."

Mathew figured Trevor was right. The two stood little chance against three armed men and on top of that he had already been shot in the leg. "If we don't make it I want you to know we've had a good run. It's been my pleasure to work the freight with you."

"Same here," was all Trevor said.

Satan had paid particular attention to the three when they came from cover and approached the campsite. When he saw the three men were carrying guns he knew this was bad. When one of the men carrying a short gun shot Mathew it startled all eight mules, the others slightly more than Satan. The big long eared critter knew things had just gone from bad to worse; men that acted that way toward other men tended to also treat their animals poorly. Satan was now worried about the other members of his hitch, he was also worried about Mathew and Trevor. The two teamsters had seen to his needs for years, now it all seemed to be at an end.

Rifle filled one of the tin plates sitting by the fire pit and stood by the fire as he crammed handfuls of beans into his mouth. After each bite he licked his fingers before scooping up another handful. The two men with the Colts used the two spoons that belonged to the two teamsters. The three ate until the last of the beans was gone. It didn't take long before the coffee pot ran dry too.

"Them was good beans, old man, I believe that might be about the best I've had in a spell. Coffee was good too. Now I believe that about does it for bragging about the cooking. Me and these other two been looking for the two of you for a couple of days now. Only description we had was two old freight hauling bastards, one oversized freight wagon being pulled by an eight mule hitch. Four pair of mules would make eight I believe. Do I have it figured about right?" Rifle asked one of the two that helped him take over the campsite.

The man looked at the mules and then started counting on his fingers. Trevor and Mathew looked at each other; both knew they were being held up by three dumbasses.

"I count eight boss, eight mules and one freight wagon," the man said.

Rifle smiled at the man, "I didn't mean for you to count the damn mules, I was just talking out loud."

Rifle looked at Trevor and Mathew. "You two got anyone else with you? Maybe hiding out in them trees with a shooter pointed in our direction?"

Neither of the two teamsters answered. Maybe if the three bushwhackers thought there was another man in the woods then it might convince them to walk away. It was a hopeful thought, at the moment the two freight haulers had very little to hope for.

Rifle stood and ratcheted a round in the Winchester. "Maybe if I shoot one of you then the other will be a little more cooperative."

Mathew figured since he was already shot the next target might be Trevor; he couldn't allow that to happen.

"We ain't got nobody else with us, mister. It's just me and Trevor here. We done gave you our supper and coffee, can't the three of you just leave us be?"

Rifle sat the gun on the ground and then wiped his filthy hands on his pants, then reached down and picked up his gun as he cast his gaze on the two teamsters. "Let's have us a look in that wagon," he said as he pointed the gun at Trevor and Mathew. The bushwhacker had the look of a cold blooded killer; it was the only way to describe the man holding the rifle.

The two teamsters slowly stood and went around to the back of the wagon. The whole load was covered with a heavy oiled tarp which was tied down with stout ropes at the corners and along both sides. As the two men began untying the knots that held the tarp in place they both tried to stay sharp; each was waiting for an opportunity to turn the tables on these three bandits.

"That's enough, now both of you step back so I can get me a look inside," Rifle said. The teamsters did as they were told and stepped toward the darkness. Both doubted they could make a run for it but if the chance came they wouldn't let it pass.

Rifle eased up the corner of the tarp and peered inside. The light from the campfire was enough for him so see that the load contained a little of everything. It looked like it was mostly stock for the general store at Clear Creek.

"Looks like we hit the jackpot, once we head this wagon south we'll stop at the first town we find and sell this loot to the highest bidder. Should be enough to see us through till spring," Rifle said.

The Trail

The two men with the Colts were also looking at the back of the freight wagon; both were shaking their heads in agreement. Each sported a nasty grin.

"What about them mailbags we was sent to find boss? I believe that pays better than even this wagon load of goods we got here," one of the two pistol packing varmints said.

At this Rifle balled a fist and hit the man squarely on the side of his face. Not a hard strike but it did get the man's attention. "You just shut up about them mailbags, we was told to get the wagon and bring it back. We was also told to not mention a word about the reason we was hired."

The man that got hit had regained his footing and was rubbing his jaw. The sudden display of violence against the man told a lot about how this was going to end, it didn't look good for the two teamsters.

Rifle again pointed his gun in the direction of the two old freight haulers. "Alright you two, hitch up them mules and be quick about it. Don't either of you worry about them animals; I plan on selling the lot, along with your rig here, when we sell off your freight. The way I see it you two ain't going to need them much longer anyway." Both men holding pistols began to laugh as if it was the funniest thing either had ever heard.

This confirmed what Trevor and Mathew suspected, they were going to be killed after they got the hitch of mules attached to the freight wagon. Neither man could have imagined this day would be their last; life and death seem to go hand in hand in this world with neither far from the other.

The two men with Colts walked over to the mules, keeping a close eye on Trevor and Mathew, Rifle stayed by the fire. The two teamsters worked slow knowing the moment the mules were in place they were going to be killed. With each passing minute both men knew time was running out. All they wanted was for an opportunity to present itself, anything that might give the two a fighting chance.

With six of the mules now hitched it just left Satan and one more mule and that would be that. Trevor grabbed the front left animal; just as Mathew was about to untie Satan his neckerchief came undone from the gunshot wound on his leg and fell to the ground. As he bent at the knee and reached for the bloody bandage one of the two men with the Colts, hoping to hurry up the process, decided to lend a hand. Lending a hand was soon to be something literal.

Satan had been alert from the moment the bandits first stepped from the stand of trees. He wanted nothing more than for Trevor and Mathew to somehow take control of the situation; that, so far, just wasn't happening.

When the man holding the Colt untied the rope and reached for the mule's bridle Satan made his move. When the man's arm was beside his face Satan turned his head and clamped down on the man's forearm with his teeth and bit hard.

With the arm firmly in his grasp Satan yanked hard. The bite was so vicious that it broke both bones in the man's forearm. Satan also managed to dislocate the man's shoulder when he jerked; a mule is a powerful animal, especially a mule that is nervous and scared.

The man screamed in pain as he fell to the ground, partly from the pain and partly from the force the mule used to yank his shoulder out of place. As his victim was going down, Satan released his grip on the arm so the man could fall free. When he hit the ground Satan reared up a couple of feet and came down firmly on the man's head with both front hooves. The crunch of bone told Satan he had just killed the man. With that target out of the way the big longed eared mule turned to see what other damage he could inflict before the other two men started using their guns.

When Satan's victim first screamed the other man with the Colt turned to see what happened. It was the opportunity Trevor was looking for. Without a second to lose the old teamster reached behind his vest and pulled his knife. When the man with the Colt turned back Trevor was ready.

He put the point of the big knife under the man's ribcage and plunged it upward at an angle that went through the heart and nearly out the man's back. With his heart cleaved in two the man never made a sound as his weight pulled him off the blade and he fell to the ground.

Mathew also took advantage of the ruckus. While Rifle was raising his Winchester to shoot Trevor, he lunged forward and picked up the Colt lying by the man Satan had just killed. Just as Rifle took a bead on Trevor the Colt fired striking Rifle squarely in the chest. The Winchester went off but the bullet went harmlessly over everyone's heads.

In less than thirty seconds all three bandits were lying dead. Trevor and Mathew both looked at Satan. The big mule was standing statue straight looking back at the two teamsters.

"I reckon Satan just earned himself a second scoop of grain Trevor," Mathew said in a low voice as if nothing had happened.

Trevor looked at the three men lying on the ground, "Hell, I might even give him a big kiss."

Mathew looked down at his leg and poked at the wound as he said, "Probably remind you of that wife of yours."

"You know, it just might," Trevor said with a chuckle.

It took the two nearly thirty minutes to put the hitch back out for the night. Satan continued to scan the surrounding area even though the three bandits had already been dealt with. Even as he enjoyed his second scoop of grain he seemed nervous. Once he got his soul spooked it took him quite a while to calm himself down, even with a name like Satan. Maybe the big mule didn't understand the implication of his name, how could he?

"Satan has still got something on his mind, Mathew. He keeps looking about like there's a hungry bear out there that wants to march in here and eat him alive."

Mathew had finally gotten his leg patched up enough where it wouldn't bleed anymore; he wasn't in the mood for any more trouble tonight. "Tell you what, how about we gather up these dead men's guns. I doubt they have any more use for 'em. I plan on purchasing me a good used Colt or Remington just as soon as we make it to Clear Creek. I always suspected we might get set upon someday by bandits, looks like today was that day."

After a moment's thought Mathew added, "Say, do you remember that old shootin' iron I've been admiring. It's the one laying in the front of that glass rack in the gun smithy's shop?"

"Yea I remember, you been looking at that rusty piece of junk for the better part of a year now. Almost every time we make it to Clear Creek you browse that shop trying to find something good that you can buy for a pittance. If you weren't such a cheap bastard you might have had a gun on you tonight, then maybe you wouldn't have got yourself shot," Trevor said with as much venom as he could muster.

Mathew looked up from the bandage on his leg and said, "Are you going to stand there and pretend all our troubles tonight were because I didn't overpay for a gun I probably never would have used anyway? Is that what you're saying, Yankee?"

Trevor stood and faced his friend, "That's exactly what I'm saying and if you don't like it then I don't care you Johnny Reb. If you liked that rusty shooter so much then you should have parted with the money and bought the damn thing. That is if that wife of yours lets you travel with any walking around money."

"That reminds me, do you remember what make of gun it was? It sure was a pretty thing," Mathew said matter of factly as if none of the mean talk between them had just happened.

"It was a Colt, a rusty old Colt and if you don't buy it this trip then I just might have to," Trevor said without a hint of anger in his voice. The two old teamsters could talk mean and kind to each other in the same sentence.

Mathew was suddenly anxious to make it to Clear Creek. Once there he was going to pay the old gunsmith a visit and see if he could buy that old Colt at a reasonable price. Just as he was thinking of his next purchase, and also dreading to part with his hard earned money, another thought came to mind.

"Say, Trevor, instead of either of us looking to buy an extra gun how bout we confiscate one of them owl hoot's guns?"

Trevor was stoking the fire with a long stick. He paused and looked up at Mathew. "Why that sounds like the thing to do. You gather up the weapons while I fix us another supper. We'll look the guns over as we eat and figure out which one we'll keep. Them bastards didn't know it but the grub they stole from me and you turned out to be their last supper."

"I figure they payed for that meal with their lives. We'll just confiscate us a gun as a bonus," Mathew said as he hobbled around looking for a piece of wood he could use as a crutch. "The gun that man used to shoot me is now mine. I figure if it didn't kill me before, then it won't kill me to own it now."

Both men settled down by the fire waiting for the next batch of beans to burn. Each examined the weapons Mathew collected. There were the two Colts, both looked to be well used but also, well taken care of. The Winchester was old, older than a seventy-three model but still looked to have some life left in it. There was also a two shot belly gun and three knives; none of the three was as long as the one Trevor carried.

As the men scraped beans off their plates something suddenly occurred to Mathew, "You know, I mentioned earlier that I intended to buy me that used Colt as soon as we get to Clear Creek. I think me and you should just keep all the weapons we took off them bandits. Law of the land and such is the way I see it."

Trevor looked at his partner and wondered if the man was losing his mind, "You done said that not more than five minutes go, what in hell is wrong with you?"

"Ain't nothing wrong with me I reckon, I just forgot. Did you hear what I just said, these shootin irons now belong to us," Mathew said, the smile on his face growing wider by the minute. The old teamster hated to spend a dime on anything. Now he had figured out a way to get what he wanted and not spend a penny.

As the two sat and pondered the events of the day a few more questions came to mind. "What do we do with the bodies Mathew? We going to take them to Clear Creek and see if there might be any reward money involved. Who knows, we might have us a little bounty money coming if them three was a dead or alive situation."

The Trail

Mathew hadn't thought about any bounty that might be collected. "As much as I would like to accommodate the law in this matter I doubt we want to take those bodies along with us. We'll be lucky if some hungry bear don't come into camp tonight and cause us some more trouble. I reckon the smell of blood is strong around here. We're maybe six or seven days from Clear Creek, we'll have every bear and cougar in the territory after us if we're toting them three bodies."

Trevor knew Mathew was right. "I suppose you're right, where would we put the three if we decided to take them along anyway? That old freight wagon is packed full." After a minute he added, "I'm just glad the smell of blood you mentioned ain't ours."

Both men had another thought about the same time, and it was the same thought. "Those three must have horses nearby; you know they weren't on foot out here this far from civilization, and in this kind of weather. A man would surely freeze to death if he was in these parts and on foot," Trevor said.

"You know, I was just thinking the same thing. You think we ought to go and have us a look? That would be at least three horses and possibly a pack animal or two. I sure hate to think of a horse out there by itself tied to a tree. That's a real scary thought. Maybe the two of us should go have us a peek at what's out there."

Trevor looked into the darkness. Leaving the safety of the fire and the wagon was a bad idea. "I reckon not, we'll scout around in the morning after first light. If there are horses out there then they'll be alright tonight. I also don't want to be roaming around in the darkness, what if there are more of them bandits about. I for one have had my fill of bandits for a while. Them three 'bout done us in." After saying this Trevor looked over at Satan, the big mule was finished with his second helping of grain and was standing straight as a tree looking back at the two teamsters.

The two old men always had a kind heart toward the old mule. After what he had done for them tonight they both were beholding to the four legged beast.

"Say Mathew, is that old curry comb still in the bottom of the side box?"

"I reckon so, what you got in mind?"

"I was just thinking about going over and giving old Satan a good brushing. After what he done for us I think he deserves it."

Mathew looked at the mule. "You brush him tonight and tomorrow it'll be my turn. That old mule might get the brush every night from now on. It's the least we can do."

Trevor was good to his word. Satan got his coat brushed and he really enjoyed it. It didn't mean he wasn't going to nab a hat from time to time but he appreciated the brushing just the same.

Mathew wanted to go tonight to try and find any horses the three dead bandits might have had but knew Trevor was probably right. "Alright then, we'll look first thing in the morning. I hope if there are any horses out there they don't get set upon by some hungry critter before we have a chance to go out and find 'em."

Trevor thought it was the only safe thing to do. "Them horses are on their own until morning. I think one of us should stay awake tonight and keep watch, just in case. Like I said, might be more bandits about and if not then we still might be set upon by a hungry bear. I don't know about the smell of blood in the air but I do know them three stink to high Heaven. I know winter is setting in but anybody can heat a pan of water and wash at least once a week. I believe them three ain't seen a slab of soap or a scrub brush in a year."

"They do stink. Wonder why we didn't smell 'em before they made it to camp? As far as the horses them bushwhackers was riding I agree, they're on their own tonight. Might not be a bad idea for one of us to stay awake tonight, like you say, might be more outlaws about. I doubt I can sleep much anyway, too much excitement," Mathew said as he cradled the Colt he now claimed was his. Both men wondered if they would ever calm enough to sleep again.

"You pull first watch and I'll try to catch me a little sleep. You hear or see anything that don't make sense then you wake me, got it? I think a little sleep right now might do me some good, remember, I was shot tonight," Mathew told his partner.

"You do that, sleep all you want. I doubt I'll ever sleep again."

Mathew took his bedroll from a side box on the freight wagon and spread it under the wagon. Both men had been using that old wagon to keep the rain and snow off them for years now; it was just what teamsters did. The wagon made a good roof and it also gave them a sense of security, albeit a false one. Even though Mathew had said earlier that he was too nervous to sleep he was snoring within minutes of crawling under the wagon. Trevor made another pot of coffee, hoping it would keep him alert during the night, it didn't.

Just as the first light of the new day ambled into camp Mathew stirred from under the wagon. The first thing he saw was a cold fire and Trevor leaning back against the front wheel of the wagon, sound asleep. He was sleeping so soundly he could have been mistaken for dead.

Mathew noticed the leg that had been shot was stiff and sore but it could have been worse, he could have been dead himself. He checked his bandage and found the wound had stopped bleeding and appeared it might just knit up on its own without the need to be sewn back together. One troubling sign was a little redness around the edges. He also felt a little feverish but not so much as to cause him to worry. The two men had been doctoring themselves for years; it was just something you did when away from town.

Letting Trevor continue to snore he went about the task of restarting the fire and filling the coffee pot, not an easy undertaking considering the stream had frozen over. There was a frost in the air; the branches of the trees were white. Kinda Christmas looking Mathew thought. As he was carrying the coffee pot back from the stream he weaved a little. He chalked it up to just getting older.

Fifteen minutes after crawling from under the wagon he had coffee boiling in the pot and bacon burning in the skillet. It didn't take long for Trevor to stir from his sleep, the smell of coffee and bacon will do that to a man.

"Well darling, it looks like you beat me up and already got breakfast started," Trevor said.

Mathew gave him a sour look. "You call me darling again and I will beat you up."

Trevor laughed as he stood and stretched trying to get the frost out of his bones. "Maybe I should go and look for them dead men's horses while you torch that bacon. I don't like the idea of them animals tied to a tree out there all alone." As he said this he looked into the distance. It wasn't a pleasant thought of walking into the timber after what walked out of the timber the night before.

"Might be a good idea at that, you go and I'll stay here and keep the coffee hot. I doubt I could walk very far on this leg of mine right now anyway. I was thinking maybe I should ride on top of the freight for a day or two and let some of this soreness leave me. All I need now is to get the damn thing full of infection. You know something like that has killed more than a few men."

Trevor knew the man was right. If he started trying to walk around with that crease in his leg then he was going to get in bad shape fast. "I reckon that's the way I had it figured too. I knew you would find a way sooner or later to ride that freight wagon like some high-handed boss, king of the entire world with me and the eight mules to Lord over."

Mathew smiled; he liked the sound of that. "Well then, if I be your king I appoint you to go and find the dead men's horses, and be quick about it lad."

Trevor headed off in the direction the three bandits came from the previous night shaking his fist at Mathew as he went. The hitch of mules was still tied out where they had spent the night. Satan gave Trevor a curious look as he went by; it was unusual for the man to leave camp before hitching the mules to the freight wagon. Ah, what the hell, men were known to do crazy things, look what happened last night. Satan knew Trevor would be back soon and then he and the other seven mules would start their day's work. On cold days Satan preferred pulling rather than standing, it tended to warm the long eared beast up.

Once past the hitch of mules, Trevor headed through the thicket of trees where the three men, now dead men, first came into view the previous night. He carried the old Winchester rifle and one of the Colts, both were fully loaded. Just past the thicket of cottonwood and fir trees was a fair sized clearing. On the other side stood three horses, all saddled and looking put out for spending the night without having the gear stripped off their backs.

Trevor stood a minute in the cover of the fir trees as he scanned the surrounding area. Nothing looked worrisome but things might not seem as pleasant as they looked. After a good ten minutes he assumed it was okay to step from cover and approach the three horses. With one last look he stepped into the open and started for the other side of the clearing.

Not more than two steps into the open and Trevor felt a tug at his coat and at almost the same time heard a rifle shot. He went to the ground and tried to see where the shooter was, he also felt the pain the bullet had caused. His entire left arm was numb and this was bad, Trevor was left handed. He knew he couldn't aim the Winchester with just his right hand so he pulled the Colt as he scanned for whoever had shot him. He knew his left arm, or maybe even his left side had been hit but for the moment that would have to wait, he needed to find the shooter.

After falling Trevor made little to no movement hoping he might avoid detection. He was well hidden in the tall buffalo grass but this wasn't much comfort, whoever had shot him knew exactly where he was. As he waited he tried to see how bad he was hit, he was starting to get a little feeling back in his left arm and hand and upon further inspection he found there was little blood, practically none at all. Maybe he wasn't hit that bad after all. He felt around as best as he could and then he touched the pocket watch he had carried for the past ten years.

The Trail

Upon further inspection he found it to have a big dent in the metal face that covered the workings and hands. There was a hole in the center of the face. Them bastards had killed his watch. The bullet that would have killed him was somewhere inside the heavy watch because there wasn't a hole in the back of the timepiece, just an outward facing dent.

As he scanned his surroundings he double-checked the Colt, it was fully loaded. This gave him little comfort; he had never fired the gun before and didn't know if it even worked. The Colt Mathew had been shot with was one of the two but he didn't know which was which. Maybe he had picked up the other man's gun. What if it was defective and wouldn't fire? He had heard of such things before, now wouldn't that be just his luck. He hoped he hadn't used up all of his luck with the pocket watch.

As Trevor lay still as a corpse, trying to not draw any attention to his position, he kept a close eye on the three horses standing on the opposite side of the clearing. He felt sure the shooter was somewhere around the spot where the horses stood. A thousand things were going through his mind. Was this new threat associated to the three men he and Mathew had killed the previous night?

"You there, if you can hear me then stand up where I can see you. If you don't then I'll pepper that spot with lead. I know where you're hiding," a voice said.

Trevor didn't want to stand until he saw what he was up against but he knew if they started shooting then he was dead. "How can I trust you, you done shot me without warning," Trevor shouted hoping to buy himself a little time to figure out his next move, his preferred next move was hopefully not to get killed.

"You ain't in no position to bargain. Stand up or die where you are, your decision," a man said as he stepped from cover near the three horses and headed in Trevor's direction. There was another man with him and both were holding long rifles as they approached the spot where Trevor had fallen.

Trevor knew he couldn't win a shooting match at this distance; he was shooting a handgun with his off hand against two men with rifles. If he stood now he was sure the two would finish the job they had started. If he didn't stand then they would be on him in no time.

"Alright, hold your fire," Trevor said as he struggled to his feet.

"Drop that gun, mister, and I mean right now," one of the two men said after Trevor made it to his feet. He did as he was told; he doubted he could hit either of the two anyway. His left arm was starting to feel about normal but given the events of the last twelve hours normal could mean anything. Nothing it seemed was normal.

The two men walked to within ten feet of Trevor before stopping. Both were thin and tall, each had the look of men that traveled the out of doors a lot. Each wore tied down guns and both carried rifles, one a Winchester and the other a Sharps.

"We came looking for three friends of ours that came through these parts yesterday. You wouldn't know anything about three riders in these parts would you, old man?" the shorter of the two asked.

Trevor needed to buy some time, he didn't know why but felt if these two found out what really happened to the three men from the previous night they would probably kill him on the spot. They were most likely going to kill him anyway.

The Trail

"I don't know anything about your friends, mister, what gives you the right to shoot me for no reason anyway?"

The two only looked at each other. After the briefest of moments one raised his Winchester and pointed it at Trevor. There was a gunshot, Trevor grabbed his chest but didn't feel any pain. So this is what it feels like when you die he wondered.

Immediately there was another gunshot and as Trevor waited for blood to erupt from his chest he noticed both men standing in front of him collapse to the ground. It was then that he noticed both had been shot. He turned to look for who had saved his life and saw Mathew standing at the edge of the trees behind him, he was holding a smoking Colt.

"Mathew, am I glad to see you," he told his partner as he turned back to see the two men lying in front of him.

Mathew limped up and stood beside Trevor. "Are they dead?"

"I think one is past dead but it looks like you only winged this other feller. I better make sure he ain't carrying a hideaway," Trevor said as he bent to search the man. It was then that Mathew noticed his wound.

"Why, you've been shot. There's some blood on the side of your coat."

Trevor looked at Mathew, "Well I figured since you got shot and all I would just even the score. The last thing I want to hear for the rest of my days is how you got shot and I didn't. Now we're even."

Trevor pulled a second Colt from the man's coat pocket. "Yeah, one of these two bastards got me when I stepped from the trees over there. Done more damage to my time piece than they did to me. I think that watch bit into my side and that's where the blood is coming from."

Trevor fished the old pocket watch from his pocket and held it out for Mathew to see. "Now look at that, busted all to hell."

"Better the watch than you. That must have been the shot I heard a little while ago. I figured you might need my help so I limped over as fast as I could. Looks like I got here none too soon either. I believe that first feller I shot was about to send you over the next rise."

"And then some," Trevor said.

After clearing the two men of guns and knives the two teamsters stood and looked over their surroundings. "You reckon there's any more of these bushwhackers about?" Mathew asked.

Trevor patted his shoulder and then his side; he had been shot but couldn't seem to find out where, other than in the watch. The blood must have come from a deep scratch near where the pocket watch had been. Still though, that watch couldn't have stopped a powerful bullet fired from a Winchester or Sharps.

"I think this here varmint you wounded might be able to answer that and I got a sure fire way of finding out. He stood over the man and asked, "You mind telling me if you got any more friends about, mister. It might make things go easier if you answer my question."

The man said through gritted teeth, "You go to hell!"

"I thought as much, mister," Trevor said.

Trevor pulled the big knife from his scabbard and slid it across the front of his pants as if he were wiping the blade clean. He knelt beside the man Mathew had shot and gently laid the knife on the man's chest and then released it, he then stood.

"Tell you what stranger; I got me a little game I used to play back in the war. You got one good arm and so do I. Now when I count to three we are both going to go for that knife. The first to grab it is to stick it clean through the other, you understand me mister or shall I explain it again?" Trevor said with an evil smile. The look on the wounded man's face changed from one of concern to one of pure hatred. "I'll be glad to play your little game fool, you say when."

Trevor smiled, "Alright then, instead of counting to three I'll just say when." After only a second Trevor said, "When!"

The wounded man reached for the knife with his one good arm knowing he could grab it and kill the old teamster before he even got the chance to bend at the knee. Trevor hadn't lied when he said he had played this little game before, just the fact that he was still alive meant he had never lost.

As the man wrapped his hand around the handle and prepared to raise the knife, Trevor, as quick as a cat, took his right foot and stomped the man's chest, the same spot where the man grabbed the knife. The force of the blow knocked the air out of the man's lungs; it also drove the knife sideways into the man's chest.

The man struggled to make a sound but finally managed to whisper, "You done killed me." With that his head rolled to the side and his eyes rolled back in their sockets. Trevor reached to pick up the knife but made sure the bandit was dead first.

"Now why do you suppose everyone we meet is trying to kill the two of us, now answer me that?" Trevor said as he wiped his knife off on the dead man's coat. "Also tell me how I got shot with a rifle and it only wounded my pocket watch?"

Mathew picked up the Sharps and examined it. "Good thing you was shot with this rather than that Winchester. This ain't more than a bird rifle."

Trevor took the Sharps and looked it over. Sure enough it was small caliber, something a man might use to shoot varmints.

"Looks like they only meant to wound me in order to get some information. That other feller was going to finish me off with his Winchester, that is until you killed him," Trevor said.

After a moment's thought Trevor added, "Now why do you figure everybody wants me and you dead and then to steal that wagon?"

Mathew rubbed his chin as he looked back in the direction of the freight wagon. "Can't rightly say, we don't have anything on that wagon that would warrant the deaths of so many men I reckon."

"Maybe not, but it seems that way. Five men dead and the two of us are still alive. Either the two of us are the luckiest buzzards this side of Hell or those five are the unluckiest," Trevor said as he picked up the guns that belonged to the two dead men.

"We better bring in them horses; you reckon that's the three that belong to the ones that tried to do us in last night?"

Trevor reached the weapons to Mathew. "That would be my guess; you suppose there are a couple of others tied out here somewhere"

"Most likely, let's go and have us a look," Mathew said. Fifteen minutes later both men were leading five horses back toward the freight wagon.

"Are we just going to leave these two here?" Mathew asked.

The Trail

"I reckon so, doubtful if they were going to give the two of us the pleasure of a burial. This time tomorrow the wolves will have cleaned up the mess for us anyway."

Both men hurried back to the freight wagon, neither liked to be out of sight of the rig for very long. Once the two broke from cover Satan gave a welcome snort. After all the mischief of the last few hours the big mule was on edge, he was anxious to get the hitch moving. Anywhere down the trail would be better than here. Less than an hour later the mules were hitched and the campsite put away. No one could tell the wagon had stayed the night, other than the dead bodies.

Mathew had managed to climb on top of the tarp that protected the freight from the weather. It was agreed he would lay prone and would be armed with the best of the long guns they had taken from the dead bandits, a seventeen shot Winchester model '73. It was chambered to use a .44-40 bullet, a potent weapon in that caliber.

It was agreed that since Mathew couldn't cover any amount of distance with his wounded leg that he would stay hidden on top of the freight wagon and not show himself unless circumstances warranted. Trevor would walk beside the hitch to give directions to the mules but it wasn't necessary. Satan knew where he was and he knew where he was going.

To Trevor's pleasant surprise the big lead mule was anxious and the pace he set was evident by this. Satan was moving at nearly half again the normal pace the hitch usually traveled. Trevor knew all eight mules were on edge; gunfire and dead bodies piling up in their wake made the animals want to get to a town, and a stable for that matter. Hell, he wanted the same thing but knew it was still a good three or four days away even at the pace Satan was going.

Nathan Wright

Silas Phillips was in a foul mood this Saturday morning. He was on his way to meet with his boss, a man by the name of William Butler. Silas was what most would consider the right hand man of Butler. The tasks he performed for his boss were, for the most part, legal, but there were a few that were not.

On more than a few occasions Silas had been asked to take care of a delicate situation, one that needed to be taken care of in the shadows of the night, not in the light of day. What endeared Silas to his boss was the fact that when he took on a job he finished it without any evidence left behind. At least not any evidence that would lead anyone back to Butler.

The suite of offices Butler occupied were situated in a nine story steel frame building with a masonry and stone exterior dubbed the world's first skyscraper. The building was located in the town of Chicago.

The offices were on the fifth floor, two floors below the offices of one of the most successful men in town, Wilbur Westbrook. Westbrook and Butler at times worked together when it benefited both men but usually their interests ran afoul of one another. For this reason there was the unwritten rule that Westbrook and his associates used the River Street entrance and Butler and his minions used the Lake Avenue entrance. Although both organizations had their offices in the same building it was almost as if they were separated by many miles. The arrangement suited both.

Silas patted the breast pocket of his jacket and felt the reassuring feeling of the Remington double Derringer hidden inside. The Derringer was a two-shot weapon and used a potent .41 caliber rimfire cartridge. The little hideaway had sufficient stopping power and could be well hidden in a coat or pants pocket. Silas wasn't expecting trouble today; if he was then he would also be carrying a second gun hidden in a shoulder holster, one that held more than two bullets.

As he made his way to the lobby for the Lake Avenue entrance a stiff breeze assaulted his face and exposed hands. The temperature this November day was twenty-five degrees, with the wind it felt more like ten. Silas pulled up the collar on his heavy coat and held a hand on his hat to keep it from blowing away; it wouldn't be the first hat he had lost in the Windy City.

When he finally made it through the double glass doors of the lobby he felt as if he was nearly frozen. "I'm getting too old for this," he said to no one in particular.

There were three men standing at the far wall, the wall where the staircase began. Silas eyed the three suspiciously, he hadn't seen any of the three before but he knew the look. As he approached the three took notice and each turned to face him. This was enough to stop Silas in his tracks. The look he was getting from the three was not accidental, it was deliberate and menacing.

Silas now had a problem, he faced three unknown men and all he had was a two shot Derringer. It was broad daylight and there were others in the busy lobby but this did little to soothe his anxiety. It wouldn't be the first time men pulled guns and started blasting away and to hell with the consequences. After only seconds, although it felt more like minutes, one of the men raised his hands, palms out, and approached Silas.

When the man was close enough to whisper he lowered his hands and said just loud enough to be heard, "Mister Westbrook would like to have a word with you."

Silas only looked at the man as he considered his options. If he refused then he wouldn't know what the powerful crime boss wanted with him. If he agreed then there was the slight chance he could be setting himself up for trouble, possibly serious trouble. Somehow though, he felt Westbrook wasn't going to do him harm today. If that were the case then it wouldn't be done in broad daylight.

"Alright, you lead the way," Silas said.

The man and his two companions turned and walked through the first floor eatery that connected the two lobbies. Once on the other side Silas took in the lobby that fronted River Street, it was his first time to be on this side of the building. The four men ascended the stairs that led from the River Street entrance to the seventh floor. The stairs were nearly identical to the ones on the Lake Avenue side of the building.

As the men climbed Silas couldn't help but pat the side of his coat that hid his gun, it helped to calm his nerves but he knew if trouble awaited then he and his little Derringer would come out on the losing end of things.

Once the four men reached the seventh floor they exited the stairwell into a lavish lobby staffed by a single man standing behind what looked like a well-polished bar, although small it was well stocked with any number of libations.

The man who had originally approached Silas downstairs stepped to the bar and said, "A gin and tonic for me, my friends here don't drink."

The man behind the bar didn't reach for a glass; he also didn't reach for the gin. What had just been said was a code which changed each day. If the order matched the code for that day then entrance to the suite of offices was granted. If it didn't then a drink would be produced and that was it. Just behind the bar and around the corner out of sight were two more men, both armed with twelve-gauge shotguns. If you gave the wrong password request then you better enjoy your drink and get out fast or you might be introduced to the two men in the back. All this caution was the first line of defense for the suite of offices, offices set up and orchestrated by Wilbur Westbrook.

The barkeep walked around the bar and proceeded to a heavy door opposite. He knocked twice and then the door opened. Standing just inside was another man wearing a fancy set of clothes and sporting a Smith and Wesson revolver in his right hand.

"Got the men Mister Westbrook is expecting out here," the barkeep said.

"Morning gentlemen, please step inside," said the stout looking man wearing a smart looking suit. He didn't offer a name, neither had the three that escorted Silas up the stairs. Even if a name had been offered it was doubtful if it was accurate. In this line of work shadows and secrecy was the norm.

Silas was impressed with the security; it was better than what his boss had on the other side of the building and two floors down. He would make sure to describe everything he saw and heard this morning.

The four men stepped inside and the heavy door was immediately closed and locked, the lock was impressive, as was the robust thickness of the door. Silas assumed this door was not the only means of either entering or exiting the suite. There was probably one more and possibly two other staircases for private use.

The four men were motioned toward a row of chairs and asked to be seated. If Silas had been worried earlier it was now replaced with an intense curiosity. He scanned the room intently, taking in every detail. He also noticed the bulge in the coat the heavy set man wore, no doubt a gun. Possibly a backup for the one he still held in his hand.

As the four sat Silas wondered what he had gotten himself into. Here he was sitting in the offices of his boss's main rival and he didn't even know why. He began to wonder if it might be possible to excuse himself but thought better of it. He had come this far, he would stay to find out what these men wanted.

Another door suddenly opened and an older man stepped out. He had the appearance of a bookkeeper, or accountant. Although he looked to be of advanced age, maybe sixty or sixty-five, he still looked to be a man that could take care of himself.

"Sorry to keep you waiting, Mister Phillips, the boss will see you now," the bookkeeper said.

Silas was surprised to hear his sir name used; these men probably knew more about him than he first thought. Silas stood and waited for his three escorts to stand, they didn't. His indecision was noticed by the bookkeeper, "The three men that escorted you here won't be joining us," he said.

Silas gave a quick glance to the three, the one that had spoken to him downstairs, the only one of the three to speak, gave him a nod. If Silas had apprehensions about what was going to happen before then they were now doubled. He turned back to the bookkeeper and followed him through this second layer of security.

The suite of offices was ornate, if such a word could be used for something as commonplace as an office. There was a wide hall that was adorned with paintings and live plants. There was an expensive rug that ran the middle of the hall and the whole place had the feel of a fine home rather than a place where business was conducted.

On a small table halfway down the corridor was a bible, it was opened to a passage but at the pace they were walking Silas was unable to identify what page, or passage, was referenced. He found it odd that a man who was noted for his rough business practices would keep a bible in the building at all. Maybe Westbrook managed to compartmentalize the different aspects of his life, a notorious business man by day and a bible toting upstanding citizen by night. The thought nearly made Silas laugh but he managed to reduce it to a silent chuckle.

Silas found the ornate walls, ceilings, and floors, to be an insult to the senses. He was a working man, although some of the things he considered work could be more properly describes as unlawfulness. All the same, Silas worked hard and in doing so had managed to improve his life to what he considered upper-class. Yet here he strode down what might be considered a palace, an ugly example of what money could do in the hands of the wrong types; he considered Wilbur Westbrook to be of the worst wrong type.

Being in this palace like place didn't suit Silas; he was more accustomed to being on the street doing the bidding of his own employer, William Butler. Most of what he was asked to do in his employment was on the up and up but on occasion he was asked to take care of a delicate situation here and there; a situation that fell on the other side of up and up.

If Silas found his days falling into a routine he took delight in the fact that soon there would be another job that might involve danger. Whether it be gun or knife he didn't care; what he really liked though was the use of his fists. Silas had grown up in the rougher neighborhoods of Chicago and in doing so had learned how to take care of himself, and others when they got in his way.

Silas Phillips was a killer. He managed to wait until he was fourteen before he killed his first victim, a policeman in the Westside Corner who had witnessed Silas coming out of a closed up shop in the dead of night. Rather than facing arrest and punishment Silas had simply killed the man. The murder was never solved by the department but the tenants of the Corner knew who did it, at least they had a good idea. Neighborhoods were filled with tenants who talked and when something like the murder of a policeman took place it didn't take long until the gossip mill came up with a suspect and it was surprising how often the rumor-mongers got it right.

Silas still had the gun he had taken from the dead cop. It wasn't anything he carried but he still had it hidden for future use, a use that had yet to present itself but the day would come, he knew it would. The weapons he used since then were of a more common variety that could be easily discarded at the bottom of a river or in the foundations of some building under construction.

During Silas's career as a fixer he had assumed any number of aliases. Once he had even dressed as a Chicago policeman in order to gain entrance to a residence that was owned by a man that had ran afoul of Mister Butler. After the deed was done all that was left behind for the real authorities was a dead body and an abandoned policeman's uniform. Silas had even thought of dressing his victim in the uniform but decided against it when he considered having to look at the man's naked body while he tried to re-dress him.

Silas lived alone, where he called home was anybody's guess. It wasn't the kind of information he shared even with those that considered him a friend. He slept better at night knowing he was just another face among the masses. He liked to consider himself as someone that blended in well among the throngs that inhabited the crowded tenements of the city.

Silas was smart and anyone that knew him knew he was a man not to be trifled with. Brains, brawn, and a skillset that suited violence were three things he possessed. Any two would make for a formidable adversary; all three made him one of the most deadly men in the city.

Silas was a mystery among those that claimed to know him. Some men felt themselves lucky to be his friend. Those that were his enemy found it necessary to avoid him, and his corner of the city, altogether. It was believed that a long ago hit on Silas, one that was never fulfilled, was still in effect. Others thought the two men that were given the job had simply taken the money for the hit and left town. The truth was that the two men had found Silas at an inopportune time, inopportune for them; their bodies were never recovered.

Silas followed the stout man down the hallway all the while flexing his shoulders to warm his muscles; if violence was in store then he wanted to be as ready as possible. The two men turned right and headed down another hall, not as long as the first but a hallway just the same. At the end was a door and standing at that door were two men, both of above average size. Silas wondered why anyone would need armed guards standing by their office door the entire day. What he didn't know was that most of the blustering being put on was being staged just for Silas. Wilbur Westbrook was sending a message, one he was sure Silas would share with his boss.

The two guards recognized the man escorting Silas and stepped to the side so the two could enter. The stout man didn't knock; he simply turned the knob and slowly pushed the door open, another thick heavy door.

The man stepped inside and Silas followed. If he was expecting Westbrook's office to be a reflection of the rest of the suite he was mistaken. The main office was manly and functional. Not to say it wasn't elaborate, it was, but it was done in a more restrained fashion.

There was an abundance of bookshelves that nearly covered one entire wall. At the end of the bookshelves there was a small bar not unlike the one at the top of the stairs. There was a door to one side which was open and revealed a lavatory, an elaborate lavatory. The two corner walls had large glass windows at the converging ends revealing an amazing view of the city, or at least as much as you could see from this height.

"Come in, gentlemen, I've been expecting you. Have a seat, Mister Phillips, while Felix prepares us a drink. What will you have?" Westbrook asked.

Silas was caught off guard by the friendly demeanor of Westbrook and the offer of a drink at such an early hour. He wasn't opposed to drinking before noon, as a matter of fact he enjoyed a stiff shot many mornings to steel his nerves for the duties he was required to carry out during the day.

"Good day to you, sir, I suppose straight bourbon for me," Silas said.

Apparently the stout man was named Felix since there was no one else in the room other than Silas and Westbrook. The man named Felix went straight to the bar and took down two glasses; this wasn't lost on Silas, Felix wasn't going to join them in a drink.

"Have a seat, Mister Phillips, while your drink is being poured." Westbrook motioned to one of the leather chairs in front of his desk. Not a minute later Felix reappeared with two glasses of which he reached one to Silas and the other to Westbrook. Both looked to have the same dark liquid but Silas wasn't sure, he now wished he had observed whether both were poured from the same bottle. He wasn't really afraid of being poisoned but in the business he was in it paid to notice everything, something he had just now failed to do. Oh well, maybe the drink was fine, why would they do away with him here in this office when it would have been more practical to make the attempt someplace else? Silas waited for Westbrook to take a sip, he would decide later if he was going to sample his drink.

After the drinks were distributed Felix took the seat beside Silas and both men waited for Westbrook to speak. Before saying anything Westbrook took a slow pull on his drink and then sat the glass on his desk. He glanced toward the window and seemed to be weighing what he wanted to say.

Finally he looked back toward the two men, Silas in particular and said, "Mister Phillips, I would like to speak frankly with you, probably more so than you are accustomed to. I would also like you to do the same with me; I feel the two of us can come to terms more quickly if we dispense with the pleasantries and just get down to business. Do you agree?"

Silas found this refreshing, he didn't like being here and if blunt talk got him back on the street faster then he was all for it. "That sounds fine with me, Mister Westbrook."

"Your boss, Mister Butler, and I have been doing business in and around Chicago for a number of years now and there has been only an occasion or two where our interests have, what word shall I use? Collided I suppose would describe it best. Are you aware of those events, Mister Phillips?"

Silas knew more than he would let on but he was sufficiently up to date to know there had been a couple of small wars over the years that had resulted in a number of deaths. "As with any venture there will always be disagreements I suppose," he said.

Westbrook smiled, he realized his information on Silas Phillips was accurate; he was slightly dangerous and extremely intelligent. "I would like to meet with your boss if arrangements could be made that would be satisfactory to each of us. Do you think something like that could be arranged?"

Silas was surprised by the request but managed to keep a poker face. In all his years and dealings with adversaries he had trained himself to have complete control over his facial muscles as to not convey what he was really thinking. "Possibly, but I would need to know the particulars of what matters are to be discussed in order for my boss to weigh the importance of such a meeting."

What Silas was most concerned about was the security of his boss while such a meeting took place. It wouldn't be the first time someone had attended a meeting and then disappeared. With the amount of money both men skimmed off the streets it would be highly advantageous for one, or the other, to meet an unfortunate end.

"The matter I wish to discuss is important, more so to me than your boss, but important all the same. It is also time sensitive, I need to see Mister Butler sometime this afternoon if arrangements could be made."

Silas was again caught off guard, how could any meeting take place on such short notice? He was confident his boss would not agree to a meeting with so little notice. "All I can promise is to carry the request to my boss. If he agrees or if he declines, I was wondering how I could get the answer to you. I doubt I would be allowed back into your offices without an escort." Silas wouldn't come back here again unless his boss instructed him to.

Westbrook smiled, "That won't be a problem. I'll have Felix Johnson here stationed in the adjoining lobby for the next two hours; he can escort you back here once you've had a chance to talk to Mister Butler. Is that acceptable to you?"

Silas now knew the full name of Felix. He tried to think, somehow he knew the name Felix Johnson but at the moment he couldn't place where he had heard the name before. "All I can promise is that I will talk to my boss. I can't even promise I will be able to give you his reply. In matters such as this I leave it up to Mister Butler as to whether I bring back his reply or not."

Westbrook figured as much, it's how he would have handled the situation if the tables were turned. "I appreciate your being candid in this matter. Tell your boss I can guarantee the time spent will be prosperous. I feel I have kept you long enough. Felix will see you to the door, Mister Phillips, thank you for your time. I look forward to a reply." With that said Westbrook stood and walked back to the window. He never offered a handshake and this suited Silas just fine.

After exiting the suite of offices Silas walked down the seven flights of stairs. He was deep in thought, mainly what could have been important enough to warrant a meeting between two of the leading crime bosses in the city, two men who at times were in fierce competition with each other. If Silas had begun his day hoping for a little peace and quiet he was now sorely mistaken.

The town of Chicago had enjoyed several years of mostly uninterrupted peace, something unusual for such a booming town with a growing immigrant population. The last time Chicago had seen anything close to a war between some of the opposing crime families in the city was six years prior. Before that little skirmish was over nearly forty men had been killed, including six police officers.

The year had been 1880; a year that started out peaceful enough but soon trouble began brewing. The friction was caused by a growing population and the dwindling availability of housing. Some of the tenement owners were allowing as many as four families to live in a three room shotgun apartment that was built for one family. The owners of several of the tenements came up with the plan of charging, not by the apartment, but by how many families lived there.

The plan was ill conceived from the beginning and tensions began to rise and soon boiled over. It wasn't the families that were causing the troubles, as one might expect. It was the owners of the properties. With all the money being made off ramshackle buildings it wasn't long before some of the more prosperous slum lords began trying to acquire buildings owned by some of their lessor competitors.

Deeds were altered at the courthouse with the ease that only a well-greased palm can accomplish. Both Westbrook and

Butler had city clerks on their payrolls; it was only a matter of how many loosely prepared deeds could be found and then altered. If a building owner didn't have the funds to litigate then he was forced to sell his property for a pittance of what it was really worth.

If the two men's connections in the courthouse weren't enough to acquire a target property then a little intimidation would usually do the trick. Most of the owners of the tenements in the city were men that weren't accustomed to violence, something Butler and Westbrook thrived on. Even the owners whose deeds were solid found themselves anxious to sell rather than face the consequences, consequences that could mean staring down the end of a gun, or even worse, a knife. Most men would rather face a gun than a knife; it just seemed to be human nature.

Silas reached the bottom of the stairs and then, rather than going the shortest route through the adjoining restaurant, he exited the building and walked to the Lake Avenue entrance by way of the street. He needed the few extra minutes this would afford him to sort out his thoughts; it had been an unusual morning to say the least.

Once at the Lake Avenue lobby he was met by two men that he considered as only acquaintances even though the two worked for the same man he did, William Butler. He knew the two but then again what he knew amounted to almost nothing. His senses were on high alert as they approached.

"Morning, Silas, Mr. Butler wants a word with you, that is if you got time after your little meeting with Wilbur Westbrook," one of the two, an unlikable fellow by the name of Onis Barnett, said.

Silas might have been employed by the same man as these two but it didn't mean he was on friendly terms with either. "If you got something to say Onis then say it. Otherwise keep your thoughts and opinions to yourself," Silas told the grinning bastard.

The look on Onis's face went from every day ugly to vicious in an instant. "You watch yourself, Silas; otherwise I might be obliged to teach you some manners."

Silas never broke his stride, he just marched up to the two men; as he drove a fist into the second man's stomach he grabbed Onis with his other hand. "I'm here right now, why don't we talk about those manners before I go up to see the boss?"

Onis tried to pull free but found Silas to be a powerful man. After a second or two of struggle he said, "I reckon you got some explaining to do to the old man once we make it upstairs. I done told him about your little meeting with Westbrook."

Silas had to strain against the impulse to beat Onis to death right here in the Lake Avenue lobby but managed to contain his anger, at least for the moment. The man he hit had managed to regain his feet and by the look on his face he wasn't anxious to go another round with Silas.

Silas released the collar of Onis Barnett and then put a finger in his face, "I don't like either of you and I don't like the implications about where I've been and what I've been doing. I have been doing the boss's work, which is more than I can say for the two of you. Both of you insult my name again and I will deal with you more harshly than I have just now. Consider this as just a small taste of what might happen the next time you cross *Me*." Silas said the word '*Me*' with as much emphasis as possible, both men knew he wasn't exaggerating. With that Silas turned and headed up the stairs followed closely by his tormentors.

Willian Butler was a man of roughly sixty years of age but still had the look of a man that could take care of himself. Most men that lived to the half-century mark usually took on the look of age, not Butler. He was fit and still sported a mop of disheveled hair that men half his age would have been proud of. His hair was still dark with only a slight graying above the side whiskers which most found gave him a grandfatherly appearance, although one that demanded respect.

Butler was standing in the front office talking to the Bookkeeper, a man with no apparent name other than the Bookkeeper. His real name wasn't known to any of the people that worked in the offices, only Butler knew his real name. This was by design rather than any oversite. Butler knew the less that anyone knew about his chief bookkeeper the better. Some of the Bookkeeper's responsibilities, if not most, regarded the handling of money. This, Butler considered, was best kept secret.

"Good morning, Silas, come in. I would like to have a word with you," Butler said with a smile.

Silas stepped into the office, one he had been in any number of times. only now realized just how plain the tastes of his boss were compared to that of Wilbur Westbrook. The office had none of the darkly stained woods or the corner bar. There wasn't a double corner window looking out over some of the more expensive sections of Chicago. In fact the single window in Butler's office simply faced out toward another building. It was functional as a means of brightening the room but afforded none of the views that could be admired from the side of the building Wilbur Westbrook's office occupied.

"Have a seat, Silas, would you like a cigar?"

Butler might not have a fancy bar in his office but he did have a selection of some very expensive cigars. Having a drink earlier in the office of Westbrook and now a fine cigar in the office of Butler was a welcome addition to the stress of the morning. Silas reached for the cigar that was offered, both men lit up and took their first puffs.

The two men that had tried to accost Silas downstairs weren't offered a cigar, they hadn't even been allowed inside Butler's office. They were stationed in the front office, both men stewed at being bested by Silas downstairs and now shunned by Butler.

After a few moments Butler decided to get right to the point. "Westbrook is an eccentric son of a bitch in my view. You've now met the man so please tell me your take on the matter, Silas."

After a couple of puffs Silas conveyed the message he was told to bring to Butler. "My chat was pleasant enough; in the few minutes I spent in the man's presence I found him to be courteous and well-mannered but that is just an observation. That opinion could change immensely if I were the one dealing with him. What we discussed was a possible meeting between you and him that apparently needs to take place this afternoon. He stressed the importance of the matter to be discussed and that a substantial amount of money was at stake."

Butler rolled the cigar between the thumb and fingers of his left hand as he listened to Silas. The news he just heard had been expected. "I knew he would want to talk, I just didn't know it would be so soon. Meet his contact and inform him I will be available to meet in two hours. As for the location, I recommend the courthouse in the chambers of Judge Duncan. I will have you attend and he can also bring someone of his choosing. As he and I both know, all four of us will be searched at the doors to the courtroom and relieved of any firearms we possess. Tell him it's the only agreeable spot that guarantees the safety of all those concerned."

Silas was impressed at how quickly Butler had formulated the plan; it was nothing short of brilliant. "I was instructed to meet a man by the name of Felix Johnson; he is waiting in the ground floor restaurant for your reply."

"Alright then, head back down and set the meeting. If all is agreeable then come back up immediately," Butler said.

Twenty minutes later Silas was back, the meeting was set for 1:00 that afternoon. It would be Wilbur Westbrook and Felix Johnson attending, along with William Butler and whoever he chose. Silas was again informed he would be going along with his boss, this suited him fine.

At one o'clock sharp the four men presented themselves at the courthouse and were immediately searched before being allowed access to Judge Duncan's chambers. The judge was glad to accommodate the two men. It wasn't often that he associated with leaders of Chicago's underworld, at least outside the courtroom. The judge had struck an arrangement a couple of years earlier in which he would steer trials one way or the other depending on which was monetarily more advantageous to the aging judge. It wasn't uncommon for the legal system to be influenced by money; it had just taken Chicago a few more years to follow the lead of New York.

Nathan Wright

The judge met the two men, along with their seconds, at the door to his chambers and offered each a seat. Once the four were seated the judge, rather than walking around and sitting at his large desk, just went to the front and sat on the edge.

Judge Curtis Duncan was a man of about sixty-five. He was tall and thin, almost to the point of being skinny. He had a narrow face and sported a full head of graying hair although it appeared to be thinning at the corners. He wore mutton chop whiskers which seemed to be the fad of the day. He wore a heavily starched white shirt with a solid black bowtie. If anyone didn't know better the judge might be mistaken for an undertaker.

"Gentlemen, I would like to thank you for discussing your endeavors in this fashion rather than the style that has been known to be used in the past," the judge said. Every man in the room knew what he was referring to when he said, *style that has been used in the pa*st, it was a reference to gunplay and murder.

"If the two of you can come to an agreement then it will most likely save a few lives and also not clutter up my docket. I also expect to benefit from this meeting, the same as before plus twenty-five percent if that is satisfactory with each of you," the judge said as he looked at Westbrook and Butler.

The two men knew they would pay whatever the judge asked. More than a few of the tenement building problems came before the Honorable Curtis Duncan and in every case he had taken care of the two bosses sitting before him today. In the rare event a case involved both men it was prearranged as to the outcome. They won alternately, this arrangement was acceptable to both.

The Trail

Now that the judge had laid out the rules in which the game would be played he walked around to his chair and sat down. He would listen to everything said between the two men. No notes would be taken at this meeting, they never were. The judge was here for two reasons. First was to establish his fee, second was to be the arbiter in case either of the two men disputed the terms of the agreement later on.

Butler turned his gaze from the judge to Westbrook. "You arranged this meeting now what is it that's on your mind?"

Westbrook leaned back in his chair and crossed a leg over a knee. "I have a situation out west that really doesn't concern you but felt if you and I worked together on this it would be advantageous to the both of us."

Butler assumed he had just been lied to. If Westbrook could do the deal without him he wouldn't hesitate. What he now suspected was that Westbrook was somehow in over his head and needed a little more muscle to get what he wanted.

"What kind of situation are you talking about?" Butler asked.

Butler could tell that Westbrook was on the spot. Something had happened beyond his control and now it appeared he needed the help of his main adversary.

"Do you know a man by the name of Raymond Dinsmore?"

Butler only took a second to respond. "I did know of him, he's dead."

"Yes, quite so. He was a reporter for the Chicago Post-Dispatch," Westbrook said.

"I am aware of who he worked for," Butler said. He was also aware of the situation of the man's unfortunate death. He had been missing for more than three months and his body was never found. He had only been declared dead the previous week and the order was signed by none other than Judge Duncan.

"At any rate, I thought you might want to hear the latest article the good reporter had been working on for the last year and a half. It pertained to organized crime in the City of Chicago and its connection to the court system," Westbrook said.

Butler noticed the judge seemed uncomfortable at the mention of the court system being mixed up in any way with a crime. Undoubtedly the good judge was mentioned in the article and probably not in a good way.

"This seems to be a matter that pertains to you and the judge here, why bring me into your plans?" Butler asked, possibly more harshly than he intended.

The judge snapped out of his momentary daze and pointed a finger at Butler, "Now see here, I will not be connected to any crime by you, Mister Butler. I also don't like the manner in which you speak."

Butler wasn't about to be preached to by a dishonest judge about tone and ethics. "Well, Judge, I really don't care what you think about the manner in which I express myself in your chambers. The way I see it the three of us are peas in a pod here. Although you stand to lose more than the rest of us because of your position. Now you can leave the judge talk out of this conversation for the remainder of our little meeting if you don't mind."

Duncan knew his little outburst was misplaced. Butler was right about the fact that he had more to lose than the two men seated before him. They were both criminals and the profession they had chosen came with a certain amount of risk. He though, was a judge and was held in high esteem by the people who had elected him. How would those same people feel about him if they saw the company he now kept?

Now Duncan went back into judge mode, anything to steer the conversation away from himself. "Gentlemen, if the two of you could stick to the topic at hand."

Westbrook was amused at the uncomfortable situation the judge now found himself in, he decided to move on.

"At any rate, Mister Dinsmore's article was a project he had been working on for quite some time. I was kept abreast of the situation and the articles progress by a couple of employees at the Dispatch. They assured me that I would be notified prior to publication. I had a standing agreement with my sources that once the article was finished I would have access to everything written, that would also include all the notes and research material of Mister Dinsmore," Westbrook said.

Now the picture was becoming more clear to Butler. Raymond Dinsmore had been primarily working on the connections between Wilbur Westbrook and Judge Duncan. There were still quite a few unanswered questions and Butler was sure he was about to hear the answers.

"Please continue," Butler said.

Westbrook cleared his throat and then continued. "One of my sources at the Dispatch double-crossed me. At the last minute the man must have let his conscience overrule his better judgement, he notified Dinsmore and told him that I knew everything and planned to squash the story before it made it to press. My second source managed to steal the work and brought it to me. Dinsmore immediately disappeared and I hoped that was the end of it."

"Dinsmore just disappeared. Now how could you accept the fact that your troubles disappeared with him?" Butler asked.

Westbrook looked at the judge; he was searching for a way to make his mistakes in these matters seem more the fault of others rather than a misstep on his part.

"I had the materials and the reporter was gone, I assumed that would be the end of it."

"The reporter was gone. How could you know this to be true, maybe he was just on a little holiday after completing such a work as you describe. That is unless you were certain he was gone, as in gone for good. Did you have him silenced?" Butler asked.

"No, I did not, but I wish I had. I hoped another of the men mentioned in the article might have gotten word of it and killed Dinsmore. After a few weeks I assumed the situation was under control. I had the article along with all the research and Dinsmore was missing and presumed dead. I now know that isn't the case."

"So what is the case?" Butler asked.

"Before Dinsmore disappeared he mailed a package. No one knows what the package contains," Westbrook said.

Butler looked at the judge and then Westbrook. He knew the implication but wanted to hear what the two men thought.

"Let me see if I understand. The journalist, Mister Dinsmore, is missing and presumed dead. Killed not by you but by another member of our little club that might be mentioned in the article Dinsmore had just finished and was only hours away from publishing in the largest newspaper in the city. The story and all the research are in your possession and I assume either locked up tight or destroyed. Do I have it right so far?" Butler asked.

"You are correct, but the article hasn't been destroyed. It contains information that might be useful in the future if you know what I mean?" Westbrook said.

Butler smiled. "You kept it to use for blackmail or bribery, whichever might be more useful to you. I understand all that, I might have done the same myself. There must be another piece to this story because what you've told me so far seems to be nicely tied up, no loose ends."

"If the story ended there then you would be correct, everything is nicely tied up. It seems though, a loose end has popped up. I managed to learn what the package contained and where it's heading. It appears the reporter made a copy of his research material along with a complete duplicate of the article he was about to run," Judge Duncan told Butler. It was the first he had spoken since being dressed down earlier by Butler.

Butler smiled, something just came to mind. "Neither of you have indicated that I am mentioned in the article. I believe this because if I were mentioned then the two of you would have brought that up earlier as a way to garner my assistance in this matter. Am I correct in my assumption?"

"You are correct. I have read the materials and also the article and you aren't mentioned. You are also correct in the fact that I would have led off with that little tidbit in order to gain your assistance free of charge. As it is, I must offer you a deal in which you stand to make a great deal of money. A deal that I would otherwise not offer in a million years," Westbrook said.

Butler wasn't ready just yet to join forces with this man, or the judge for that matter. He still didn't have all the information or what was expected of him.

"If you know what's in the package and where it will arrive then why is this a problem? Just have someone take possession of it when it arrives."

Both Westbrook and the judge looked uncomfortable. "As you know I have contacts out west, you and I have been competitors long enough to know quite a bit about each other's operations. My contacts in the west seem to not be up to the job. More than one of my, let's say employees, has made the attempt to intercept the package and have been unsuccessful."

"I assume there have been some deaths involved?"

Again Westbrook and the judge took on the look of two men that would rather not be here discussing their misdeeds and missteps. "Let's just say I've used some of my best contacts out there against what I assumed to be easy targets and have not gotten the results that I expected." Westbrook said.

Now the judge leaned forward, elbows on the edge of his desk, and said, "Every man he's used out there is either dead or locked up. I had hoped this issue would have been resolved long before now but it hasn't. The only reason you are here is because we are out of options. I still don't like sharing this type of information with a man like you, Mister Butler, but as I've said, we have no choice."

Westbrook stood and walked to a cabinet at the back wall of the judge's chambers. He opened a drop wing door to reveal a small liquor shelf. The door was held in place by a small chain on each side to make a small shelf. Westbrook looked over at Felix Johnson and said, "How about fixing a few drinks? Please include yourself and Mister Phillips."

The Trail

As Felix stood and headed toward the liquor cabinet Westbrook walked to the judge's side table and opened the lid to what looked to be a very expensive humidor. Inside he noticed several varieties of cigars, again what looked to be an expensive selection. After choosing one he looked at Butler, "Would you join me in a smoke? The judge keeps a very nice selection and I'm sure he won't mind."

Butler looked at the judge who didn't seem to be put out in the least. It was apparent that Westbrook spent some time in chambers with the judge discussing topics that otherwise should be discussed in the main courtroom in front of a jury.

"I believe I would like a cigar. Please choose the same as you're having," Butler said.

As Felix made the drinks Butler took in the office. It was his first opportunity since entering the room to take in the surroundings made available to a judge. The room itself was adorned in a darkly stained wood not unlike the main courtroom. This of course was part of the building and paid for at taxpayers' expense. What Butler really wanted to see was the personal effects of the judge to determine his station in life.

The drinks Felix was preparing was being poured from a selection of bottles none of which seemed to be of a cheap variety. There were at least three types of Kentucky Bourbon and this Butler knew to not be cheap.

The humidor on the side table was of a style that looked imported, possibly from Spain, or maybe Italy. The judge's clothes were of the finest quality and cut. Even the derby hanging by the door looked to be of the highest quality and most likely imported. In the judge's right front vest pocket hung the links of a gold watch chain. The watch wasn't visible but going by the other items the judge kept in his office Butler assumed it was hand crafted overseas just like so many of the judge's other belongings.

Butler was startled back to the here and now by Felix who was reaching him a drink. The glass looked to be of crystal, not unaffordable by any means but still expensive none the less. In the glass sharing space with the amber colored liquid was not less than three ice cubes. Either the judge had his ice chest stocked just for this meeting or he had ice on a daily basis. Probably the latter.

Only the judge, Westbrook and Butler had the option of a cigar. Felix and Silas did each have a drink but no smoke. Butler assumed it was to limit the amount of cigar smoke in the room. With three of the things going it would still be a bit smoky, but smokers really didn't mind.

"So now that I have all the particulars, or at least all you feel comfortable sharing with me, what is it you propose?" Butler asked.

Westbrook took a puff of his cigar and then exhaled mightily toward the ceiling before saying, "This is my suggestion. You use your contacts out west to acquire the package and find Mister Dinsmore. The package and all its contents are to be returned safely to me. Mister Dinsmore is to remain out west, indefinitely."

The word *indefinitely* was said slowly and with emphasis. The meaning couldn't have been made clearer.

"The west is a big place. Do you have a location?"

"I do, but before I give you any more details I need to know if you are interested in my proposition." Westbrook said as he took a sip of his bourbon.

"Before I agree I would like to hear of my compensation. You mentioned it would be substantial."

The Trail

"As you know the two of us control a substantial portion of the tenements in Chicago Proper. If you deliver the two items mentioned earlier then I am willing to turn over control of everything in the southwest corner from Seventh North over to Wisshier Street. This will put you on par and equal footing with me in that quarter of the city," Westbrook said.

Butler didn't smile, he didn't frown either. He kept a poker face as his mind did the math. As was mentioned earlier the opportunity was a nice one. The area mentioned would increase Butler's holding in that section of town by more than fifty percent. But, if Westbrook was willing to give away so much then wasn't it possible he was willing to give more?

"Seventh North won't quite cut it for me. I am satisfied with the boundary at Wisshier Street but feel Eighth North would be a more reasonable offer," Butler said.

Without hesitation Westbrook stood and stuck out a hand. "You have got yourself a deal. Now assuming you keep your end of the bargain I will sign over control of every building within the agreed upon boundaries once I have the packet and assurances that Mister Dinsmore is resting comfortable in his grave."

Butler stood and the two men shook. Judge Duncan raised his glass and drained it. No sooner was it empty than he stood and went to the liquor cabinet and refilled it. There was no way of hiding his delight at having a plan in place to deal with something that could possibly have ended his career and sent him to prison. At his age any sentence above ten years would be a life sentence.

After refilling his glass he walked back to where Westbrook and Butler were standing and said, "Gentlemen I propose a toast." The other two quickly retrieved their glasses and the three held their drinks aloft. "To success," Duncan said as each man took a sip.

"The location where the package was sent is a hole in the wall little town by the name of Clear Creek, Colorado. No telegraph, no rail depot, not much of anything really. It does have a town sheriff who is assisted by one deputy. Both men are honest and as far as I can tell above corruption. Believe me we have tried.

"We got one man locked up there now and as far as we know he hasn't talked. How he got locked up is anybody's guess but I assume he got himself drunk and then got himself arrested. The mail to that little out of the way place is delivered by freight wagon and the trip is, to say the least, brutal. No less than eleven or twelve days at best.

We had a man in the town of Bristle Buck where the freight wagon was loaded but he was unable to access the mailbag, of which there are three and the package could be in any one of them. There are two teamsters driving the wagon and they've been taking care of that job for five or six years now. Honest men is what I'm told, both up in years but still capable. Both fought in the war so each have skills of the type that makes them dangerous characters when backed into a corner.

"I've got eight more men trying to intercept the wagon but don't know if they have been successful or not," Westbrook said.

Butler thought there was more information here and he needed to know everything if he was going to have any success. "How is it you have information this current if the trip from Clear Creek to the nearest town with a telegraph is eleven days away?"

The Trail

"The eleven day trip is for the freight wagon, it's the only road suitable for wagons. There is a pass through the mountains, a pass suitable for a rider on horseback only. Two days if a man pushes it and has a spare horse to switch out every few hours. A little less than two days actually. I got four men riding that trail, two each day so my news is always less than twenty four hours old," Westbrook said with a bit of pride in his tone. It was apparent this was at least a bit of organizational skill the Westbrook operation could crow about. So far it was about the only thing Westbrook's men had done right.

Butler was growing tired of the meeting. Not that he wouldn't benefit from the deal, he would. He had other things to attend to and now for some reason this new deal would take front and center stage. It wouldn't be a bother; it was a challenge, a challenge with a substantial reward at its conclusion.

"Timeframe?" Butler asked.

"Yesterday wouldn't be soon enough," the judge said.

Butler suspected as much but there was one last thing that needed to be worked out before he left the judge's chambers. "The titles to the tenements in question, how and when will I acquire them.

The judge opened a side drawer to his desk and pulled out a sheaf of papers, titles and deeds by all appearances. "Every title previously mentioned is here Mister Butler, I have reviewed them myself and I can assure you that all are here."

"How can they all be in that bundle Judge? The original offer was everything to Seventh North, Mister Westbrook and I agreed to extend the deal to Eight North," Butler said.

The judge started laughing. "Thanks to your alteration to the original deal I now owe Mister Westbrook a C-Note. He told me you would insist on this exact change to the original deal and I bet him hundred bucks that there was no way he could know that. I lost."

For the judge to have just lost a hundred dollars, not a small amount of money no matter who you were, and was laughing about it indicated the judge was reaping a huge profit from his dealings with Westbrook.

Butler looked at Westbrook who was smiling. "Glad to know I'm that predictable," Butler said as he also started laughing.

Once the men got hold of their emotions they stood and headed for the door. Butler and Silas headed for the front door of the courthouse while Westbrook and Felix headed for the back. Neither wanted to be seen coming out of Chicago's main courthouse building together.

Butler went straight to his office and began making plans on how to proceed. The judge and Westbrook were correct in their assumptions that Butler had a network out west. He had been cultivating land agreements and taking over proposed right of way needed by any future railroad expansions in the territory. All the most attractive routes heading west would need to go through at least a portion of the properties Butler held. Even if he didn't own a property outright he managed to purchase options as first bidder. If a railroad approached a landowner they had to deal with Butler before they could acquire a clean bill of sale. Nothing about this was illegal; it was actually something politicians practiced every day.

The first thing to do was find out who was the closest to the town of Clear Creek and get them there fast.

The Trail

Around three in the afternoon two men rode into the town of Clear Creek, Colorado, looking tired and nearly frozen. Both men wore heavy dusters against the wind and cold, it appeared the dusters barely did the job. With hats pulled low and gloved hands on the reins both men scanned the town, a place neither had ever had the opportunity to visit before. The deterioration in the weather, added to the fall in temperatures the previous day, was starting to feel like a deep freeze, maybe one for the record books.

The two men rode stout horses and led another horse that was used as a pack animal; the three horses didn't seem to mind the weather. What they did mind was the trail they had traveled for the last week, it was wintertime barren and sparse to boot. Now a horse likes to nibble, it likes to nibble during the night when not on the trail and it likes to nibble during the day, pulling tasty tidbits whenever the opportunity presents itself. This late in the season, and this far north, meant the pickings were meager at best. All three horses looked the town over, same as the two men. They each knew the sight of a town usually meant a stall, along with hay and grain. At the moment the three horses were doing their thinking with their stomachs.

The two men who rode the horses knew the horses had suffered during the last week. Both men, while on the trail, tried to find campsites that offered good water and a stand of winter sage, they had little luck. The spots where they bedded down during the frigid nights had little in the way of forage for the three horses. There was still some grain in the sack on the back of the packhorse and this did allow the three a half scoop apiece each evening. Now a horse really likes a bite of grain each day but that doesn't take away the need to forage.

The older of the two men that rode into town on such a frigid day was a man by the name of James Arthur Pack, he hailed from Arizona. His companion was Leroy Cobb, a man that hailed from nowhere in particular. If Cobb called anywhere home then he didn't mention it often enough for those that assumed to know him to remember. Maybe this was by design; it wouldn't be the first time a man disappeared into the vastness of the west in order to escape memories, or troubles, that dwelled back east.

"Cobb, what do you say we get these horses set up at the livery before we search out a hotel for the night? I think Samson here has had about enough of the short rations he's been getting lately," Pack said.

Cobb was looking the town over as he answered, "Good idea, Pack. Old Sidestep here has been whispering lately about how she would like a week or two off to get her figure back in shape." Cobb always acted as if the mare could really talk. Sometimes on the trail he would ask the horse a question and then tell Pack what her answer was. It was just a little good natured humor riders used at times to entertain themselves. Sometimes acting a little crazy kept a man from really heading in that direction.

Cobb's horse had gotten the name 'Sidestep' because of the way she trotted, a little sideways. No amount of coaxing could convince Sidestep to march straight. If you tried to pull her head around for too long while trying to straighten her out then you were at risk of getting bitten while you rode, and if not now then you were sure to get the teeth at the next opportunity. Cobb had finally given up on trying to make the horse trot normal, after a couple of severe bites he thought going sideways suited him just fine.

At the downwind end of town was a building with a gambrel roof, always the sign of a livery stable. There was a small carved wooden sign on the front but the distance was too great for the men to read what the sign said. As they approached Cobb mumbled, "Buster Adam's, Livery and Blacksmith."

"That looks like the place to be in this kind of weather Cobb," Pack said. Anywhere with a roof was the place to be in this kind of weather Pack thought.

Cobb snorted, "If you are a horse or mule it might be. I myself prefer a mattress and a meal. And I prefer it sooner rather than later. My aching bones tell me I'm getting a little long in the tooth to be out in this kind of weather. I need hot food and stove warmed air. I figure maybe one more year and I'll have you trained well enough that I can settle down on my place and watch the world go by from the front porch. I would have already been there but you're taking a little longer to learn the ropes than I first expected." Cobb began to laugh after saying this. Pack was the older of the two and also the one with the most experience.

"Did you figure that all by yourself or was it something Sidestep told you?" Pack asked.

"I reckon Sidestep mentioned it a day or two back. She said if you were a little bit smarter then she could have already been back on the farm keeping her pasture grazed down. Said she really misses her stall and pasture, said you was a dumbass." Again Cobb laughed.

Pack looked at the horse and then at Cobb. He laughed himself.

"I agree with most of what you said. I also believe between you and Sidestep she's the one with the brains. We'll ask about a hotel after the horses are settled in. We might need to be here at least two days to allow the three some feed and rest," Pack said. He knew the three horses needed rest as bad as he and Cobb did.

"That's what I'm saying, feed and rest. I believe I could use it as much as the horses. Bedding down on frozen ground and scorching one side of my trousers at a time against a camp fire gets old real fast," Cobb told Pack. The two had ridden together for the better part of a year and Pack had grown accustomed to the blunt talk of his friend. One reason he tolerated it was the fact that Cobb always seemed to say what was already on Pack's mind. Sometimes he it even sounded as if Cobb was repeating him.

Pack chuckled. Living out in the open this far north and this late in the year was not only inconvenient, it was downright dangerous. It was times like these when men went missing without a word or a trace. It wasn't uncommon for a man to freeze to death out in the wilderness. Hell it was dangerous enough in summer when the sun shined bright and the temperatures moderated. Even if the weather didn't kill you then there were a hundred other ways for a man to die.

Both men stepped off their mounts and tied them to the hitch rail outside the livery. Upon closer inspection it appeared the water in the big trough used for watering horses was frozen solid, not just on top but maybe all the way to the bottom. Before either man could step onto the boardwalk that ran in front of the building one of the big doors swung open a little and a man stuck his head out.

The Trail

"Thought I heard a horse or two sneaking up the street. You two looking to stable those horses you got tied up behind you?" The livery man asked. The smile on his face indicated he was happy at the prospect of a little business on such a cold day.

"We would be at that, are you the man whose name is on the sign?" Pack asked as he approached the door.

"I am, names Buster Adams. Just bring them three in and we'll see 'em to a stall," Adams said as he looked up at the clouds and the flakes of falling snow that looked as big as half-dollars. As he held the door he pulled the collar on his coat up, it did little good against the wind and snow.

Two minutes later and all three horses were safely inside, each placed in a separate stall. "You want to help strip the three down? I got a tack room at the end of the last stall where you can store your gear," Adams said.

Cobb and Pack assisted the lanky liveryman with the gear and the pack saddle. The supplies the two men had started out with a few days earlier were now meager at best and didn't take long to carry back, or much space for that matter.

"How much for a day or two for the three horses," Pack asked.

Adams looked at the two men. It was apparent he never had a set price and charged by how much he thought his customers could pay. "Charge a half buck a day each for the three. Includes a little oats in the evening and hay the rest of the time, and it's all the hay they can eat. By the looks of them three though you might want to spring for a little extra, they look to be in need of a good brushing and maybe some grain to go along with the oats."

Cobb didn't think the price was fair, he thought it was too high by half. "I'd think for a half dollar a day they would get a brushing and some grain anyway."

Adams squinted at the man that had just spoken. "Not the way I brush 'em. When I get through with these three I doubt if the two of you will recognize 'em. The brush and extra grain will be a quarter more per day, and that's for each," Adams said as he rubbed his stubbly chin and looked over the three animals. He had already sized up the two men and decided they would pay his price. They looked like they might even pay a little more considering the weather.

Pack thought the price was a bit steep but didn't feel like arguing. He would be reimbursed in full by his employer when the job was done. "I'll pay your price, Mister. That pack horse has a loose shoe that needs looked after. You the smithy too?"

Adams smiled, "I am, I'll be glad to check out all three if you like."

Pack knew he would probably be overcharged for the smith work too but figured it had to be done. The last thing he and Cobb needed was for one of the critters to go lame while out on the trail. "Check 'em all three out then. I don't rightly know if we will be here one day or maybe even two or three so we can settle up when we leave if that's suitable with you?"

The wind picked up suddenly, a strong gust rattled the two front doors in their frames. "I think you should stay at least until this storm blows through. The town has a good hotel and three saloons where you can take your meals. Not many travelers this time of year so the hotel has spare rooms available, I'm sure of it," Adams said. There was a small window across from a wood burning stove. Outside the wind swirled the snow in what looked like tiny tornadoes.

The Trail

The way the liveryman was pushing for them to stay Cobb wondered if he got a cut out of the fees charged at the hotel. If not then he should, he seemed to be one fine salesman.

"We might just do that. Can you point us in the direction of the sheriff's office first though?" Pack asked.

The liveryman looked suspiciously at the two. "You two ain't bounty hunters are you?"

Cobb was now the one looking suspiciously at the liveryman. "Would it make any difference if we were? Bounty-hunters got to make a living too."

"I reckon not. The sheriff's office is one street back; it's close to the hotel, as a matter of fact the two buildings sit across the street from each other."

Pack and Cobb grabbed their Winchesters and saddlebags; then bid the liveryman good afternoon. Down a short distance and one street back they found the sheriff's office. It was a solid enough looking affair but seemed to be old, possibly twenty years old, maybe more. This meant the town was at least that old with the jail probably being one of the first structures built. It always amazed Pack that these western towns always attracted the rougher sort and it never took long after a town sprang up before the townsfolk found the need for a little law and order. Law and order meant a good strong jail. It sent a message that if you misbehaved they had a place to lock you up.

As the two approached the jail they noticed how the day had grown dark and gloomy, not so much from the time but from the falling snow. Pack could see a glow emanating from the two windows in the front of the building, one on each side of a heavy door. Pack twisted the knob and pushed his way inside. He and Cobb were met by stove warmed air, it felt good.

Sitting just inside the door on a ladder-back chair that was leaned against the wall was a man, probably a deputy, sound asleep. Pack slammed the door just loud enough to wake the man. The chair fell forward as the deputy reached for his gun; he did a lousy job of it.

"What the hell?" the deputy said as he dropped his Colt to the floor. He must have been sleeping soundly.

"You the deputy around here?" Pack asked.

The man reached for the gun that had managed to bounce underneath his chair, he was glad it didn't go off when it hit the floor. "I am, names Amos Wells." Amos managed to get to his feet after he realized these two were probably just looking for the sheriff, or maybe a place to warm up, rather than shooting a sleeping deputy.

"Pleasure to meet you Amos. Sorry if we woke you up when we came in," Pack told Amos as the deputy stretched and headed for the coffee pot.

"Oh, don't pay no never mind to that. I was out early this morning checking to make sure no one passed out on any of the streets after leaving one of the saloons last night. Had a feller do that last winter, froze to death by the time he was found about nine the next morning. After that me or the sheriff does a walk around town three or four times a night to try and prevent a tragedy like that from happening again," the deputy said. "Froze to death while drunk, I don't know if that would be painful or not," Amos said more to himself than to Pack or Cobb.

"Is there a sheriff or a town marshal I can talk to this evening?" Pack asked.

Amos finished filling a tin cup from the coffee pot and then added a little cream from a small pitcher. As he stirred he said,

"Got a town sheriff, names Parness Bevins. He's over to Doc Ramey's place checking on a wounded feller we took over there earlier today."

Both Cobb and Pack looked at each other. "A wounded man you say. Was he shot by someone in town?" Pack asked.

"Neither, he came into town this morning and collapsed right over there on the boardwalk, looked to have been stabbed. He ain't come to I reckon, so we don't know much more than that. Don't know who he is, where he hails from, or who tried to kill him," Amos said as he sipped his coffee. He hadn't offered any to the two strangers that had roused him from his nap; this wasn't lost on Pack or Cobb.

"When do you expect the sheriff back? I got some business here in town and it might involve your boss," Pack said.

Amos looked at the stranger with suspicion. "You ain't in some sort of trouble are you?" Even as the deputy asked this he realized how foolish the question sounded. Why would a man in trouble search out the sheriff?

"Nope, neither me nor my friend here are in trouble. We work for a company back east; name of the outfit is the Baldwin-Felts Detective Agency. Ever hear of it?"

Amos rubbed his stubbly chin, as he did he glanced out the front window. "Looks like the sheriff is on his way back now. That's him across the street."

Both Pack and Cobb glanced out the other window. A tall man wearing a wind-flapped duster was hurrying down the street. He had one hand clamped on his hat to keep it from flying off in the strong wind. A few seconds later the door flew open and the sheriff rushed in slamming the door shut behind him. The storm had picked up considerably, the sheriff had to stomp the snow off his feet and then knock it off his duster with his hat.

Sheriff Bevins went straight to the stove paying little attention to the two strangers. As if an afterthought he asked Amos who the two men were.

"These two came in a few minutes ago, Sheriff. They say they're with a detective agency from back east," Amos said.

Bevins looked at the two and noticed they were probably as cold as he was, especially if they just come in off the street. "You two be interested in a cup of coffee? It ain't the best in town but it's hot."

Pack and Cobb headed for the stove; both were dying for a cup but hadn't found the need, or the gumption, to ask the deputy for it. "Thanks kindly, Sheriff. Me and Cobb here have only had campfire warmed coffee for the last few days. Coffee just seems to taste better if it comes off a stove." Both men grabbed a tin cup; the sheriff poured both cups nearly to the top.

"What brings the two of you to Clear Creek in weather like this," Bevins asked as he put the pot back on the stove. Before Pack or Cobb could answer his question he said, "Amos, how about pouring the grounds out of that pot and start us a fresh one?" The deputy jumped to his feet.

Pack sipped his brew, it wasn't bad but the sheriff was right, it wasn't that good either. "We're here to meet the freight wagon from Bristle Buck. When do you expect it to arrive?"

Bevins looked out the window, the storm and the wind driven snow was mesmerizing. "It should have been here day before yesterday but ain't made it yet. I for one will be relieved when old Trevor and Mathew pull into town. Weather like this ain't fit for hauling freight. They got a tough hitch of mules but I still worry about them two. Even a strong mule team can let a man down in this kind of weather."

This sounded ominous to Pack. "You expect they might have run into trouble Sheriff?"

"Not really, they sometimes show up a day late. Naw, I ain't really concerned, what I'm really waiting on is some of that new coffee I ordered. It's called Arbuckle and I reckon it's about the best coffee this side of the river." The river Bevins was referring to was the Mississippi. In the west most folks considered the river to be the dividing line between those that lived in the east and those that lived here.

Pack and Cobb both knew about Arbuckle Coffee. Both had sampled the brand but found it hadn't made it this far west, at least not until now.

"Can you tell us anything about the route the teamsters use? Maybe tell us something about the men that run the freight company?" Cobb asked.

"The trip from here to Bristle Buck and back takes nearly a month. From what they've said it takes eleven days in either direction with usually a four day layover at each end to allow for the transfer of their freight, and to give the hitch a few days' rest. Them two been running freight between here and there for a few years now."

"I can see them bringing freight here but if they are heading back empty wouldn't that shorten the trip by a couple of days?" Cobb asked.

"You'd think so but they never go back empty. We got us a family here that makes some of the finest furniture you've ever seen. They send back a full load to Bristle Buck every trip. The money Trevor and Mathew make hauling the furniture is nearly as much as what they get out of freighting and hauling the mail and supplies for the general store," Bevins said.

Now this got the attention of the two Baldwin men. "Well Sheriff, it's the mail that has us here in the first place."

"You two expecting something in the mailbag," Amos asked as he finished refilling the coffee pot.

"We aren't expecting anything but there is something in the bag that shouldn't be there. We've been sent here to apprehend the parcel and see to its safe return back east," Pack said.

Now the sheriff was curious, he knew if something in the mail was of interest to these two strangers then he would need to know what it was and why he should allow them to take possession. Mail was to be delivered to whoever's name was on the envelope or package, no one else.

"Is the parcel addressed to you?" Bevins asked as he took another sip of his scalding coffee. He wondered sometimes why he wanted the higher quality Arbuckle brand; he drank it so hot he couldn't taste it anyway.

"We couldn't tell you who it's addressed to Sheriff. What we do know is the item in question was sent to the town of Clear Creek a little over six weeks ago. It originated from back east," Pack said.

Bevins sat down at his desk still cradling his cup of coffee, more to warm his hands than anything else. "This parcel you are expecting to arrive, do either of you know what the package contains?"

"Neither of us were told. I'm not even sure it's a package, it might be something as simple as an envelope," Pack said. "We were dispatched here and told it was urgent. After a few days I began to wonder why the parcel was sent to such a remote location. No rail service and no telegraph. It could be the location has as much to do with what we're looking for as the parcel itself."

Just then the door swung open and the man who had been known as Stank walked in. He looked at Pack and Cobb, he recognized both immediately. "James Arthur Pack and Leroy Cobb, what in hell are you two doing here in this armpit of nowhere?" The question was asked in a tone that didn't represent a warning or threat but implied a pleasant surprise.

"Clarence Walker, you might be the last person on earth I'd expect to find here," Pack said as he extended a hand. After Walker shook Pack's hand he did the same with Cobb.

"You two just get into town?" Walker asked as he looked out one of the front windows at the swirling snow.

"We did, came here on business. That's what we were just talking to the sheriff about." Pack wondered if the unexpected appearance of Walker might have something to do with the parcel he was sent here to intercept.

"If you and Cobb are here on business then I assume you both still work for that detective agency back east."

"Still work for the same outfit, going on ten years and counting," Cobb added.

Walker walked to the stove and lifted the lid on the coffee pot, it was full but the pot was luke warm, closer to cold. He turned to look at Amos, "You in charge of the coffee this evening, Deputy?"

The deputy, who had just sat back down, jumped to his feet. "I reckon I am, Stank, and you ain't running this place last time I checked. I just put that pot on and it'll be hot when it decides to get hot and not a minute sooner."

Amos knew he had overreacted, he still couldn't wrap his mind around the fact that the filthy drifter that had once been known as Stank Collins was now supposed to be treated with respect just because he told some story about being a lawman back east. Walker didn't respond to Amos's outburst, he just grinned at the sulking deputy.

"Stank, did the deputy just call you Stank?" Cobb asked as he first looked at Amos and then back at Walker.

Before Walker could answer the sheriff spoke, "Walker here has been masquerading as the town drunk for the last little bit. I still ain't sure how I feel about that but he has been handy with the stabbing we had. Got a man over at the doc's that might not pull through."

Just then there was a shout from the back where the cells were located. Amos was glad for the distraction after his outburst at Walker. "I'll go see what the prisoner wants, Sheriff."

"Who you got in the back, Sheriff, if I might ask?" Pack asked as he took another sip of his bad coffee.

Bevins stood and went to the window. "Don't know and he won't tell us. I was going to let him out yesterday if he would tell me his name, he wouldn't do it. I never let a prisoner go until I check him out against the dodgers I got in my top desk drawer. For all we know he might be as innocent as a spring daisy, or he could be wanted for murder. Anyway, he was locked up for drunk and disorderly and until he tells me who he is I'm keeping him here."

Just then Amos came from the back; he was shaking his head in disgust. "Our fine prisoner back there wants to know who we got out here doing all the talking, said it sounds like a party. He also is complaining about it being cold in his cell and the quality of the food. I told him we ain't running no hotel and to shut the hell up."

"You got a man locked up back there and you don't know who he is?" Pack asked.

"That's right, he wouldn't say. It makes me think since he won't tell us who he is that he might be in some sort of trouble with the law. He can rot back there for all I care," Bevins said.

Pack stood and went back to coffee pot. As he poured he asked the sheriff, "Is there any way I can talk to your prisoner? I ain't got anything pressing just now, other than waiting on that freight wagon."

This wasn't expected. "Now why would you want to talk to the prisoner? You're not from around here and I doubt you would know the man."

"Let's just say he's got my curiosity stirred a little. I'm here to intercept a parcel of mail that shouldn't even be heading this way and you got a man locked up that refuses to talk. Might be nothing, then again, it might be something. Wouldn't hurt anything to let me talk to him. I just need to make sure I check out all the possibilities."

"That parcel you're waiting on must be of some value for your employers to send you all this way. I suppose it wouldn't hurt for you to see the prisoner. Amos, how about leading him out here so we can have another talk with him?" the sheriff said.

Pack quickly refilled his cup and went to the opposite end of the room. He wanted to be behind the man when he was brought from his cell.

It didn't take more than a minute for the deputy to bring the prisoner out. Here you go mister 'ain't got a name.' Grab that chair right in front of the desk there," Amos told the man.

The man seemed to be anxious to get to the front office where the temperature was at least twenty-degrees warmer than it was back where the cells were located. There was a potbellied stove back where the cells were but the sheriff decided to keep the fire back there as small as possible until the man finally decided to give his name. Maybe when he lost the feeling in his hands and feet he might decide to talk.

As he was heading for the chair he noticed Walker by the front door. "Now hold on a minute, Sheriff, you ain't planning on allowing that big feller to hit me again are you?"

"That all depends, are you ready to tell us your name?"

"You don't need my name. I've served my time for that little charge you and your deputy stuck on me. Tell you what, you seem so intent on keeping me here then go right ahead. By the looks of the weather outside I believe right here is the place to be. Say, how about you putting an extra log or two in that stove in the back since you're not letting me out. It gets damn cold back there. All you gave me was that one thin horse blanket to cover up with at night."

"As soon as spring shows up I plan on buying another cord or two of wood. As of right now though I plan on using even less wood back there. I figure as long as the water don't freeze in the mop bucket then it's plenty warm enough for the likes of you," Bevins said.

"Hello, Gravitt, fancy meeting you here," Pack said.

The prisoner nearly fell out of his chair at the mention of his name. It was apparent to everyone in the room that the man's name was Gravitt by the startled look on his face.

Pack hadn't been seen until he spoke. He was leaning against the back wall and his presence was partially blocked by the still open door to the cell room.

The Trail

"I always hoped to cross paths with you again," Pack said as he marched forward and kicked the chair out from under the prisoner. Gravitt fell to the floor; with surprising speed he got back to his feet and took a vicious swing at Pack. This was expected by the Baldwin-Felts man but what happened next wasn't expected by either Gravitt or anyone else in the room.

Pack stepped to the side and allowed the swing to simply chop the air. After Gravitt's arm was fully extended pack grabbed the man by the outstretched arm and drove a knee into his groin. The blow was mostly silent; the only sound heard was the air being driven out of Gravitt's lungs. As the prisoner started to fall Pack grabbed him by the shirt and held him up so the two were face to face.

"You got some explaining to do as soon as some color returns to your face, Gravitt. After you and I have us a little talk I intend to take you back to St. Louis so you can hang. You understand me, Lem?" Pack asked.

When he was finished he stood the chair back on its legs while still holding Gravitt with one hand. When he got the chair where he wanted it he roughly placed the prisoner back in his seat. No one in the room had said a word during all this and no one attempted to interrupt the rough handling of the man now known as Gravitt.

Pack went to the stove and poured another cup of coffee and reached it to Gravitt, "Here, drink this while you think about that hanging I just promised you."

Gravitt cautiously took the coffee. He had been in this same chair two days in a row and he had taken a beating on both days. He was now sorry he hadn't given some sort of name the previous day and now maybe he could have been miles away.

Sheriff Bevins, who had sat patiently while he watched the show, asked, "So, Pack, I take it you know this man."

"I do, Sheriff, me and Cobb both know him. We had a run in with this varmint and a few of his friends last year. A bank holdup resulted in a couple of people getting shot. Cobb here, and myself, were the closest Baldwin men to St. Louis so it fell to us to apprehend the outlaws. The firm we work for represents the folks back east that owns a majority interest in the bank that was robbed. They don't like it when someone walks in and starts killing their customers."

"Why would that task fall to private detectives? Wouldn't a marshal and some lawmen have been sent to do the job?" Bevins asked.

"Normally that would have been the case. As I said the bank in question was owned by some clients of the firm we work for. A judge signed the warrants and we were sent in pursuit. Three days later we found the three. Two of them decided to put up a fight so I killed one and Cobb killed the other. Old Gravitt here was holed up in a house of ill repute with a lady by the name of Wynette Crockett, part time school teacher, part time lady of the night, if you know what I mean.

"Well, it seems Ms. Crockett liked the finer things in life, things that cost more than an honest woman could afford with only a teacher's pay. For this reason she not only sold her body to the highest bidder but was also in the habit of collecting rewards on some of the criminals she called customers. She turned in old Gravitt here before he had time to button his trousers.

"We found Gravitt passed out on bad whiskey. You might say that bad whiskey and a bad woman turned out to be his downfall," Pack told the men.

The Trail

Bevins sat looking at the man seated across from his desk. "You got a first name, Gravitt?"

The prisoner knew he was in a bad spot. "Name's Simm, Simm Gravitt. You might know my face but you still got the wrong man. I've never been to St Louis in my entire life, not even close."

Bevins looked at Pack who was standing behind the seated prisoner. Pack was shaking his head.

"How is it these two men identified you and now you say you ain't the man they say you are. Help me out here Simm, my mind just don't work all that well in cold weather," Bevins said.

"I got me a twin brother, me and him went our separate ways a few years back. I ain't seen hide nor hair of him in at least five years, maybe even a little longer."

Bevins looked at Pack, he could tell the Baldwin man was considering what he had just heard. If this man Simm had instilled even the tiniest bit of doubt in the Baldwin-Felts detective then it might just be possible that what the prisoner said was true. Bevins would need more proof before a decision could be made as far as releasing or continuing the incarceration of the prisoner.

"The man you arrested for the bank robbery, what was his first name?" Bevins asked.

"His name was Lem Gravitt. This story about a twin brother could be real, but it could also be a lie. How long would it take to get a wire to the authorities in St. Louis?"

"Take a while, closest telegraph is a three day ride from here, in this weather maybe six. Most folks in Clear Creek simply send letters when they need to correspond with family or tend to business," the sheriff said.

"What do you intend to do about your prisoner now? You still don't know his name, at least his real name. He might be here for months," Pack stated.

Sheriff Bevins had some thinking to do. He still couldn't turn the man known as Gravitt loose; what if his name was really Lem and he had just lied about a twin brother with nearly the same name. "Got no choice but to lock you back up Gravitt. Might take a few weeks to figure out what to do with you. Got a storm brewing outside and the closest wires are three days from here, that is in good weather and it ain't good weather. A letter to the authorities back east could take upwards of a month and a half. Even then I don't know how anyone in St. Louis can shed any light on who you really are. It might come down to you being held here until someone can escort you to the authorities in St. Louis."

Gravitt smiled when he heard this. It was apparent he would rather spend the next few weeks holed up in Clear Creek than being transported anywhere else. That is if they didn't let him freeze to death in his cell.

"Amos, put him back in his cell. You can add a small log to the stove back there if you like," Bevins said. He figured there was a slim chance the man was telling the truth but he doubted it. One thing was for sure, he was going to keep him alive until someone could tell him what in hell was going on.

After the prisoner was gone Walker looked at Pack. "You done stepped in it now. How on earth are you going to prove he is who he says he is, or who he ain't? It sounds like old Gravitt is either innocent or a hell of a liar."

"Not my problem, I think Sheriff Bevins here makes the decision on what to do with Gravitt now. Cobb and I already have a job and that's the acquisition of the package coming in on the freight wagon. I have strict orders to intercept the mail bag and return the contents to a yet undisclosed location," Pack said.

Amos thought this sounded silly, "How can you return anything to an undisclosed location. That just doesn't make sense."

Pack decided to humor the deputy. "Once we have what we're looking for we are to head to the nearest town with a telegraph and send a wire. We'll be told then what to do and where to go."

Cobb looked outside again and realized they had spent too much time in the sheriff's office. The last thing he wanted was for the hotel to be all rented out and have to sleep at the livery. "We best be making arrangements for our rooms tonight. Maybe after that we can go to one of the saloons for a little supper. All I've ate for way longer than I want to talk about is trail food. Beans and bacon are starting to get a little old if you know what I mean."

Pack pulled a pocket watch out and looked at the time, it was nearly three o'clock. "Might be a good idea, what is the best hotel in town, Sheriff?"

Without a moment's hesitation he said, "That would be the York. The couple that works the place also owns it. The rooms are reasonable and clean."

"Would that be the same place the liveryman told us about?" Cobb asked.

"Probably, it's the only hotel in Clear Creek. Got a couple of boarding houses but they are mostly for folks that rent by the week or the month," Bevins said.

"Well, I guess the York is the spot for us. Say, would any of you like to join me and Cobb for supper, it'll be my treat? Or should I say it will be the treat of the Baldwin-Felts Detective Agency," Pack said.

At this Amos frowned. He knew he couldn't leave the jail as long as a prisoner was locked up. He figured he was about to miss out on a free meal, a meal that was most likely better than what he usually scrounged up for himself.

The look on the deputy's face told the story to anyone that cared to notice. "Sheriff, the invitation goes to you, Walker and Amos. And I'm serious about me buying."

Bevins looked at his deputy, he really hated for the man to miss out on a free meal at the saloon. "Amos, how about you put another log on the fire back there and then light a lantern in case our fine prisoner is afraid of the dark. I think Gravitt will be alright for an hour or so while we go eat. A good supper in this kind of weather might lift all our spirits."

Amos nearly ran trying to get to the cells in back; five minutes later he was standing out front pulling on his heavy coat. Pack assumed the man never got to eat at any of the saloons in town. Most men that worked as deputies didn't earn a lot of pay; most never earned a lot of respect either.

"Amos, how about you heading over to the York and letting Mister Hatcher know we got a couple of fellers that are in need of two rooms. Tell him they will be over as soon as we get through eating at the Tavern," Bevins told his deputy. "Don't you worry none, Amos, we'll wait for you. I'll have us a table in the back near the kitchen."

Amos tipped his hat and hurried off down the street. Bevins took a key from a pocket and locked the door to the jail. The wind hadn't picked up from earlier when the men were out, it didn't have to. If it had warmed up any during the day it wasn't apparent. With the frosty air and swirling snow the scene on Main Street looked like something you might imagine out of one of those Alaskan dime novels you could see at any number of general stores.

The place the sheriff had mentioned was down a ways and one street back. As the men approached, the sound of piano music could be heard emanating from the first floor entrance. The Tavern, as it was called, had the usual batwing doors but they were buttoned to two full length doors that were needed this time of year to keep out the weather. The four men pushed their way through the swinging doors and were instantly assaulted with the strong smells of tobacco, beer, and whiskey. The stove warmed air was a pleasant surprise from the frigid air outside.

"The dining room is located off to the left over there. It'll be considerably quieter and the smell of food should overpower the smells from the saloon. Let's head over and see what kind of business they got on such a day as this," Bevins said.

Pack stepped to the side to allow the sheriff to lead the way. There was another set of doors and these led into a room that was nearly as large as the saloon. Bevins gave the dining room a once over and then headed to a large round table near a corner in the back. There were five chairs and this would work out nicely once Amos made it back from the York Hotel.

Walker took the seat directly against the wall; Bevins took the one beside him. Cobb and Pack knew what the two were doing; they were positioning themselves to watch over the room. Not a bad idea if you represented law and order in a town this far west. It didn't bother the two Baldwin men; they were strangers in Clear Creek and doubted anyone would give them a second look.

No more than twenty seconds went by before a middle-aged woman appeared from a side door, undoubtedly the kitchen. She was pleasant looking but had the look of a person that worked long hours but probably enjoyed her job just the same.

"Evening, Sheriff, I'll bet you're glad to be in here instead of walking the streets looking for lawbreakers on such a cold day. Are the four of you looking for supper, or maybe just coffee?"

"How about coffee and supper, Mae, and there are five of us. Amos will be along in a few minutes after he does a little deputy business."

"Well how about I get five fresh cups and some cream and sugar? Maybe Amos will be here by then," the woman named Mae said as she turned and headed back toward the kitchen.

"That's Mae Halstead. She's been working here for the better part of a year now. She had to take up working after they found her husband about a mile out of town. Somebody killed that man while he was on his way back from some business down near Bristle Buck," Bevins said.

This struck Pack as unusual, more so than a normal killing might. "Killed you say, on the same road you said the man was on who stumbled into town yesterday morning with that knife wound?"

Bevins looked at Pack, up until now he hadn't thought about the previous murder and the death of Mae's husband. "That's right. It wasn't more than a hundred feet from where me and Walker here found the spot we think the stranger over at Doctor Ramey's was attacked."

Just then Amos walked in and looked around. It didn't take him more than a second to see the four men sitting in the back.

He hurried over and pulled out the last of the five chairs. "You men ordered yet?"

"Not yet, Amos, you get things squared away at the hotel for Pack and Cobb?" Bevins asked.

"I did, got two rooms saved, both are upstairs. Good thing you sent me over there when you did because it was the last two rooms they had. He told me he ain't been this busy in months and with the weather and all he found it a mite unusual. Said folks needed to be at home rather than out traveling," Amos told the men.

The sheriff wondered what the hotel owner found unusual about folks trying to get in out of the weather, especially weather that was as bad as this.

"Why did Hatcher think that was unusual Amos? I would think that in weather like this more people would be staying at the hotel," the sheriff said.

"He said nearly everyone that came in was carrying long guns and nearly nothing else. I told him most men don't like to leave their Winchesters in a livery; the moisture ain't good on a shooting iron. Anyway he told me he had five men check in this afternoon and all were packing the same thing, long guns and practically nothing else."

Now Pack thought of something that Amos said that needed explaining. "You saying he told you these men didn't have saddlebags and bedrolls, Amos? Is that what this Hatcher feller said to you?"

"That's what he said. Come to think of it why would anyone be out traveling in this kind of weather with only a long gun? A man out and about might just find himself frozen solid to the ground if he weren't careful," Amos said.

Pack noticed the sheriff and even Walker were thinking the same thing, why would anyone be traveling without the items needed to stay safe? Blankets, saddlebags, food, extra clothing, it really didn't add up.

"All I can figure is these folks that filled up the hotel must have left their horses, along with all their gear, at the livery. Maybe after we finish our supper I'll go over and talk to Buster Adams. Surely those men would have left their horses and trail gear at the livery," Bevins said.

Pack looked at Cobb; both men knew they were going to go along with the sheriff to see what news he found at the livery. Something about the happenings in the town of Clear Creek just wasn't adding up. Maybe it was nothing but the detective in both men was starting to peak a bit.

Just then Mae came from the kitchen with a stack of coffee cups. She sat a cup in front of each man and then hurried back and grabbed the coffee pot.

"Any of you like cream with your coffee? We got the best cream in the whole territory I've been told. Cold weather seems to make the cows over at the Johnson farm turn out sweet cream. Different in the summer, don't know if it's to do with the temperature or the grass but it just seems wintertime helps them cows make the best cream," Mae said.

"I'll try a little cream and some sugar too if you got it," Amos said with a smile. It was apparent by the look on his face, and the sound of his voice, that he was really looking forward to the meal he was about to get. The other men at the table took eating at a diner, or saloon, as just something that you did when you were hungry. The deputy acted like this was the first time he had been inside the diner and for all they knew it might just as well have been.

Mae hurried to the kitchen and brought the cream and sugar. "Here is a pitcher of cream and some sugar. You try that cream and see if I wasn't exaggerating, best in the territory! Now, what can I get you men for supper?"

Sheriff Bevins spoke before anyone else, "What's the special today, Mae?"

"Oh, I think you'll like it, Sheriff. Jimmy cooked up a big pot of stew, matter of fact he just finished cooking the second pot, the first one got cleaned out about thirty minutes ago. There seems to be a lot of strangers in town this evening. Anyway, we got either biscuits or cornbread to go with it, along with sweet potatoes for dessert if that suits you?"

"Sweet potatoes you say. I haven't seen a sweet potato since last summer. Didn't know they would keep this long," Bevins said.

"Oh they keep real good, Sheriff. Just put em in the cellar and don't fan the door too much. We got cinnamon to sprinkle on top if that suits your taste. Try that with some fresh butter and I guarantee it'll put a smile on your face. We got the best butter you ever tasted, comes from them cows over at the Johnson farm," Mae said.

Pack started to think the cows over at the Johnson farm must be pretty talented going by all the praise Mae was heaping on them.

"I think the special along with sweet potato dessert sounds just about right for me," Bevins said as he looked at the other four men at the table. Each of the other men decided to try the special.

"Sheriff, if you don't mind I would like to go along with you when you check out the livery. Me and Cobb might like to hear what the hostler has to say," Pack said.

Bevins looked at the Baldwin man with suspicion. "You expect something might be up, Pack?"

"Not really, Sheriff. I just like to keep my eyes and ears open when I'm in a strange town. Something seems to not add up according to the man that owns the hotel. I just don't want to get caught off guard, especially if I'm sleeping in the same building with these strangers."

The sheriff thought about this. He could see how a man that worked for a detective agency might be of the suspicious type. "I reckon if I were in your shoes, Pack, I would want to know myself. After we finish up and you pay the tab I say we go down there and ask a few questions. Maybe Buster can shed a little light on things. I believe at the moment I'm just about as clueless as the rest of you fellers."

Just then Mae came from the kitchen followed by another woman, this one much younger than Mae. "Here you go Sheriff, nice and hot to warm a man's insides on such a cold day."

The two women sat a plate in front of each man and then headed back to the kitchen. Wasn't a minute until they were back carrying five more plates, each held a big sweet potato split down the middle with a dab of butter in the center. On top of that was sprinkled what had to be cinnamon. The smell was nearly enough to make the men forget the stew and head straight for the dessert.

"There you go, how does everything look?" Mae asked.

By the look on the deputy's face it was apparent the meal would suit the man just fine. Probably the best meal he could have imagined. The other men nodded as they each picked up a fork.

"Thanks, Mae, you might bring a wedge of cornbread if it ain't too much trouble?" Bevins said.

The Trail

Mae raised a hand to her mouth, "My goodness Sheriff, I plum forgot the cornbread. I'll get it right away; maybe you would like a little butter for that too." As Mae headed back toward the kitchen she said, "It's the best butter around; we get it from the Johnson's farm. Them cows of theirs sure do fine work when it gets cold."

Walker looked at Bevins, "The way she goes on about them cows over at the Johnson farm makes me want to ride over there and see such magical beasts."

The other men at the table didn't respond, each was too busy chewing. By the looks on the men's faces you could tell the food was good, really good.

The table was quiet for the next thirty minutes with the only sound being that of Mae refilling the coffee cups. Once everyone was finished Pack paid the tab and on top of that he gave Mae a fifty cent tip. By the look on the woman's face you could tell a tip was a rare thing for her.

With the bill paid and the dishes cleared away Amos went about the task of rolling himself a smoke. Just as he struck a match a rifle shot went off from somewhere outside. The bullet came through one of the big front windows and struck the wall between Bevins and Walker. Just as the men around the table went to the floor for cover there was another shot, this one hit the wall too but not before going through Amos's shoulder. The deputy grunted as he was knocked to the floor. As he went down his head struck the edge of the table knocking him out cold.

Pack and Walker both crawled on hands and knees toward the front window to return fire if need be. By then both figured whoever had done the shooting was probably long gone. Cobb stayed put on the floor next to the table with his Colt drawn and the hammer cocked. It was apparent both he and Pack had been shot at before by the way Pack cautiously proceeded in the direction of the shooter while Cobb stayed behind and gave cover.

Bevins hustled around the table on hands and knees to check on Amos. He first thought his deputy was dead but soon realized it wasn't as serious as he feared. The bullet hole in the shoulder, although not life threatening, bled at an alarming rate. He needed something to stop the bleeding so he grabbed the edge of the tablecloth and yanked it off the table, then ripped it into strips to use as a bandage..

"You see anything moving out there, Pack?" Walker asked as both men tried to peek out the broken window without getting shot themselves. .

The way the snow and wind was coming through the broken window, and as dark as it was out on the street, it was damn near impossible to see anything outside.

"Not a thing. We can't stay here waiting for whatever happens next. Tell you what, lets fire a couple of shots at an angle that won't hit any of the building across the streets and see if whoever's out there fires back. My guess is the bastard has lit out," Walker said. Both men fired two shots each and waited for a response, none came.

With no return fire it was guessed that whoever had fired the shots was gone. The two men rose and stepped through the double front doors with guns at the ready. Nothing could be seen but swirling snow. Just when it looked like the excitement might have passed another shot went off. The door frame just behind Walker burst into splinters from the impact of the bullet.

The Trail

Walker saw the muzzle flash, even as the bullet was impacting the frame he was raising his gun and stepping to the side where the light shining through the saloon door wouldn't give the shooter an advantage. He went to a knee and fired at the spot where he suspected the shooter stood. Walker fired three shots, one center and one each a little left and right. He was rewarded with the sound of a man letting out a grunt of pain.

"Cover me, Pack," Walker shouted as he sprinted from the boardwalk into the darkness and swirling snow.

There was little Pack could do, if he fired he was just as likely to hit Walker as he was to hit the shooter. Still though he tried to look into the darkness to see if there was anything he could do, there wasn't.

"Hold your fire, Pack, I'm coming in," Walker shouted. Moments later Walker came into view, a second man was limping along as best as he could being led along with Walker's Colt pointed at him.

"Found this skunk across the street, looks like I hit him in the leg." With that said Walker shoved the man roughly onto the boardwalk in front of the saloon.

"Let's get back inside, Pack, before my hand freezes to my gun" Walker said.

Once back inside the two noticed Amos lying sprawled on the floor beside the table. "Is he dead?" Walker asked.

Bevins looked up and answered, "Not yet, he'll be alright I think. We need to get him over to Joe Ramey's so he can look at this shoulder," Bevins said.

Just then they noticed the man Walker and Pack brought through the door, they also noticed the bleeding leg the man sported. Bevins stood and looked the man over.

"You got a name mister?" the sheriff asked.

The wounded man didn't speak; he just looked at the deputy he wounded with his wild shots earlier. Bevins walked to where the wounded man stood. Without any warning he drew back and hit the man squarely on the jaw with his fist. The action caught both Walker and Pack by surprise.

The man didn't collapse to the floor; the force of the blow was strong enough though to knock the man back through the door onto the boardwalk outside.

"Well, Walker, let's go out and bring him back in," Pack said.

Once back inside Bevins approached again but was stopped by Walker.

"Hang on there, Sheriff. I don't think killing this man with your bare fists is going to get us any closer to knowing who he is or who he works for."

Bevins looked at Walker and almost took a swing at him. Walker stepped forward and put a hand on the sheriff's chest. "You better calm yourself, Sheriff. I understand you're upset that Amos got shot by this Bushwacker but what you're doing isn't helping us right now. We need to get the deputy over to the doc's and get him looked after. After we get some answers out of this bastard then you can beat him silly, that is if he doesn't bleed to death from that leg of his I shot.

Bevins took a deep breath and then rubbed his knuckles, the same knuckles he had just used so effectively against the wounded Bushwacker.

"I suppose you're right, let's get these two over to Ramey's." Bevins looked at the injured man and added, "I don't know how bad you're hurt but I can guarantee you that my deputy, the one you just shot, will get treated before you do."

The Trail

As he said this he was poking the man in the ribs with the forefinger of his right hand. Walker knew that was the sheriff's trigger finger; if he couldn't shoot this man with it then he would just poke.

Just then Amos began to stir. The first thing he did was grab his gun and try to get it out of the holster. "Hang on there deputy, the danger is past," Bevins said as he ran over and took the gun out of his hand.

Amos felt the pain in his shoulder and protested. "The hell it has, some dry-gulchers done shot me," he said through gritted teeth.

It was only now that Mae and the other woman got the courage to peek out of the kitchen. When the two saw Amos lying on the floor with a bloody tablecloth tied to his shoulder they realized how bad it was.

"Sheriff, Amos has been shot," Mae said.

Bevins looked up at the woman, "Thanks for letting me know that, Mae. I first thought this was a result of your cooking."

Mae suddenly realized how foolish her remark must have sounded. "Is he going to be alright?"

"I think so, we'll need to get him over to doc's place."

Amos looked at the tablecloth tied around his shoulder and arm and realized that this was the only injury he had. "Help me to my feet, Sheriff. I can walk if you promise I won't get shot again."

After Amos got to his feet he reached for his hat. As the two men headed for the door two other men that had been eating at another table grabbed a tablecloth with the intention of nailing it over the broken window. It would just have to do until more permanent repairs could be made.

Walker and Pack led the way, escorting their prisoner, while the sheriff followed, all the while making sure his wounded deputy didn't topple over from loss of blood. Cobb followed at a reasonable distance all the while scanning for any more trouble.

Doc Ramey had been in the kitchen of his place trying to figure out what he was going to fix himself to eat for the evening when he heard a hard knock at his door.

"Open up, Doc, it's the sheriff," Bevins shouted.

When the door opened Bevins and Amos were looking at the hollow end of a double barrel shotgun. Once Ramey saw for sure it was the sheriff he stepped back to let the men in. When the last of the six were inside Ramey closed the door.

"What happened to Amos, Sheriff, he get shot or something?"

"He did at that, Doc. Somebody shot through the window over at the diner and hit him in the shoulder. I think it ain't that bad but you might want to have a look for yourself."

Ramey gave the sheriff a sour look. "You say it ain't that bad, how in hell would you know? Of all of us in this room I believe only one of us could be considered a doctor," Ramey said.

"Well what the hell got you so feisty this evening Doc? All I said was I didn't think it was such a bad injury," Bevins said as he helped Amos to a chair.

"I'll tell you what's got me so riled, Sheriff, it's that damn patient you left here yesterday. He came to about an hour ago and damn if that ain't the most foul mouthed human I've ever met. And let me tell you, I've met a few."

"Did he say anything useful, Doc?" Walker asked.

"Only if you count cussing as useful." It was only then that Ramey noticed the other wounded man. "What happened to you stranger, you get shot by the same man that shot Amos?"

"This is the man that shot Amos. Walker and Pack ran him down outside the diner. After you patch up my deputy you can take a look at him, that is if he lives that long." The sheriff only said this to torment the Bushwacker.

Walker looked at the sheriff and made a suggestion. "If the man that got stabbed a few days ago is awake maybe we should go and talk to him.

Bevins had been so wrapped up in the wounding of his deputy that he had completely forgotten about the patient with the knife wound.

"Doc, I think me and Walker are going to go talk to your other patient," Bevins said.

"Help yourself, Sheriff. Spend all the time you want in there. See if I wasn't exaggerating about the language that man uses."

Walker and Bevins went down a short hall and entered the last room on the left. The man in the room was sitting on the edge of his bed. When the man saw the sheriff and Walker walk in he stood on wobbly legs.

"Who in hell are you?" he asked.

It was all Bevins could do to keep from hitting this man the same way he hit the Bushwacker back at the diner.

"I'm the sheriff and this is a friend of mine, his name is Walker. Let me explain something right off the bat. I've had one hell of a bad day and if I hear any more disrespect out of you then I might just shoot you where you stand so I can go back to my office and drink a cup of coffee. Now if you don't understand any of what I just said then nod your head right now so I can explain it a little more forcefully."

The man retreated until his wobbly legs came in contact with the edge of the bed. He looked down and then back up at the sheriff. "I understand exactly what you said. What in hell gives you the right to come in here and threaten me like this?"

"Because I'm in a threatening mood right now so sit down and shut up. This is the way things are going to work. I ask a question and you answer it truthfully. Then I ask another question and you answer that question truthfully and so on. Do you understand me?"

The man sat on the edge of the bed and looked at the sheriff. "I reckon my hearing didn't get stabbed, it was my ribs so go ahead and ask all you want."

"First of all I would like to know who I'm talking to."

The man suddenly found interest in his feet. He stared down as he considered whether to answer the question or not. And if he did answer he wouldn't use his real name. After a little thought he said, "Names Jess Runyon."

Both Bevins and Walker figured they had just been lied to. It was the way the man hesitated before giving his name. it was also the way he said it with his tone trailing off and the fact that he didn't make eye contact when he told his name.

"Alright, Mister Jess Runyon, how did you get that knife wound?" Bevins asked.

Runyon looked down at his bandaged chest. He really didn't feel that bad now that he was warm and out of the animal hides he was using for clothing. "Got jumped outside of town. It was a day ago. Naw wait a minute, I think it was maybe two or three days ago."

The Trail

This could be true, Bevins knew for a fact that the man had spent at least one cold night leaned against a tree not more than a mile outside of town.

"You say you were jumped. That sounds like it was random. Was it random, Mister Runyon, or do you know who did this?" Bevins asked.

Runyon thought long and hard. "No Sheriff, I can't say I had ever seen that man before. He came out of nowhere, just all at once. I tried to fend him off." At that last statement Runyon held up his right hand and looked at the bandage the doc had applied.

Both Bevins and Walker noticed the man's language had become much less homey and now took on the accent of someone that lived farther north and also farther east.

"The last thing I remembered was stumbling back away from the bastard that was after me. Just as he was ready to finish me off I fell backward down a steep rock face. I thought I was dead until the slope caught me and I slid. Felt like I slid a hundred feet. When I came to I was at the foot of a ravine. Looking up I figure I must have fallen sixty or eighty feet. If I had fallen off the cliff ten feet in either direction I would have been a dead man. As it was, the spot where I stumbled off the edge was a spot where the sloping base was made up of loose gravel.

"Anyway when I gathered my wits I looked for the man with the knife, he wasn't around and he wasn't looking over the edge of the cliff. I didn't know how bad I was hurt but I knew I needed to put some distance between me and my attacker. I ran as best as I could. After maybe ten minutes I looked back and got a better view of the place where I fell. It went in both directions as far as I could see. It would take some time before my tormentor could find a way down so I felt some relief. The only problem was where to go and who could I find to help me before I either bled to death or froze to death."

Bevins was ready to continue the questioning, that was until the doc came back in. "I reckon you've got all the information you're gonna get for a while. This man needs rest. Let him be for a spell and then you can question him further."

Runyon looked tired. Neither Bevins nor Walker had noticed due to the story being told, they were fascinated by it.

"Alright then, you get yourself some rest, Runyon, and then we will talk some more. A word of advice, you try to run then you'll die out there. You give the doc any trouble and I can promise you more trouble from me. We understand each other?" Bevins asked.

"You got no worries, Sheriff, I'm a peaceable man. Just because of what happened and the shape I'm in doesn't tell the story of me."

Walker and Bevins headed out the door and back toward the sheriff's office. As they walked both pondered what they had just been told and wondered if it was all true or if any of it was true.

"Say, Walker, you feel like a little trip?" Bevins asked.

"You planning on checking out that man's story about the fall and the cliff and all?"

"Damn right I am. I know the spot he just described. It's there alright. If things happened the way he said it did then there might be evidence of it to back up his story. There might even be a few clues left if the snow ain't covered everything up."

The Trail

"Alright, count me in. The way he described it though I doubt we will be able to check out the top before nightfall," Walker said.

"Oh I think we can check out the top if we hurry. I know where a break in the face leads all the way up. Can't use the horses but we can climb it on foot. We can tie the horses up at the base while we check out the top," Bevins said.

"Sounds risky, Sheriff. I don't like leaving the horses unattended in this kind of weather. There's also the fact that whoever attacked Runyon or whatever in the hell his name is might still be lurking around. He takes the horses then he has a way out of this and the two of us are stuck outside in a damn blizzard."

Don't worry I got a plan for that. We're taking Buster Adams with us. He can stay with the horses until we check out the top and then we'll head back to town. Shouldn't take more than a couple of hours which should put us back in town right at dark," Bevins said.

Walker looked at the sheriff. "You think Adams will go along?"

"He will I'm pretty sure. He helped me with a little deputy work late last year. He's good on a horse and he knows how to use a gun. He'll go along."

Thirty minutes later the three men rode out of town in the direction of the cliffs. As soon as they made it to the end of Main Street they were met by Pedro. The big dog had already made his rounds and polished off every scrap of food left out of doors in the entire town of Clear Creek. He saw the men on horseback and decided he would just tag along, might help to settle his supper.

"That dog got a name, Sheriff?" Walker asked.

"Names Pedro. Come to think of it he showed up here about a year ago, which makes him more of a citizen in this town than you. I do believe though for the last year he took better care of himself than you did. How is it you been here two or three months and never heard what that dog was called?"

Walker looked over at the sheriff. "Most folks wouldn't talk to me; I think you already know that. I stayed to myself and that suited both me and the townsfolk just fine. I saw that dog almost every day, just didn't think he had a name is all."

"Well tell me this, Walker. What on earth convinced you to masquerade around town looking the way you did? You ain't running from something are you?"

The three men rode in silence while Walker thought. Finally he said, "Maybe I am, Sheriff. That gunfight back east took some getting over."

"You killed three men that needed killing; why would that throw you off your moral compass. You was a lawman and from what I heard a damn fine one."

"Long story, Sheriff. The short version is that one of the three took a little boy hostage and tried to bargain his way out of town. I knew if he got to a horse and left with the boy then most likely he would kill the child as soon as he got out of sight. I took a chance."

Both Bevins and Adams looked at Walker. "What kind of chance," Adams asked. He was as mesmerized by the story as Bevins.

"I drew on the man. Hit him with the first shot. I thought the shot was doable but as it worked out I nicked the boy. Nothing serious, only a scratch but still," Walker was quiet for a few seconds before he continued. "I still shot a child."

"Did the child recover?" Adams asked.

"He did, as a matter of fact he was out playing with his brothers two days later. His maw and paw told me they thought what I done probably saved the little boy's life. That helped but for some reason I couldn't get that moment out of my mind."

"What moment was that?" Bevins asked.

"The moment when I drew down on that man. It was as if I saw the entire episode in slow motion. My gun clearing leather, my thumb pulling back the hammer, my finger pulling the trigger. I knew as soon as the gun went off I missed my mark by a fraction of an inch. In my mind I could see the bullet traveling toward the two, an outlaw and a little boy.

"In my mind I willed the bullet to move away from the child, at least that's the way it felt. I saw it all. The exact moment his little shirt tugged just below the shoulder. The moment it entered the outlaw's chest. The moment the force of the slug caused the man to release his grip on the child. The moment I saw the blood on the little boy's shoulder. The look on the child's face as he felt the shot, he was looking at me."

The three men rode in silence as each replayed the story in their heads. Both Bevins and Adams couldn't imagine the pain Walker was feeling right now.

"You said the child was only grazed, Walker. That's something to be thankful for. If that outlaw had made it out of town then much worse could have happened," Adams said.

"I suppose so. Still though, I was shaken by it. Didn't know if I could ever draw on anybody again. In my line of work you can't have second thoughts. Decisions are made in less than a heartbeat. If you pause you die. If you react too fast then innocent bystanders get hurt," Walker said.

Nothing more was said until the three men made it to the cliff. Adams was left to guard the three horses. He was armed with a Colt the sheriff had loaned him just for the job. He was also sporting a deputy's badge; it was the one Amos wore. Bevins figured the injured deputy wouldn't mind if someone else borrowed that badge for a few hours.

"What's this place called, Sheriff? I doubt a rock like that can go many days before somebody gives it a name," Walker said.

Bevins grinned, "Lover's Leap, I figured you could have guessed that."

Walker looked up at the rock face and tried to figure out just where a man could fall off backwards and hit the bottom with a little life still left in him. "Over there, Sheriff," Walker said when he found what he was looking for.

The two men walked to the base of the cliff and searched the loose rock for any sign of disturbance. "That looks like the spot right over there, Walker," Bevins said as he headed in the general direction he was pointing.

At a spot where the slope was a little more gradual they found a few drops of blood. Looking up they could see where a man had fallen from the top. Not more than ten or twelve feet from the main top the hill went from vertical to a steep slope that became more gradual as you got nearer the bottom. The slope was made of loose gravel and shale that had built up over the years as it chipped away from the rock face and tumbled to the bottom.

"Would you look at that? Looks almost as tame as Runyon described it. Reckon why the man that attacked him didn't follow him down the same way?" Bevins asked.

The Trail

Walker continued to look at the slide. "We are looking at it from the bottom. I'd imagine from the top that looks twice as high and ten times as dangerous."

The sheriff kicked a few of the pebbles that represented the stuff that the slide was made of. I believe a man could fall down that and if he was lucky he could make it all the way down here without getting hurt. That is if he was real lucky."

"I think that's about right Sheriff. Remember he was dressed in animal hides, which would have offered a measure of protection. Where did you say that cut in the rock face is located?"

"As best as I can remember it's about a hundred yards to the left," Bevins said.

The two men walked to where the rock face had separated from the main body of the cliff. There was a narrow gully that had developed up the side that ran all the way to the top. The grade wasn't steep and it didn't take the two more than ten minutes to make it to the top.

The terrain was flat for about a quarter mile with scrub and skinny trees dotted here and there. There were also numerous boulders about that ranged from small to as large as an outhouse. The two walked back to where they figured Runyon had fallen and looked over. At the bottom in the distance they could see the three horses and Buster Adams looking up at them. He waved and Bevins waved back in acknowledgement.

The sheriff and Walker looked over and found the spot where they figured Runyon had slid to the bottom. The loose gravel had been disturbed; it was obvious even with the light snow that stuck here and there.

"You're right, Walker, from here this looks way more dangerous than it does from the bottom," Bevins said.

Walker didn't reply at first, he was studying the base of the cliff where Runyon had slid to a stop. "You know Sheriff, there might be another reason the man that attacked Runyon didn't feel the need to get down there and finish the job. Maybe he thought Runyon had been killed with the combination of being stabbed and falling off this cliff?"

Bevins continued to look over the edge. "How do you figure that?"

"Look where he landed. Got a couple of scrub cedars and a few large rocks scattered about down there. It ain't fifteen feet to the edge of the larger trees and scrub. From here, if you take into account the amount of dust that must have been thrown up by Runyon's slide down the hill, I doubt if the attacker could have seen exactly where he landed. And it is highly likely Runyon staggered into the trees before the dust settled enough to see him from here. For all the attacker knew the body might have been covered by the rock slide."

"That makes sense. Runyon had been stabbed and then fell off backward down this cliff. He was dead and that was that except he wasn't dead and now we got him over at the doc's place. We might be able to use that knowledge to help capture his attacker."

"Let's look around a little. I really don't want to be caught out of doors in this kind of weather," Walker said.

Both men headed straight back for the trees and scrub. They found where a horse had been tied up. They also found where a second horse had been gathered and led away. Whoever attacked Runyon took his horse when he left.

The Trail

"Runyon didn't say anything about a horse. I was just getting to that when the doc came in and ran the two of us off. We need to know what the horse looked like and get a description of the saddle and anything else Runyon might have been carrying. Say, Walker, how well do you know those two men that came into town? Pack and Cobb if I remember correctly. They came in on two horses and were leading a third."

Walker started laughing. "You ain't telling me that you suspect Cobb and Pack of this crime?"

Bevins knew he had said something silly. "Not really, but you know I had to ask."

Walker started back toward the break, "I know, I would probably have thought the same thing. It is some kind of peculiar though; them showing up when there are so many unanswered questions around town."

The two men eased back down the break. Buster Adams was waiting with the three horses. "You find anything unusual up there, Sheriff?"

"We did; looks like our stabber took Runyon's horse. Now we know to look for a rider leading another horse that's saddled. Don't believe I've ever seen that unless the second horse was hauling a body over the saddle," Bevins said.

Adams thought about this as all three climbed in the saddle and turned their horses toward town. "Say Sheriff, you ever figure out anything about that varmint at the jail? The one with the gruesome saddlebags."

"Not much, why do you ask?"

"Not really sure. I remember him when he came to the stable that night. I told you he was mostly drunk and quite a smartass. Well, when I first asked him if he needed to stable his horse he said how much for two. I told him how much and then he said he was mistaken, how much for one. That was when he said he wouldn't pay it and I told him if he didn't I would just keep his horse. You remember me telling you that, Sheriff?"

"Yea I remember, Adams, but not the part about him first saying he needed to stable two."

"When you asked me I didn't feel the need to repeat the words of a drunk, now I wish I had," Adams said.

"You think that man has the second horse tied up somewhere?" Walker asked.

The three rode in silence for a while as Adams thought about the question. "I do, I believe that man has a horse tied up somewhere while he's lying over in that jail."

"How long has he been in jail, Sheriff?" Walker asked.

"Tonight just after dark makes four full days. Can a horse survive four days without water, Adams?"

"If it was summertime and the weather wasn't too hot that would be tough but the horse could survive." Adams looked around as he thought of an animal tied out all this time. "In this weather and these low temperatures I just don't know Sheriff. We get back to town I think I'll put on another pair of gloves and a thicker hat and have a look around town. I doubt I could sleep a wink tonight unless I tried to find that animal."

"Tell you what, how about the three of us head over to the jail and ask a few questions. If that bastard doesn't want to talk then I might just beat the hell out of him," Bevins said. It was evident by the man's tone and use of foul language that he was disturbed at the thought of an animal being left out of doors to die.

The three found they were riding a bit faster. They would still be in town a little before dark but if they didn't get any information at the jail then they would be forced to search outside of town in the dark. It didn't matter, the three would gladly search the entire night if they had to.

They tied up outside the jail and the sheriff went straight to the back and unlocked the cell containing the prisoner with no name. He marched him out front where the light was better and the air was a bit warmer.

"What's the matter with you, Sheriff, you look all put out," the prisoner said with a chuckle.

"You got another horse tied up somewhere outside of town?"

The man didn't respond, he just looked at the three men standing before him. He recognized Buster Adams as the man from the livery where he stabled his horse.

"I got my horse stabled with that man standing right there. Go ahead and ask him."

Thinking about the danger the horse was in, Adams walked over and grabbed the man by his shirt collar and lifted him clean out of his chair. "I got no time for this. You tell me right now or I promise to beat you to death with my bare fists." After he said this he dropped him back into his chair and then balled both his fists as he stood over the startled man.

The livery man was strong, real strong. Working as a blacksmith, and also doing all the work that a livery can generate, will build some muscle on a man. Adams had the muscle.

"I got only the one horse, Sheriff, I promise." The man said to the sheriff but didn't take his eyes off the liveryman.

Adams drew back and hit the man squarely on the jaw. He, and the chair he was sitting on, were knocked over backward. No sooner had the man hit the floor than Adams grabbed him up and held him off his feet. "You will die right here tonight unless you tell me where that horse is. If you doubt me on this then it will be the last doubt you will ever experience," Adams screamed at the man.

Both Bevins and Walker were startled at the violence the mild mannered liveryman just exhibited. They were also impressed with the strength Adams was exhibiting.

"I believe I'd tell him, mister. If you don't then he'll kill you right here in my office," Bevins said.

"You can't let him do that, Sheriff. It's your job to uphold the law," the man said as he dangled in the air.

"The only witnesses you got are me and Walker. The way I seen it play out, it was you who attacked Adam's and he was only defending himself. In the process you got killed," Bevins said with a smile.

The man knew he had to think of something fast because at the moment he feared the liveryman was going to kill him.

"Alright, alright, put me down. I believe I do remember something about a horse."

Adams roughly put the man down but didn't release his grip on his shirt. "Talk, you damn nuisance, and remember, if it ain't what I need to hear they will be the last words you ever speak."

The man nervously looked at the sheriff and Walker. He couldn't make himself look Adams in the eye; he was way too scared for that.

"Well let's see, I was riding into town a few nights back. It was past dark and I was in a bit of a hurry, you know with the weather and all. Anyway as I was hurrying toward the lights of town I uh, well I heard a horse. Yea that was it, I heard this horse and since it sounded close I changed direction a little and rode to where I thought it was.

"Well, when I got a little closer I saw it was a horse and it was tied to this tree. It was tied to a tree and I figured that whoever owned it was near so I trotted on into town and stopped at a saloon. After a few drinks I went and stabled my horse with this man here that just threatened to kill me. After that I got arrested for drinking, they said I was being arrested for public drunkenness, and well I think you know the rest of the story."

All three men knew the story they just heard was a lie but right now all they wanted was to rescue the horse.

"Where was this horse you spotted? And if it's a lie then I can promise you I'll be back to finish what I've started," Adams said.

The man looked at the sheriff, and then at Walker, he still didn't have the nerve to look at Adams.

"I believe I'd tell him if I was you mister. I've seen the blacksmith do some terrible things, if you know what I mean," the sheriff said.

"North of town at a spot where the creek combines with a little stream coming off the mountain. The horse was maybe fifty feet downstream from the forks and ten feet from the water. It was tied to a big cottonwood with a long lead, long enough for it to reach the water."

"Alright then, head your sorry ass back to your cell and make it fast. The three of us are going to go find that horse," Bevins said.

Before the man could take a step Adams grabbed him again and roughly pushed him toward the cells in the back. As he slammed the iron door he said. "You better hope that horse is where you said it was. You better also hope that horse is okay because if it ain't I plan on heating me an iron and coming back here and branding your sorry ass."

With the prisoner locked up the three hurried outside and saddled up. They were headed in the direction they were told the horse would be. Not more than fifteen minutes later they came to the fork in the stream. Both Adams and Bevins knew the area pretty well and it didn't take long to find what they were looking for.

Tied to a tree ten or fifteen feet from the edge of the creek was a horse, a horse that was looking put out and hungry. She had heard the sounds of the men as they approached , she had also gotten the scent of the three horses the men rode even before she heard the noise the three made.

"There she is, you two stay back and let me approach on foot. Try not to make any noise," Adams said as he reached the reins of his horse to Bevins.

As he got off his horse he pulled two apples out of his saddlebags, something he grabbed from the sack lunch the sheriff had sitting on his desk. Bevins at first protested but then realized what it was for and gladly agreed.

As Adams slowly approached the horse he held one of the apples in front of him. The horse went from being mildly agitated to being anxious; she wanted that apple in the worst way.

"Here you go, girl," Adams said as he grabbed the bridle and reached the apple out, being careful to not lose a finger to the hungry horse. She snatched the apple with her teeth and bit it in half. After quickly consuming that half she bent her head to the ground and picked up what was left and quickly devoured that as well.

The Trail

The horse knew Adams had one more apple and she wanted it. Again she took the apple from Adams and quickly made short work of it. Without releasing his grip on the bridle the liveryman led the horse the short distance to the stream. She drank but not a lot. Apparently she had drunk her fill during the three or four days she had been here.

"Well Adams I believe you saved that horses life by threatening the life of that sorry son of a bitch I got locked up. I doubt he would have talked out of the goodness of his heart," Bevins said.

Adams was leading the horse back from the water as he said, "I might still kill that bastard. Look at this horse, she ain't had nothing more than a few blades or winter sage and some twigs she pulled of the trees around here."

The sheriff and Walker looked the place over. The rope used to tie the horse out was maybe eighteen or twenty feet long. The area out from the tree the horse had been tied to was picked clean; even the bark on some of the trees had been gnawed on. The only good thing they found about the place was the fact that the rope was long enough for the horse to make it to the water.

Adams couldn't undo the knot in the rope where it was tied to the tree. The powerful horse had the knot pulled so tight all the liveryman could do was take his knife and cut the loop in two.

"Would you look at that bridle, it's damn near pulled apart at the seams," Bevins said. "What would have happened if we hadn't found her, Adams? Could she have freed herself?"

Adams was inspecting the bridle. It was well made and strong to boot. "I think in another day or two she would have been so hungry she might have been able to pull free. The leather was starting to stretch a bit and the rivets at the seams were starting to give way. She is a stout animal and deserves better." Adams said as he rubbed the horse's ears. "We better be getting back, I need to get her in a stall with lots of hay and a little grain."

The three had been so glad to find the animal that none of them had given much notice to the fact that she was wearing a saddle and carrying saddlebags.

"I'll strip the gear off her when I get her in a stall. She's probably tired of that saddle and this bridle for that matter. I'll need to check to make sure it hasn't hurt her back. A saddle can wear on a horse after a day, and this has been way more than a day. A good brushing will fix her right up." Adams was in full liveryman mode now, thinking of what the horse needed. "You know, she probably got a little cold and lonely out here all by herself. Now you think of the kind of weather we've been having and this poor animal tied up out here all by herself." There were quite a few trees around and even a few cedars, this undoubtedly helped to block the wind and give the horse a little protection. The stretch of water where the horse took her drinks was fast moving and this helped keep it from freezing solid, another bit of luck for a horse that had ran shy of it.

"Let's get back to town. Damn glad we found her. Sheriff, I got a question for you," Adams said as mounted and turned his horse toward town.

Bevins wondered what the liveryman wanted now. "What's that?" he asked.

"I'd like a few minutes to talk with your prisoner again if you don't mind?"

Walker looked at Bevins; both thought that would be a bad idea. "I think you should stay away from the man for a while. At least until you cool off a little. He told us where the horse was but still maintains he only stumbled across her on his way to town. Let me do a little thinking on how to handle things from here. All I need is for you to go in there and beat the man senseless."

Walker looked over at the liveryman. The look on his face told the story; he was going to do exactly what the sheriff suspected. If given the chance he would probably kill the man outright.

Fifteen minutes later and all three men were at the stable. The horse was led to a stall after getting the gear stripped off. As Adams went about the task of feeding and watering the animal, Walker and the sheriff looked over the gear.

The saddle was of poor quality and pretty old. The look and feel of the leather indicated many years of use in all kinds of weather. The bridle was better made but was now nearly useless after being practically pulled apart by the horse.

"Let's put the saddlebags on the table and see if we can get any clues from what it contains," Bevins said.

The pair of leather bags were not that different than the saddle. They had seen too much time in both rain and sunshine. The leather was worn and shiny, even cracked in places. The sheriff opened the first bag and poured its contents on top of the table.

The first item they noticed was a velvet pouch which contained a pipe. If the saddle and saddlebags led them to believe the owner was down on his luck, the pipe told a different story. It looked expensive, the carving on the side said London. Another pouch contained the tobacco for the pipe. This also looked to be expensive.

"Whoever rode this horse spent more on his tobacco than his tack? I never seen such ratty gear," Bevins said.

Along with the pipe and tobacco pouch were half dozen cigars. They were wrapped in a cloth that undoubtedly helped to keep them from drying out. It looked to be some sort of cheesecloth. A box of matches and a paper sack of beef jerky rounded out the contents of the first bag. Bevins slid the items to the side and then looked in the second bag, it contained more than the first. Rather than just pouring the contents out he decided to dig the stuff out an item at a time.

"Looks like whoever this stuff belonged to wasn't unarmed after all." The sheriff pulled out a brand new Colt. It was of .38 caliber, there was also a box of shells for the gun.

"Whoever owned this wasn't much of a man for guns. A .38 is a good gun but not heavy enough for some of the critters you might run into out in the wilds. Both two and four legged," Walker said.

Bevins slid the gun and ammo to the side and looked back in the bag. The next item out was a leather wallet with brass snaps. Inside was a wad of bills, mostly of the hundred dollar variety.

As Walker watched, Bevins counted out twenty-one hundred dollar bills and an assortment of lesser amounts. "Now why a man with this kind of money would be seen with such a worn out saddle and saddlebags, is a mystery to me?"

The leather wallet was also of high quality and looked to be nearly new. There was also a leather coin case again with a brass snap. Bevins opened it up and whistled. He looked up at Walker as he poured gold coins onto the table. Seventeen fifty dollar and thirteen one-hundred dollar gold coins glistened in the lamplight. The leather coin wallet couldn't have held a single coin more.

"Say, Adams, you got anything around here to write on?" Bevins asked.

Adams closed the stall door after getting the horse all situated with a little grain a little hay and a lot of water. "I got to be careful of that mare. She needs to be brought back to food real slow like. I got a few pieces of paper and a couple of pencils in that cabinet on the wall there, what you two figuring on writing down anyway?"

Just then Adams saw the loot lying on his table. "Well would you look at that, how much money was in them saddlebags anyway?"

"Ain't sure yet, I need the paper and pencil so we can get an inventory on all this stuff. After that I plan on putting it in the safe over at the bank," Bevins said.

Without taking his eyes off the money Adams said, "I doubt that little bank has that much money in it now. You might just be doubling its assets."

Bevins laughed, "You might be right about that. Walker, how about you and Adams getting a count on this, designate gold and paper money separately and list the denominations of each. Also include the other items we found. Might be handy if anything is ever said. This is also evidence. I don't know when or where the evidence will be needed but it's best to be prepared.

Adams grabbed the paper and then pulled out a chair. "You want to count while I write the items down Walker? Or do you prefer to do the writing?"

It didn't take the three long to inventory the contents of the two saddle bags. They also included one saddle and one bridle. There was also the horse and a gun boot, the boot was empty.

"If anybody comes and claims the horse I need to talk to them. If they ask any questions try to remember everything they say. Write everything down if you need to. Actually write everything down regardless and then find me or Walker here," Bevins said.

Adams looked at Walker. "Tell him? Sheriff, I don't believe I need to be talking to Walker, he ain't no deputy. This might be part of a crime that's been committed and I should tell everything I know or find out to a lawman.

Bevins rubbed his stubbly chin before saying, "Walker, I now deputize you for the town of Clear Creek. Adams, you are the witness. Now I'm heading back to my office." With that the sheriff turned and left the livery.

Adams looked up and grinned at Walker. "Ain't you going to follow him, Deputy Walker?"

Walker stood and grunted, "Damn sure beats my previous name."

Trevor and Mathew traveled the remainder of the day without any more trouble from outlaws and bushwhackers. Mathew spent his time riding on top of the load keeping a sharp lookout for any more trouble. Both men continued to think of the happenings of the previous night. Five men dead, and for what reason. Neither man could figure out why they were set upon the way they were. Even Satan was keeping a close watch as he rushed the hitch along. He wanted to get as far away from the previous night's campsite and he wanted to do it as fast as possible.

"Say, Trevor, how about tossing me up a piece of jerky from the side box. Maybe that canteen and a wedge of cornbread to go along with it. I'm starting to get a hunger pain," Mathew said around two in the afternoon.

Trevor figured it was about time for a little grub himself. He stopped the hitch of mules and set the wheel lock on the big wagon. He looked up to see Mathew poking around on his leg.

"How's that gunshot wound of yours looking? You keep nosing around like that and it might start to bleed again."

Mathew pulled the bandage to the side and made a frown. "Alright, alright. I reckon it's just a little red is all. I feel real bad about riding the top of the wagon like this, but I really don't know how far I could walk with the way this leg is looking."

"You just said it was looking fine now which it is?"

"Fine I guess but I don't like the way it's getting red and all. I might even feel a bit feverish to boot," Mathew said as he continued to poke and prod at the wound.

"Here, can you catch or do I need to climb this stuff up to you?"

"I can catch, Yank, can you throw is the real question?

"You know calling me names ain't going to get you any lunch so shut the hell up if you want this cornbread."

Mathew caught the canteen, and then his cornbread and jerky. As he and Trevor ate they both kept a close watch on their surroundings. Getting nearly killed the night before, and again this morning, will make a man cautious.

"Trevor, grab one of them rifles and keep it with you while you eat."

Trevor stood up and looked around, "You see something?"

"I thought I caught a glimpse of a rider about a half mile up the trail. He came out from some trees and then he was gone again."

Trevor grabbed one of the long guns and then checked to make sure it was fully loaded. "You see him again?"

"Naw, just the once. Maybe since the two of us are now set for guns we might just use the money we was going to spend on a new shooter to buy us a spyglass. It would be real handy right now," Mathew said as he held a hand over his forehead to try and reduce the glare.

"That might be a good idea. Always wanted me a spyglass."

"Maybe the two of us should detour a day and head over to Hartman Station. I could use something for this leg of mine, it's starting to give me a bother. Seems the more I think about it the more it hurts."

"Well I got a cure for that, just don't think about it," Trevor said. He turned his gaze from the trail to Mathew. "You sound like a man that's getting the spooks. A day is something I'd rather not spare right now. I want to get to Clear Creek and get shed of this freight. The quicker we get there the quicker we can warm our hides against a hot stove instead of a weak little campfire."

Mathew wouldn't have any of it. "A day won't kill either of us and the mules might appreciate a stall for the night. We can pull in there about dark and leave first thing in the morning. I might get that little Indian wife of his to make me up a poultice or something for my leg. Might even spring for a bottle of whiskey. I'm starting to feel poorly and a shot of whiskey might help. I've never known a time when a shot of whiskey didn't help."

The Trail

"That injury of yours is starting to hurt me a little too. Just listening to you whine is about more than I can stand right now," Trevor said as he released the wheel lock and headed for the front of the hitch. He felt a little bad about jumping on to Mathew but decided it wasn't worth worrying about.

Billy Tucker rode his horse at a steady trot for the better part of twenty minutes and then slowed her for a cool down. Ten minutes later he entered the camp the four men had used for the last day and a half. He got off and walked the horse the last twenty feet and tied her up with three others. The four men didn't have a pack horse, all they carried was what would fit in their saddlebags. Grub was getting thin, real thin.

"Damn sure took you long enough, Billy. You fall asleep on the job or something?" Anderson said.

Billy didn't answer, he just walked to the fire to get a cup of coffee. "Why you three done let the fire go out."

"Can't be using a fire in broad daylight you damn nuisance," Anderson said. "You want them two teamsters to see us a mile before they get here?"

Anderson was of the loud sort. He was also big, standing at six feet five inches and that was in his stocking feet. Anderson wasn't of the type to make friends easily, he found it easier to make enemies and that was something he did often. The only reason anyone tolerated the loudmouth was because he was the one who always managed to get the jobs. The job they were on now was to intercept a freight wagon being driven by two old relics from back in the Civil War. If the war hadn't done the two in then this trip surely would.

Anderson had been contacted four days prior and told to get to the trail as fast as possible and intercept the wagon. They were to kill the two drivers and burn the wagon, that was after they removed the mail bags. They were given a rough description of the parcel they were to intercept. After that they were to burn all the mail except the parcel and enough letters to partially fill one bag. If they were intercepted then whoever bested them wouldn't know which of the articles in the bag held any importance.

"That coffee pot has been sitting in the ashes ever since you been gone. It might not be hot but it's still coffee. Now what did you find out?" Anderson asked.

"Wagon's about four miles back. One of the teamsters is riding on top of the freight. The other is walking the lead mule."

Anderson smiled, "Good, good, they'll be here in a couple of hours. We got maybe an hour before we need to take up our positions."

"There's one more thing boss. They got five horses trailing the wagon, no riders just empty saddles," Tucker said.

"Five saddled horses you say. Sounds like them other fellers we was to look out for might have gotten themselves killed. But that don't make sense, how could two old men have killed five of the likes as we was told about?" Anderson said as he peered into the distance. He knew by the description he was given that the two old men were more than capable of taking care of themselves, but two against five seemed to be a stretch.

The two remaining men of the four were a couple of troublemakers Anderson had rather not have hired but on such short notice they were all he could find. One of the two was a man by the name of Claude Dingus. Dingus wore a beard, an extremely shaggy beard and wore a Bowler hat. The only reason he wore the Bowler was so people could make fun of it. It was then that his skills as a brawler came into play as he pummeled whoever had disrespected his hat.

"I knew two of them men, they weren't men to be handled as easily as you say. Either of the two I know would have been more than a match for the two teamsters. Maybe the two are dead and the wagon is already in the hands of your rival Anderson. If that's the case then I still expect to be paid for my four days' work. I could have been in some warm saloon right now and avoiding this weather," Dingus snarled.

Anderson had heard of the reputation Dingus carried with him. He also wasn't about to be tongue-whipped by the Bowler wearing fool. "Maybe you don't know them two as well as you say. Maybe you should just shut your mouth and leave the thinking to me," Anderson said.

Dingus bolted to his feet and advanced on Anderson. Before he got three feet he was looking at the dangerous end of a Colt. It stopped him cold.

"Now, I'll be glad to discuss the particulars of our deal at a more opportune time but for now we got a job to do. That is unless you want to finish up right here and now?" Anderson said.

Dingus might have been of the mean sort but the sight of the Colt and the speed in which Anderson drew it caused him to take pause. "I reckon I can wait. After this job is done and I get my pay maybe you and me can have us a little talk without the interference of a gun? You know, man to man."

Anderson holstered his Colt as he said, "Be my pleasure. We get this job done then I would like nothing more than to teach you what I think of that little hat of yours." Anderson added that last part to let the Irishman know what he thought of him and his ways. He would now need to keep a close eye on the redheaded troublemaker, just in case.

The four rode to the trail to a spot they had picked out earlier. It gave good cover and offered even better firing positions. It was the plan to just shoot the two teamsters and drag their bodies off the road and into a shallow ravine. It would be easy to cover the bodies with the loose sandy soil at the base. They would then lead the team and wagon off the trail so they could go through the contents. Not only did they want the mail bags but they also needed to replenish their meager rations. There would undoubtedly be food on the wagon and they would simply take what they needed.

It was Anderson's intention to simply cut the mules loose and let them wander the territory and graze. Dingus wanted to put a bullet in each just for the fun of it but Anderson couldn't allow such cruelty. The mules would be set free along with the five horses. If any of the saddles the five carried were of their liking he would allow any of the men to switch.

The stretch of trail where the ambush was to take place was a half mile after the road split. The other road led to Hartman Station. Anderson would have rather made the ambush before the trail split but there wasn't a suitable location that would conceal them before the wagon got there.

It was unlikely the wagon would alter course from Clear Creek to the Station anyway. The load, and the mail they carried, was for Clear Creek.

The two teamsters hadn't gone more than a mile before Mathew hollered down from the top of the freight wagon. "We get to the split in the road I think we should head to the

Station. I'm starting to feel poorly. What I need is a bottle of whiskey and a poultice for my leg. I done heard your complaint about it slowing us down but the way I'm feeling right now makes me not care about the inconvenience."

Trevor knew Mathew was right. He had climbed up and took a look at the gunshot wound before the two had started back on the trail. It was getting red around the edges and it looked like Mathew was getting a fever. Infection was something that could kill a man and Trevor knew it.

"That's about a three hour distance but the way Satan is making the team pull I'd say two would put us there. We'll detour and get that leg of yours looked at. Good thing I'm an understanding sort."

Mathew heard what Trevor said but was feeling too bad to respond. He was glad they were taking the detour. He knew Hartman's Indian wife would be able to fix him up. The whiskey would help too.

"You sure you spotted that wagon where you said it was Billy? They should have been here by now," Anderson asked as he peered down the trail. He was anxious and wanted to get the wagon in his possession. Once he got the job finished he would hole up somewhere until the weather improved.

"It was right where I said it was and they was ready to pull out. They stopped for some grub. I watched 'em eat and when I left they was fixing to get started. Give it a few more minutes, they'll be here."

The four men continued to watch the road. They were looking for dust from the hitch of mules. They were also listening, a wagon and eight mules weren't all that quiet. After thirty more minutes Billy was told to back track and see what he could see. He was also told to try and not be seen himself.

Billy trotted his horse back up the same trail looking for the freight wagon. He went as far as the turnoff for Hartman Station. He could see where the heavy wagon and hitch turned west. Just to make sure he wasn't wrong about things he went as far as where the teamsters had stopped to eat. Now he was sure of it, the wagon was heading for the Station.

Trevor and Mathew were less than a mile from the Station when Mathew hollered from the top of the load. "Looks like four riders coming up behind us, they look to be riding hard." The old man might have been feeling the effects from his wound but he was still smart enough, and determined enough, to keep a sharp lookout.

Trevor stepped out from the hitch where he could get a better look. "I see 'em, they sure do look to be in a hurry don't they?"

"They do at that. You think they're associated with the business from last night and this morning? I think until we get to where we're going we need to treat everybody we see as someone wanting to cause mischief."

Trevor had already thought the same thing. He reached over and tapped Satan with his walking stick. The big mule had sensed the four riders about the same time as Mathew had seen them. It didn't take any coaxing for the lead mule to start pulling harder and in doing so the other seven followed suit. Within a minute the eight mules were at nearly a trot. Satan suspected trouble and wanted no part of it. He had been on this road before when the two teamsters had dropped part of a load at the Station on a previous trip. The big mule knew where it was and he knew how far they needed to go to get there.

As the mules picked up a little speed the freight wagon began to jostle Mathew. It was enough to make the ride unpleasant but at the moment the old man had the same thoughts as Satan, get to the Station as fast as possible.

"There they are, come on boys let's give chase," Anderson said to the other three riders.

The four spurred their mounts as they tried to catch the wagon before it got too close to the station. If they could catch it in time then they could do away with Trevor and Mathew and then turn around and head back the way they came.

Trevor was nearly out of breath trying to keep up with the hitch. Satan was doing what he knew best, command the other mules and at the moment that command was speed.

"There's the station, Trevor, better slow Satan down a bit before he runs you into a grave."

Trevor was more than glad to accommodate his partner. He took a few paces at a full run and caught up with the lead mule. Satan resisted at first but after a little coaxing from Trevor he began to slow. The other seven mules, along with Trevor, were glad he did, they were nearly spent. They were now less than a half a mile from their destination and in clear sight of it if anyone cared to look.

"Better slow a little boys. Wouldn't pay to go chasing that wagon into the station. As it is we just look like someone looking for a meal and a place to bed down," Anderson said.

"Fine by me, it'll just add another day's pay to what you already owe me," Dingus said. Anderson was really starting to hate that guy.

Lance Hartman was a German by birth. His parents had immigrated to America when he was a young boy. Although they never spoke the language with any degree of success he managed to speak without any German accent at all. He could also speak German with no hint of an English accent. Hartman had traveled west after both his parents were killed in a boating accident in the sound. The small steamer they were traveling in simply blew up halfway across the harbor. There were any number of small steamers working the water as ferries and on more than one occasion a boiler simply over heated and exploded.

With no other ties to New York, and nothing other than bad memories to keep him there, the then eighteen year old Hartman packed up his meager belongings and headed west. He finally landed in Colorado and went to work for a couple of the ranchers in the area. He worked hard, it was his German ancestry kicking in, and soon had enough money to open up his little out of the way station.

After fifteen years he had built it to a substantial operation. He sold to the trappers that came down from the mountains twice a year to trade their furs for ammunition and supplies. Hartman in turn sold the furs for a profit.

The station had a large barn and corral where horses could be stabled during the night. He had ten rooms he rented by the night or week depending on the weather. His was a location where some hunting guides would meet their paying customers before heading into the Colorado wilds in search of game. These folks were usually of the moneyed type and spent freely when at the Station.

Meals were prepared and served in a large room that was attached to the only saloon for fifty miles in any direction. The kitchen was run by another German that Hartford had sent for when he finally had the place up and running and making a profit. Hartman had his own freight wagon, one pulled by a six mule hitch, that he sent once a month to the same place where Trevor and Mathew picked up what they were taking back to Clear Creek. At times he contracted with the two teamsters for any empty space on the big freight wagon to help keep his trading post stocked. Between Hartman Station and Clear Creek the town of Bristle Buck was getting a fair amount of business.

Hartman was heading back to the trading post from the stable when he saw Trevor and Mathew coming down the trail. He noticed Trevor running trying to keep up with the hitch and wondered where Mathew was, the two never worked the route alone. When he finally spotted the second teamster on top of the wagon he was even more confused. Then he saw the four riders and they looked to be trying to catch the wagon.

Hartman went into the Station and got his double-barrel Greener and a handful of shells. There was another man that helped Hartman work the trading post, his name was Lewis Hagans. Hagans had been working for Hartman for the better part of seven years and had proven himself to be dependable. Hartman suspected the name the man used was an alias but he really didn't care. Men came west all the time to escape troubles back east. Hartman suspected there was a rougher side to the man but until now that side had never shown itself.

"Where you going with a shotgun this late in the day?" Hagans asked his boss. He knew Hartman liked to bird hunt from time to time but he knew you couldn't shoot birds at night.

"Looks like Trevor and Mathew are coming into the station and they got four riders following them. I just thought I'd see what gets said after they show up. You see me needing help then grab that other Greener," Hartman said.

"I'll do that, boss, you need help I'll be there." Hartman never doubted for a minute that Hagans would back him up.

Hartman went out and across the road that bisected his operation. He was standing in front of the barn when Trevor stopped.

"Howdy, Trevor, you and Mathew look to be a little lost," Hartman said.

Trevor pulled a dirty neckerchief from a pocket and mopped his forehead. "We might be at that."

Mathew managed to climb down but with great difficulty. Hartman noticed the bandaged leg and the five saddled horses. He now knew bringing out the Greener was a good idea.

Mathew hobbled over and shook Hartman's hand. "I might need that woman of yours to look at my leg. I think I got an infection building up." Mathew looked feverish and was sweating something awful.

"Sure thing, Mathew, why don't you go into the trading post there and let Hagans know. You might tell him to go ahead and load that other Greener and be ready."

Mathew tipped the brim of his hat and hobbled inside. Trevor went to the side box and grabbed one of the

Winchesters and then made sure it was loaded. He joined Hartman beside the wagon. "You know them men coming up the road there?" Hartman asked.

"Trevor stood behind the front wheel of the wagon and ratcheted a round into the Winchester. "Can't say as I do but this could be associated with some trouble me and Mathew had last night and this morning."

"By the looks of them five empty saddles trailing the wagon I take it there's been some killing?"

"Yep, it was looking like it was me and Mathew going to be gittin' killed until old Satan over there saved our bacon. I'll tell you all about it over a beer a little later. I need to see what's on these gent's minds first." The four riders were now at the station and were slowing their mounts as they approached the two men. The four noticed the two men with long guns and wondered how they could know what they were up to.

"Hello the wagon. Me and my boys here need to have a talk with the man that runs the freight," Anderson said.

Trevor stepped clear of the wagon. "That would be me mister. What is it you need to know?"

Before Anderson could answer Dingus got involved with the conversation. "Them horses belong to some friends of mine. You mind telling me what you're doing with their horses and saddles?"

"You say them was friends of yours?" Trevor asked.

"That's what I said, old man, now answer up."

"Well if they was friends of yours then all I can say is you need to find yourself some new friends."

This made Dingus lose his temper, something he barely kept under control on the best of days. "I say you're a horse thief and I'm here to take you and that other old man back to town to stand trial. And if I find the men that owned them horses have been killed then I might just string you up myself, before we even get close to a town."

Trevor pulled the hammer back on the Winchester as Hartman did the same with the Greener. Neither had pointed the long guns at the four yet but it was only a matter of time. "Doubt you and your men got the authority to do anything mister. I don't see no badges."

"Throw up your hands, we'll be taking you and the wagon now," Dingus said as he eased his hand over the butt of his gun.

Just then the door to the Trading Post opened and Lewis Hagans walked out holding a Greener, it was identical to the one Hartman was holding.

No sooner had Hagans made it out than Mathew limped out the door carrying a Colt. It was the same one he had used to shoot the two men that had tried to kill Trevor that morning. Even during the war a pistol had been the weapon of choice for the old teamster. Needless to say he was good with that type of weapon.

James Anderson had listened to the remarks made by Dingus in disbelief. It had been agreed that if the wagon made it to the Trading Post then the four would simply pass themselves off as travelers needing a place to take a meal and rest the horses. Once Dingus started shootin' off his mouth that plan had gone out the window. Anderson needed to reign in Dingus and decided to shut the man up before things got any worse.

"Hold on there a minute, Dingus. We don't want these two men, just the wagon and the stolen horses," Anderson said.

Dingus had other intentions. He planned to kill Anderson before this was over and decided this was as good a time as any. He twisted in the saddle and drew his Colt at the same time. Anderson was astonished that one of his men would draw down on him. Before he could even go for his own gun there was a shot. Everyone expected to see Anderson topple from his horse but it was Dingus who fell forward and then toppled out of the saddle. He was dead before he hit the ground.

Everyone looked back to see Billy holding a smoking gun. He had seen what Dingus was about to do. Before he drew down on Anderson, Billy, as quick as a cat, drew and shot the man. He had saved Anderson's life.

Billy Tucker hadn't liked any of the happenings since hiring on four days back. He wasn't a killer but he was fast with a gun. He never intended to let the other three shoot Trevor and Mathew down in cold blood. As it worked out he had just eliminated one of the men in the gang. Tucker backed his horse a few steps as he held the gun.

Anderson looked at the young gunman and said, "Good work, Billy. I never liked that Dingus and it was a mistake for me to hire him on."

Billy turned the gun toward the man. "Keep your gratitude to yourself and keep your hand away from that gun. Sloane, you and Anderson keep your hands where I can see them."

"Now you wait just a minute, Billy. You know who I work for and once he finds out what you did here today he'll put a price on your head," Anderson said.

"I know who you work for, a man by the name of Wilbur Westbrook. As it works out Mister Westbrook lost faith in you."

"So Westbrook hired you," Anderson said.

"No, I don't work for Westbrook. The man I work for is none of your damn business."

Sloane was the fourth man in Anderson's group. He was slow witted but dangerous just the same. Instead of complying with the demands put forth by Billy he went for his gun. Before it cleared the holster Billy put a bullet in the center of his chest. He fell and joined Dingus in the dirt.

With two of the four now dead and Billy holding the fastest gun Anderson had ever seen he decided to do as he was told. Billy trotted his horse over beside Anderson's and took his gun. He also got the hideaway the man carried.

After disarming Anderson Billy put his Colt back in its holster and turned to the two men by the freight wagon. "Trevor, I don't believe you know me I but can promise you, I intend no harm to you or Mathew." He trotted his horse over and reached the two guns he had taken from Anderson to Trevor.

Trevor lowered the Winchester a little, but not much. "That's good to know. In the last twenty-hours I was beginning to think everybody we came across had the intention of killing me and Mathew. Now before I put away this rifle I'd like for you to tell me what in hell is going on."

Billy pulled up the collar on his coat as he stepped from his horse. "I'd like to help you put away that hitch of mules if you would let me. I think Mathew there needs to sit and rest because of his busted up leg. Maybe we can talk over supper?"

Trevor looked over at Mathew, "I like this kid already." He looked back at Billy. "You can help me with the mules but I feel obliged to warn you. You see that big long eared beast up front on the right. That's Satan and you better let me tend to him. He's a bit skittish when it comes to strangers and dead men lying all over the place. Hell, he's down right mean on the best of days," Trevor said with a chuckle.

The Trail

"Satan, can't say as I've ever heard that name used before on a mule. There a reason he's got a name like that?" Billy asked.

"There are several reasons, one is lying in a shallow ravine near where we made camp last night."

Hartman told Trevor to put the mules in the corral and he would come out and feed them later. He wanted to haul the two dead outlaws off the road before anyone else rode up. If he could make room he would put the eight mules in the barn later. He suspected the animals had been driven hard and needed a place out of the weather.

"You intend on burying them two or just leaving them out for the wolves?" Trevor asked.

Hartman didn't really have an answer for that. "Grounds frozen too hard to dig a grave. Tomorrow morning I'll put them in a wagon and haul them to the ravine about a mile or so from here. I'll shove them in and then say a few words. Might be able to use a pickaxe to chip away enough topsoil to cover them. I don't know what kind of men they were but I have a feeling they lived their lives closer to hell than heaven."

"Sounds like the thing to do, might ease a few folks conscience. If it was up to me I'd leave them out in the woods, wolves need to eat too," Treavor said.

"How about we just store the bodies in one of the empty stalls tonight? Don't want to leave them beside the road," Hartman said.

After the bodies were placed inside the barn Trevor went inside to check on Mathew. He found him in the tavern sipping on a beer. He looked a lot better than he had at any time during the last twenty-four hours.

"I thought you was going to get that leg looked at?"

171

Mathew turned from the bar and pointed to the bandage on his leg, it looked new. "Done had it fixed up. That missus of Hartman's made up a poultice and got me doctored up real good. She said it was a good thing we came in because by tomorrow, or the day after, I would have been down with the fever. Said never to mess with an infection. She also said I should have a beer or two to help my nerves."

Trevor believed everything he was being told, right up till the part about the beer. "Well in that case I think I might need to lend a hand with the beer."

After the two finished their beers they went into the dining room and took a table near the back. They hadn't been seated more than a minute until Billy Tucker walked in. When he spotted the two teamsters and headed their way.

"You two mind if I join you for supper? I ain't had much more than trail food for the last three or four days, and it was gittin real thin at that."

"Why we don't mind at all, I reckon if you can stand us then we can tolerate you. Grab that chair and set yourself down," Mathew said.

"What kind of food does this place serve?"

The two teamsters looked at each other. It had been at least a couple of years since they had been there and couldn't remember how the food was.

"I reckon it's good if you're hungry. Thought you said all you had for the last few days was trail food and little of it to boot," Trevor said with a smirk.

Billy held up both hands, palms out. He started laughing and when he finally stopped he managed to say, "Ouch, didn't know you two was such grouches.

The Trail

Mathew started laughing himself. "See, Trevor, I've told you for years that you are one hateful old cuss when you ain't had no supper. All the kid wanted was to find out how the food was."

"Well I'll tell you the same thing I was gonna tell him. I don't know but it will be a damn sight better than anything you can find over a camp fire with the wind howling down your shirt collar," Trevor told him.

Mathew looked at Billy and asked, "You sure you want to sit with us. I don't think I want to sit here the way that Yank is acting."

Trevor knew Mathew was right. "I was just pulling your chain. The food is good but it's been a while since we was here last."

Just then a lady came out and headed for their table. "You want supper or just coffee?"

"I'll have both," Trevor said. His tone was much improved in the presence of the lady. "I'm really looking forward to something other than trail food."

Mathew asked, "What's the special?"

"Elk Stew and cornbread. Got peach cobbler for dessert if anyone likes? The peaches are from a can. Not many peach trees in Colorado," the woman said.

Both Mathew and Billy ordered the special and also said they were interested in the dessert. Trevor ordered beans and bacon along with skillet bread.

Mathew looked at his old trail partner and said, "You just said you was tired of trail food and then you come in here and order trail food."

"It ain't the same, this is made in a kitchen and served on a plate. Why in hell do I find myself trying to explain everything to you, Reb?"

Mathew took no offense to being called a rebel, he actually liked it.

"I take it you two fought on different sides during the war," Billy said.

"That's right. I fought on the right side and he fought on the wrong side. Sometimes at night after a long day of hauling freight I dream of lining my sights up right between his eyes. Good thing me and him never met up during that little conflict or the south would have been short a Reb," Trevor said as he looked at Mathew.

"From what I heard you was a cook during the war. I've tasted the stuff that comes out of your skillet. Seven wonders the north didn't lose the war because every one of you Yanks was in the outhouse trying to get over your cooking," Mathew said.

Trevor grunted. "I am getting ready to eat and you go and bring up an outhouse. You are about as much a redneck as I've ever seen."

"Redneck is a compliment," Mathew muttered.

Billy listened and wondered how the two had managed to work the freight this long and not kill each other. As the two old men bantered with each other he wondered how the killing of Dingus and Sloane was going to affect the job at hand. He only hired on with Anderson in order to stop what the men were going to do, kill the teamsters and steal the parcel.

As the men waited for their supper Hartman came in and sat down. "Got the mules all situated in stalls. I paired them up but decided to just leave Satan in the main hallway. Figured he would like it better and I also figured he would stop anyone from coming in and messing with that wagon or the two bodies we put in that front stall. He was content to be out of the weather and knee deep in hay."

"What did you and Hagans do with Anderson?" Billy asked.

"Let him go," Hartman replied.

"You let him go. Now why did you do something like that for?" Trevor asked.

"What did you want me to do? I got no place on the property to lock him up and anyway, what would I lock him up for?"

"I guess you're right. Can't lock a man up for chasing the freight wagon but if he had gotten his way he would have killed me and Mathew just as sure as I'm sitting here now," Trevor said.

"Where is he now?" Billy asked.

"Once he figured me and Hagans wasn't going to hogtie him he climbed on his horse and lit out from here. I say good riddance. If he comes back then me or Hagans will take care of it."

"What about the two men I shot earlier? I can't say it was self-defense because Dingus wasn't going to shoot me, he was going to shoot Anderson," Billy asked.

"Maybe Dingus wasn't aiming at you but Sloane sure was. The way I see it is you did what you had to do," Hartman said.

"So you think I'm not in any trouble?" Billy asked.

"Not as far as I'm concerned. If anybody comes around asking questions then I'll tell it the way it really happened. After a month or two I doubt anyone will wonder what happened to those two. And anyway, a man's memory starts to get a little muddled after a while, if you know what I mean," Hartman said.

"Thanks, Mister Hartman. I was worried I might be in trouble with the law. As far as that wagon goes I'd like to ride along if the two of you would allow it," Billy said as he looked at Treavor and Mathew.

"You know that might not be a bad idea. A man on horseback tagging along with that big freight wagon might help ward off anybody else trying to cause trouble," Hartman said.

"I got a better idea if anybody cares to hear it?" Mathew said.

Trevor just shook his head. "It would be the first idea you ever came up with."

Mathew made a sour face as he said, "Would you shut up a minute, Yank, so I can talk. Anyway, I figure maybe since we got, let's see, seven horses already saddled and the owners all dead maybe I'll pick out a suitable one and also ride to Clear Creek on horseback. I think I can do more to protect that load if I ain't stuck on top of the freight. Now what do you think of that plan? Pretty good ain't it?" The other three men at the table thought it was a great plan.

"I got one thing to add, Mathew, we take two horses. I believe it might be a good idea if Trevor had a mount in case things go south," Billy said.

Mathew looked at Billy. "What was that, did you just say something about the South?"

"It's just a saying, nothing to get angry about. I also got a good idea. How about the two of you not getting fighting mad every time anyone says something you don't like or don't understand?" Billy said.

The Trail

"Well, I don't think the three of you need me anymore unless it's to referee. Billy, if you do decide to ride with these two try not to get in any arguments about the North or the South. Last I heard that conflict was settled years ago." With that Hartman got up and headed toward the bar.

Trevor looked at Mathew and said, "Now that was just plain rude. What about old Hartman thinking me and you don't get along?"

"Some people are just the troublesome sort, Trevor," Mathew said.

Again Billy couldn't help but laugh. He figured if the three of them didn't get killed by anymore of Westbrook's men on the trip to Clear Creek then at least the conversation would be entertaining.

The food arrived and the three managed to eat in peace. Billy noticed that if food was around the two teamsters took a pause from their verbal abuse of each other. When the food was finished the waitress brought Mathew and Billy a big bowl of peach cobbler, it looked good and smelled even better.

"Say, miss, you got any more of that in the back. I believe a bowl of them peaches and bread would suit me just fine," Trevor said.

The woman walked back and looked Trevor in the eye. "You ordered trail food, since when does peach cobbler constitute trail food?"

Trevor didn't have an answer but he really wanted that peach cobbler. The waitress only let him dangle for a few seconds before she patted him on the shoulder. "I was just having a little fun out of you. Sure you get peach cobbler." After that she turned and headed for the kitchen.

Trevor watched her go. "You know, if I didn't have me such a fine looking wife waiting at home I'd ask that little gal to marry me on the spot. Ain't it something what the promise of peach cobbler will do to a man's thinking?"

Hearing the description Trevor gave his wife caused Mathew to get choked on his food. A minute later and another bowl of steaming peach cobbler was sitting on the table. All three men were quiet as they polished off their meal.

"How should we split the tab?" Trevor asked as he finished his dessert.

Both the teamsters were looking at Billy when he looked up. He suspected the two expected him to pay for all three meals. He wasn't opposed to the plan they had in mind, especially since he would be reimbursed in full by his employer. He figured it might help to get the two to trust him.

"How about I pick up the tab for this fine food we just enjoyed. You two don't really know me and I figure a good way to break the ice is with a meal. Now how does that sound?"

The look on the two teamster's faces told it all. "Well young feller, that is mighty kind of you. I suspect I might get to like you after all," Trevor said.

"Well, you got no reason to not like me, especially with me going along to ride shotgun the rest of the way to Clear Creek."

Trevor looked at Mathew. "You see, there are some good folks left in the world besides me and you."

The lady came back out and Billy asked how much they owed her.

"Well, let me see, three dinners and three desserts comes to a dollar eighty." After she said this she looked at the three to see if they thought they were being overcharged.

The Trail

Billy reached into a pocket and pulled out two dollars and two quarters and then reached the money to her. "That extra is for you for taking such good care of the three of us." She smiled and then headed back toward the kitchen. Billy wondered if anyone ever left the woman a tip, probably not.

"If I didn't know better I would swear you was making eyes at her Billy," Trevor said.

Billy smiled and said, "Well, I reckon I might want to have breakfast here in the morning. Never hurts to get on the good side of the folks that are taking care of you. And that goes double for the folks that handle your food."

"You said it, son, and I believe every word of it," Trevor said.

Billy doubted the old teamster ever paid a compliment to anyone in his entire life. As a matter of fact he would probably bet money on it.

The three left and went to find Hartman, they needed rooms and figured Hartman was the man to see. He said he had a few rooms left and asked how many they needed. Billy looked at the two, by the look on their faces they were hoping he would pay for the rooms too.

"Just one for me I suppose. I'll grab my saddlebags. Where do I get the key?" Billy asked.

"The man at the bar handles the rooms. Just settle up with him and he'll give you the key. I took the liberty to put that horse of yours, along with the others, in the shed out back of the barn. I would have liked to use stalls in this kind of weather but the mules have everything filled up. The shed will keep them dry and help block the wind. I put fresh water and feed there for each. They should be able to take their water before it freezes solid. I'll go out around midnight and change pails so those that don't get water now will have a second chance."

"Thank you kindly, Mister Hartman. What time does the Trading Post open in the morning? I'm plum out of supplies for a journey of the sort we're about to undertake. Besides grub I'll need an extra box of ammunition for my Colt and Winchester. You got anything like that," Billy asked.

"Got almost any kind of ammunition you need. Just knock, when Hagans hears you in the morning he'll open up. It's the way we been doing business for years. Some folks leave real early and we aim to accommodate."

"Thanks again, see you fellers in the morning," Billy said as he turned and headed for the bar.

Hartman looked at Trevor and Mathew. "What will it be men, one room or two?"

"I suppose two, I ain't slept in a room in nearly a month," Mathew said.

"Probably be the best. Mathew snores like nothing you ain't ever heard before. Say, Hartman, you got hot water for that bathhouse attached to the rooms? It's been a spell and I'm starting to get a little gamey," Trevor said.

"Just tell the man at the bar. He'll see to it that the tub is filled. He will change the water after whoever goes first is finished. There's soap and a scrub brush in there too. He'll give each of you a big fluffy towel. There's also a shaving mug in there in case either of you take a notion to lather up them whiskers."

The two teamsters nearly raced to the bar to buy their rooms and pay for the use of the bathhouse. Trevor won that little footrace, probably because of Mathew's sore leg.

The Trail

"You hurry up, Trevor, I'll be needing my rest tonight. If you ain't noticed I got shot yesterday."

"You can have a beer while I soak in the suds a while, the wait might be good for you," Trevor said.

"That's fine, just don't fall asleep and leave me out here at this bar all night." If Mathew spent his whole evening and night at the bar it wouldn't have been the first time.

It only took ten minutes to fill the tub with warm water and twenty minutes after that Trevor came out as shiny as a new penny. "Well, how do I look?"

"You look as bad as ever but the smell is now tolerable. Why didn't you shave that scraggly beard of yours?" Mathew asked.

"Figured I'd take care of it in the morning. I knew you was in a hurry so I did a rush job. Now get yourself cleaned up. I'll bring in our stuff from the side box on the wagon and set yours outside your room. I want to see how old Satan likes sleeping in the hallway of that big barn. Wouldn't want that sorry cuss to go soft on us."

Thirty minutes later and Mathew was just as proud of his looks as ever, he even shaved while in the bathhouse. The two old men were used to rough living and the little they spent on the two rooms and bathhouse seemed to cheer each of them up. This was considered city life for the two, whatever that was.

When the two finally left the bar and locked the doors to their rooms they fell asleep almost instantly, they weren't as young as they once were and at the moment sleep was what the two needed most. After the two old men left the bar Hartman went in to find Hagans. He was in his bunk in the back of the trading post sound asleep.

"Hagans, you asleep?"

Hagans had been sound asleep but managed a "Yeah, I'm awake boss. You needed something?"

"Sorry to wake you up but I'm worried about the way things been going around here today. Two men killed right out in front of the trading post and a wagon pulled inside the barn that has something on it that is valuable enough for men to kill for. I think me and you need to post ourselves as guards during the night. You up for that?"

"You know, boss, I was thinking the same thing right before I fell asleep. You want to take first watch or do you want me to?"

"Hell, I'm wide awake after a day like today. Tell you what, I'll take first watch and you can relieve me around four in the morning. I think Trevor and Mathew are planning to head out early so they'll probably be waking you up anyway. I think Billy needs to make a purchase or two before they pull out."

Hagans put his head back down and wondered why Hartman woke him up if he was going to take first watch. No matter, he was so tired he knew he could fall back asleep.

After leaving Hartman's Station Anderson rode hard to the forks in the road and then turned left and headed toward Clear Creek. It was good and dark so he slowed his horse to a slow trot. He had no intentions of riding all the way there; just a little ways would work just fine. A man on horseback can make the eleven day trip that it takes Trevor and Mathew with the big wagon in only three if he rides hard.

The Trail

Just after daylight the next morning Anderson thought he smelled coffee and wood smoke in the air. He knew he would need to be careful.

Another half mile and he knew he was close. "Hello the camp."

"Anderson, is that you?" Came a voice he recognized.

"It's me, I'm coming in."

Anderson trotted his tired horse into camp where three men stood waiting, each holding a Greener. "Howdy, Anderson, where's the rest of your men?"

Anderson tied his horse to a low hanging cottonwood limb and then headed for the fire. He wore heavy leather gloves but the ride had nearly frozen his fingers. He picked up a tin cup, one that hadn't been washed since it was manufactured, and poured it full of coffee. He didn't taste the strong brew, he held it in his hands to warm his fingers.

"Dingus and Sloane are dead," he said as he finally turned up the cup and took a sip. The taste was strong and bitter, not bad he thought.

"Dead you say, what about Billy? Is he dead too?"

"Nope, Billy's alive and kicking. He's the one that killed Dingus and Sloane. Say, you got any bacon or biscuits around here. I hit the trail without any supper last night."

"Eddie, get that skillet and bring it to the fire." The skillet had what looked to be frozen food left from the night before. It was the habit of the men in cold weather to put the skillet off the fire and just let the leftovers, if there were any, freeze solid. The next morning they would just sit the whole thing back on the fire and then add to it. The skillet, like the coffee cup was in need of a good cleaning but none of the men seemed to mind.

A man by the name of Owsley stood over the fire warming the front side of his pants. He looked at Anderson and said, "I didn't trust that Billy Tucker from the moment I laid eyes on him. If you remember correctly I warned you not to hire him."

"I remember, he seemed to be alright when I talked to him. Guess I was wrong." Anderson looked at the man. "And that will be the last I want to hear of it. Right now I need to know how many men you got and what preparations you've made."

Owsley snorted as he stepped from the fire, his pants had steam coming off the front. "I got four besides me and you; most are good men, at least better than that damn Tucker. We put in here about two days ago and looked the place over, it's good, real good. Got a couple of spots where we can put men with rifles and two or three more places near where we'll waylay the wagon. Already picked out a good sized tree we can block the road with. All we need to know is when."

The skillet was starting to warm up and the smell of bacon was strong in the air. One of the other men was stirring up some flour and grease along with a little water to make a batter for skillet bread. It was so cold the batter was starting to get stiff as the water froze.

"They detoured to Hartman's Station late yesterday. I figure they will head out at first light or shortly after in order to make it to that little spot where they like to camp two nights this side of Clear Creek, which is about a mile from here. They'll be tired when they make it this far and looking forward to making camp. That's one reason I picked this spot. We'll bring down the tree today around four and all we got to do after that is wait. Make sure the fire is out long before that so no wood smoke is in the air. No coffee after noon today either. I could smell it over a mile from here. You damn varmints just as well put up a sign saying you're here and waiting."

Wasn't long until the men were enjoying breakfast. Rough weather and a rough trail makes even the worst of food taste better. They ate fast before their food froze, along with the coffee.

"Now if you don't mind I believe I'll bunk down for a couple of hours. If I manage to sleep as long as noon then make sure that fire is good and out." Fifteen minutes later Anderson had his ground cover and bedroll out and in place. It would be a cold sleep but he didn't mind, he was used to the comforts of winter.

Trevor woke at five the next morning and true to his word he headed for the bathhouse to shave. Ten minutes later he was back and banging on Mathew's door. "Wake up you damn nuisance. No wonder you and them other Johnnie Rebs lost the war sleeping every day till noon."

Mathew woke and threw a boot at the door. "Go away before I come out there and skin your hide, Yank." Trevor grinned, it was going to be a good day.

Trevor walked into the dining room wondering if it was even open, it was. Sitting at the same table as the night before was Billy. He was reading a newspaper while he waited for breakfast.

"Morning, Billy, is that really a newspaper?"

Billy lowered the paper to find Trevor heading his way. "It is. Hartman gets the latest papers when he makes his supply run every three weeks. This one is current, printed less than two weeks ago. I didn't figure you to be of the reading type, Trevor."

"Yeah I read. As a matter of fact I was a school teacher back in Boston before the war. I reckon that damn war changed a lot of lives. It ended a lot more," the old man said with a hint of sadness in his voice.

"You taught school, I find that to be a surprise."

Trevor looked sideways at the boy. "Watch your mouth, sonny. I was teaching before you was even born and being a nuisance to your maw and paw. Taught English and math. I really liked math, still do. I'm not like Mathew going around putting on airs and all, so most folks find it hard to believe, but it's true."

Just about then Mathew walked in and joined the two. "Morning fellers, breakfast about to be served? That was a real good supper we had last night but it seems the better the supper the more I want breakfast the next morning."

"Don't know, no one has been around yet. Trevor says he used to teach school. What did you do before the war Mathew?"

"Politics I reckon. First a lawyer and then county judge. Can't say as I really found a home in that world. I was doing alright though and then the war came along. Almost lost my life a time or two. Funny how rubbing that close to death changes a man."

Billy dropped the paper on the table and just looked at the two. "You two pulling my leg or what? I find it hard to believe one of you used to be a school teacher and the other a lawyer."

Just then Hartman and Hagans walked in. Both looked tired from their night of vigilance.

"Morning boys, anybody came out from the kitchen yet?"

The Trail

Billy picked up the paper and unfolded it again. "I heard some pots and pans back there rattling around. I ain't seen anyone yet though. The oil lamps were lit when I came in so I decided to wait until someone noticed me."

Trevor looked at Hartman. "How about telling Billy here what me and Mathew did for a living before that awful war interrupted us."

Hartman had stood up for the two before. It was just about impossible for anyone to believe them when they told about their prior lives. He pointed a finger at Trevor and said, "School teacher." Then he pointed at Mathew and said, "Lawyer."

Billy looked at the two in amazement. "I couldn't have guessed that in a million years."

"Yeah, we get that a lot. Both of us are educated men but decided we like our freedom. Some day when we retire that old wagon out there I plan to settle down in a cabin somewhere nice and warm with that pretty little wife of mine. Mathew says he'll probably do the same. I got me a list of books I want to read before I die. And let me tell you, it's a big list," Trevor said.

"Same here. We used to carry a couple of books on the wagon but could never find time to turn the pages. We work the freight from daylight till dark. Only time we could read would be at night and a campfire ain't no way to enjoy a book. Plus, by the time we get the mules situated and then burn our supper we're just too exhausted to even think about reading. We stopped carrying books about three or four years back," Mathew said.

"That paper have a financial section, Billy?" Trevor said as he took it from the boy's hand.

"Reach me a section of that if you don't mind. It's been more than two months since I've had my hands on a paper," the other teamster said. Billy leaned back in his chair as he tried to figure the two old men out. Appearances could sure fool a man.

As the two separated the paper and took the sections they wanted a lady came from the kitchen with a pot of coffee and a tray that held five cups.

"Good morning, Mister Hartman. Good morning, gentlemen," she said as she looked at the other four men.

"Is the eggs and bacon about ready, Julia? Me and these men have a lot to do this morning," Hartman asked.

"Irene is fixing it now. I was told all the rooms were rented last night so we figured we would be busy this morning. We both came in a little early and lit the lamps and stoked up the stove."

"All of us will have the same thing along with some biscuits. I reckon anything you got that's fast will suit us just fine. Maybe a little butter and honey also if it ain't too much trouble," Hartman said.

Julia sat a cup in front of each man and then poured the coffee. Once finished she hurried back to the kitchen.

"Mister Hartman, I don't want to seem nosey but you got quite an operation here and a lot of people on the payroll, six or eight I count. Are there really that many people traveling through here?" Billy asked. In his opinion the station was about as out of the way as it could get. He had seen other people eating in the restaurant the previous evening and there were eight or ten men in the saloon. He wondered if it was called a saloon. It had been referred to as just the bar beside the restaurant the previous evening.

Hartman put a spoon full of sugar in his coffee and stirred. "That is a good question. A couple of years back it wasn't this busy. Most folks just take the road straight to Clear Creek. That was before a couple of silver strikes a few years back up in the mountains a little north of here. Now we get prospectors in here on a daily basis buying supplies. It's getting so good I might have to buy another wagon so I can double my supply runs. My wagon is only about half the size of that boat Trevor and Mathew use. I only use four horses to pull it when the load is light. I got a six mule hitch we use when the wagon is hauling heavier supplies. If I do get another wagon I'm going to try and buy four or five more good mules. Mules just seem to work better at pulling.

"I also buy the silver and have it transported back to the railhead at Bristle Buck. There's a bank there that foots the bill and reimburses me along with a nice little profit. I got four men that make that run on horseback at different times to throw off any attempted robberies. I wouldn't want to see anyone try though, them are four that can take care of themselves.

"About a mile from here I got another big barn and corral. I got some cabins there, more like bunkhouses really, that the miners stay in for free when they come off the mountain. I let them stable their horses there and make use of the bunkhouse free of charge as long as I get their business at the trading post. I also get the privilege of brokering their silver," Hartman said.

Just then Julia and Irene came from the kitchen, both carrying a tray of food. "Got you men all fixed up," Julia said as she sat five plates on the table. There wasn't any need to be particular on which plate went where, they were all the same. Bacon, eggs, gravy and biscuits. There was also a small dish of butter and a small white porcelain pitcher that looked to be filled with honey.

As the five looked over the food Julia hurried back to the kitchen to grab the coffee pot. Not more than a minute later and every cup was full to the brim. "You men enjoy. I'll be back in a few minutes to check on you. If you need anything in the meantime just let us know."

As the men began to eat the door to the diner swung open and four men walked in, rough looking men. It was evident by their clothes and shaggy appearances that they were prospectors. The shagginess led most to believe they were heavy on the prospecting side and short on the striking the mother lode side. There didn't look to be a dollar between the bunch.

The four picked a table, two over from the one where Hartman and the other four men ate. They roughly slid the chairs out from the table and flopped down. After being seated the mangiest of the four loudly slapped a hand on the table and declared he was there and ready to eat. He shouted for someone to get out there and get him some food.

Julia heard the ruckus and hurried from the kitchen. She looked at the four newcomers and as she walked by she gave Hartman a worried look. Trevor and Mathew continued to eat but both suspected these four were going to ruin their breakfast.

Julia walked up and greeted the four with a good morning and asked if she could take their orders for food. The mangy one looked her up and down and then whistled. "Boy if you ain't the best looking thang I've seen in quite a while. How about sitting here in my lap while we figure out what we want to eat." As he said this he reached for her. Julia stepped back; she wanted nothing to do with mangy and his sort.

The Trail

"Well now, darling, no need to be unfriendly. You might not be able to tell by the looks of us but we are now the richest sons-o-bucks in the whole territory. Why I might just buy this dump and then you would be working for Me." Again he looked her up and down. "And when you're working for me I might need more than just breakfast."

This was more than Hartman could tolerate. "That will be enough, Furman. Julia can take your food order if you're hungry but other than that you watch your language."

The man named Furman took his eyes off Julia and looked at Hartman. "Now there's the man I want to talk to. Me and the boys here have us a good strike up on our claim. I want you to advance me my next month's supplies. You grubstake us and we'll make you rich. It wouldn't be the first time some storekeeper got rich by letting hardworking men make the money while he kept his own hands clean."

Hartman didn't like what he just heard. Furman was a bully and a loudmouth. "No, I won't be doing any grubstaking this trip or any in the future. You four eat and then head on out of here."

Furman looked at his three friends and then said, "Now I don't believe you heard me, Hartman, I'm expecting a little cooperation from you. I been coming in here for the better part of a year now and I don't think you should be talking to me that way."

"You been coming in here for the better part of a year, that's true. You also cut out of here the last two times and didn't pay for your meals. I also know you been using the corral and bunkhouse but not buying from the trading post here. You been buying off that carpetbagger Fields. You know the rules, you stay in my bunkhouse then you trade at my establishment, no exceptions. Not for you, not for any of the other men sitting with you."

Fields was a peddler that traveled around the mining camps and sold cheap goods and cheap liquor out of the back of a rickety wagon. He got the name carpetbagger because just after the war that's what he did for a while. Hartman hated the man.

"One more thing, Furman, you can pay for your meal this time before you get it, that goes for all four of you," Hartman said.

Furman wasn't a man to be buffaloed, but he was hungry and decided he would take care of his stomach before dealing with Hartman.

"We got two dollars total, that's all we got. Will that buy the four of us breakfast?" Furman asked.

Hartman looked at Julia who was now standing next to her boss's table. "Grab their two dollars and then bring them some food. That is if they keep civil tongues in their heads."

Julia smiled, she felt better knowing her boss was in the room. She didn't like the way Furman and his bunch looked at her. She took the two dollars and then quickly headed back to the kitchen.

"Wait a minute there, good lookin, we ain't told you what we want yet," Furman said. Julia didn't even slow down.

"Now wait a minute, Hartman. You done took our money, how do you know what we want to eat?" Furman shouted.

"You only paid two dollars. That makes you a little lite on the paying side. For that you get biscuits and gravy and all the coffee you can drink. We still need to settle up for the last two times you and your lot ate here and ran out without paying."

The Trail

Furman decided to continue this conversation after the biscuits and gravy arrived. His hunger was overpowering his temper, but not by much.

Hartman turned back to his own breakfast. He was mad and could barely contain his emotions. This wasn't the first time Furman had come in and caused a problem. Hartman knew the man was trouble but thought it might be better to tolerate the trouble rather than confront it head on. Today was the first time he felt the need to stand up to the oversized bully. He knew if he didn't then the abuse would only get worse as time went by.

Trevor looked at Hartman and knew the man was angry, hell he was angry and it wasn't even his place. "That big feller over there, he some kind of troublemaker or something?"

"Yeah, he's something I guess. At first he was tolerable, but just barely. With each visit he gets worse. The way he talked to Julia was more than I could stand. If my wife found out he was talking to her that way then she might come in here and confront the man." The way Hartman said that last part left no doubt that his wife had a temper.

"Maybe after they get a little food in their hides they'll calm down a bit?" Mathew said. It wasn't to be.

Julia and Irene hurried and brought the four men biscuits and gravy, along with coffee. They didn't stay long, one minute later and both women were back in the relative safety of the kitchen.

It didn't take long for Furman to realize that biscuits and gravy just wasn't going to do the job this cold morning. He noticed what Hartman and the others at that table were eating, it looked way better than what he had.

Furman got to his feet and walked to Hartman's table. Without asking he reached down and took a piece of bacon off Mathew's plate and shoved it in his mouth. A mouth that had gravy running out the corners.

Mathew looked up at the enormous man. "I reckon that one's on the house friend. Don't do it again."

Without hesitation Furman reached down and snatched another piece. Mathew gently laid his fork down and then, as quick as a cat, stood and shoved Furman away from the table.

"You remind me of an old dog I used to have; I had to push him away from the table during every meal. But there is one difference, that old dog didn't smell half as bad as you," Mathew said.

This didn't seem to bother Furman in the least because he promptly reached down with his dirty fingers and took the last piece of Mathew's bacon.

This was more than the old teamster could stand. He drew back and hit Furman as hard as he could. The big prospector barely moved from the blow. He smiled and drew his fist back to hit Mathew.

Before he even got his arm all the way back there was the sound of a Colt being cocked. As if to come out of nowhere there was Billy's gun above the table and it was pointed between Furman's eyes. The big man didn't move, he didn't even blink.

"Don't move a muscle, Furman. That man is a friend of mine and if you strike him I'll sent you straight to hell," Billy said.

"Why you little bastard. Why don't you put that gun away and let's talk about this outside, you know, like men," Furman said.

The Trail

"I plan to do just that but first we are going to finish our breakfast. Now why don't you go back and sit with your sisters over there. They look lonely for your fine company."

The other three men at Furman's table had watched the whole thing with a degree of amusement. But now to be called sisters was more than they could stand. As the three got to their feet Billy stood, he now pointed his gun at them.

"Just sit back down nice and slow. I reckon I'll have time for you three after I deal with this big bastard that says he's your boss. You know, I think you need to find a new boss." Billy quickly put his gun back in its holster but not before doing a couple of figure eights with it around his trigger finger.

Billy sat back down and picked up his fork. Before he resumed his breakfast though he looked Furman in the eye, "You still here?"

Furman turned and went back to his table. It had been a tense situation because all four of the prospectors were wearing guns; it was just something prospectors did. Furman and the other three decided they better eat before they took things to the next level.

Hartman took a little ease now that the danger had seemed to pass. "You seem pretty good with that gun. I doubt them four wanted anything to do with you after seeing how you could handle it."

Billy looked at the other men at the table. It was obvious they wanted an explanation on how he had gotten so good. "Back home I did a little trick shooting at some of the county fairs. I found I was good and it helped me put a little food on the table. I can't ever remember not winning first place. The prize money always afforded me ammunition to practice with, along with a little extra. Some said I was just a natural with a six-shooter."

Trevor looked at Mathew, "I think he might come in real handy if we have any more trouble between here and Clear Creek. Here, take a couple of pieces of bacon off my plate."

Mathew didn't answer but he did shake his head in the affirmative as he grabbed two thick slices. Julia had seen what happened and soon brought out a heaping plate of bacon and sat it between the five men.

"Thanks, Julia. I'll be paying for the five of us this morning. Could you bring out the rest of that peach cobbler from last night. Dealing with rowdies makes a man hungry," Hartman said.

"I'll be glad to, Mister Hartman. Irene will heat it up and then we'll bring it right out."

Furman saw the big plate of bacon, he also heard the mention of peach cobbler. He and his rowdy friends had finished their biscuits and gravy. They had also emptied their coffee cups and were waiting for more. As Julia and Irene carried out five plates heaped with peach cobbler the men's mouths began to water. The smell of the warm peaches soon filled the room.

Hartman saw what was about to happen and decided to head it off, or at least try. He and the others at his table had finished with the bacon on the plate Julia had previously brought out, it was still more than half full. Hartman picked up the plate and carried it to Furman's table.

"You men be interested in the rest of this bacon? If you are then I'll see that a few more biscuits gets brought out along with some more coffee."

The Trail

It's amazing how a plate of bacon and the promise of more biscuits completely changed the four men's composition. Furman, who only a minute before was ready to tear the place apart, now smiled as he snatched a piece of bacon even before Hartman had the chance to set the plate down.

A minute later and another plate was on the table, this one containing eight big cathead biscuits. There was also a smaller plate that held butter. The four completely forgot about being rowdy and piled into the extra food. Hungry and stupid could make for a dangerous situation Hartman thought.

"You done a good thing there, Mister Hartman. Them men was about to cause some trouble and you took care of it with a biscuit. Maybe now we can enjoy this peach cobbler in peace," Mathew said.

Hagans hurried and finished his breakfast and then stood and took his coat off the back of his chair. "Thanks for the breakfast, boss. I'll be getting over to the trading post now. I need to stoke up the fire and try to warm the place up a little. Billy, you come on over when you're finished and we'll get your supplies ready." With that the man turned and left the room.

"I told him you needed to do some trading this morning. He'll be waiting on you when you get there," Hartman said.

Trevor put down his fork and leaned back in his chair. "I guess me and you need to get over to the barn and start getting that hitch ready for the day's pull. I don't want Satan to start thinking he is some sort of barn stud."

Mathew laughed. "You know when me and you retire in a few years I wonder which one of us that big mule is gonna want to stay with?"

"The way I see it he'll probably spend winters with you and summers with me. I know for a fact that big long eared beast likes to mix it up from time to time."

Hartman pushed back from the table and stood. "I got a few things to see to in my office. Before you leave I got a letter I need to send to Sheriff Bevins in Clear Creek."

The three men looked suspiciously at Hartman, he noticed the look. "I just want to send an explanation of how them two men lying over in one of the stalls came in here and drew down on me. I also want to let him know if it weren't for Billy Tucker I would probably be dead. Thought it might be best to get my story out there before rumor put the wrong thoughts in the sheriff's head."

Billy wiped his mouth with the cloth napkin beside his plate and then stood. "Thanks for breakfast, and thanks for that letter. I wouldn't want to be indicted for killing them two. The way I see it they needed killing."

Trevor and Mathew stood and also gave their thanks to Hartman. It was the best breakfast the two had eaten in months. "Well, let's get on over to the barn and say hello to Satan. I expect he's up and dressed by now and waiting on a bite of grain. Them other seven might like a taste too." The two old teamsters went out the door laughing.

Once the five were gone it left Furman and his three troublemakers in the diner by themselves. Julia and Irene decided to stay in the kitchen rather than give the men a reason to cause trouble. Hopefully the four would leave, after all they were well fed.

"Hartman is wrong if he thinks we can be bought off with a plate of biscuits and a piece of bacon. I came in here and offered him a chance to grubstake us. I offered that bastard a chance to get rich and he treated us poorly over two meals I figure should have been on the house anyway," Furman grumbled.

Trevor and Mathew grabbed their saddle bags from their rooms and headed for the barn. They found Satan standing just inside the big front door, he looked ready for some oats. There was a small trough in each stall and one in the long hallway. These were nailed on the side of the walls. The nine mules in stalls got a half scoop of oats apiece. Satan got a full scoop all to himself.

As the two old teamsters checked the wagon and were preparing to bring out each mule to start the hitch one of the big doors swung open and Furman walked in followed by his three rowdy friends. Trevor looked at Mathew as if to say, "What now?"

"Howdy again, boys, thought we might be able to strike a little business deal with you two," Furman said as he looked at the big mule standing in the hall licking the bottom of his trough. Satan was looking at him and wondering what kind of meanness these four had in mind? The big mule could size up a man in only seconds and his first assumption was usually right.

"Doubt me and Mathew got anything to talk to you about friend. Now if you don't mind we got to hitch up these eight mules. We got a job to do and we can't afford to waste time."

Furman stepped between Trevor and the long hitch bar. "Now, it's them mules we want to talk to you about. The way we see it you don't need eight mules, you only need six. Me and my partners been needing us a good pair of mules for some time now. We'll take two of our choosing and give you two old teamsters a portion of our silver strike next time you pull through here. I figure you are getting the better part of the deal but I'm just a generous man that way."

Trevor took a step back as the other three men approached him and Mathew. "You'll do no such thing. These mules are like family to us and we treat them as such. We got no intention of selling any of our mules, not even for cash money."

Furman took a step forward and with a big smile said, "Well, we done struck the deal, I ain't letting you back out now."

"What damn deal are you talking about Mister?" Mathew asked as he stepped up beside Trevor. The two old teamsters weren't a match for the four but that didn't mean they wouldn't put up some kind of resistance.

Furman took another step toward the two men. He poked Trevor in the ribs as he said, "The deal we made when I walked through the door not more than two minutes ago. And I ain't letting you back out of it."

Furman looked at his three men. "Let's get two of the mules and head on back toward the claim. I need the two biggest they got. It'll take a couple of strong brutes to do the type of work we need done."

Mathew stepped forward and hit Furman with all his strength. He had about the same results as he did back at the diner, the big man barely moved.

Furman shoved Mathew hard and it put the old man on the ground. It had as much to do with the sore leg Mathew had as the fact that he outweighed the old man by a good hundred pounds.

The Trail

Trevor stepped over Mathew and swung hard at the big bastard. Furman had seen it coming and easily stepped aside. He then shoved Trevor backward. He tripped over Mathew in the process and fell flat on his back.

Satan saw the whole thing and decided he was about to get involved. Furman turned toward his three partners and said, "Take that big one in the hall there and then pick out another one at least the same size."

Satan continued to clean his trough as he waited to see what damage he could do, no need to waste that last bite of oats if he didn't have to. As one of the three came toward him Satan did what any frightened, or in Satan's case, mean, mule would do. He kicked, and what a kick it was! He caught the man with both of his back hooves sending the startled prospector crashing across the hallway into the adjoining wall.

"What in the hell?" Furman said as he turned to see what all the commotion was about.

Lying on the floor of the wide hallway was one of his men, he didn't appear to be breathing. After checking on the man he was shocked to see what looked to be his entire chest caved in, the man was dead.

Satan hadn't been tied while in the long, wide, hallway the entire night. He was left to roam up and down the length of the barn where he checked on the other seven mules of the hitch. Up until ten minutes ago it had been a peaceful night with the only thing out of the ordinary being the two dead men occupying the front left stall.

The big mule knew he would now pay a terrible price for what he had done to the man on the floor. The remaining three would exact a vicious payment for the death of one of their own. With that thought in mind the big mule decided to do as much damage as he could before the three did him in.

The next closest man was no more than ten feet away so Satan decided that he would be his next target. He went after the man with teeth bared and as he did he let out a snort that sounded almost like a growl. The man saw what was about to happen so he did the only thing he could do, he ran.

Satan was on him in less than two steps. He head butted the fleeing man in the back. The man stumbled forward and fell, sprawled on the floor and defenseless. This was the chance the big mule wanted, he reared and came down hard on the man's back. The blow didn't kill him, it was something far worse, it broke his back. The man went numb from the hips down, never to walk again.

That only left Furman and one other man to face the fury of the big mule. Furman went for his gun but luckily he was tackled by both Trevor and Mathew. As big as the prospector was it was all the two old teamsters could do to drag him to the ground. Once on the ground Trevor managed to wrestle his gun away and point it at his face. Furman stopped struggling when he saw his own gun pointed at his nose.

Mathew jumped to his feet to try and do something about the last man, but it wasn't necessary. The fourth man, having seen two of his group dead or severely injured by the big mule and the third now held captive by his own gun decided to give up if that were possible. But how could he give up to a mule.

Satan had other ideas. He backed the man into a corner then head-butted him into the wall. The man fell to the floor, knocked out cold. After that he went back to his trough to see if he might have left a few crumbs of oats. Satan wasn't one to waste any of his breakfast.

The Trail

"Slice me off a piece of that rope over there Mathew so I can tie this bastard up. About four or five feet ought to do the trick." Trevor tied Furman's hands behind his back while Mathew held the gun on him. The two men then took the other three guns the men on the ground carried.

"Looks like me and you are getting quite a selection of guns Mathew. That Smith and Wesson you took off that one lying over there looks to be nearly new. Let's check their pockets and see if they have any hideaways."

Furman was looking at the damage the big mule had done to his friends. He might have been an oversized bully but his brain was definitely a bit undersized. He was trying to figure out how a day that held so much promise had gone to hell so fast. He then looked at the mule, the one the two old men called Satan, and realized he had been bested by a dumbass mule.

"We better tie that one up over there in the corner, I believe he's just knocked out," Mathew said.

The man that had his back broken was moaning and complaining about not being able to feel his legs. He was lying in a funny position, not normal unless something was broken.

"I can't feel my legs. I can't feel anything," the man said. He was having difficulty breathing.

Trevor knew the man was in a bad way. He had seen one other man back in the war with a broken back caused by an explosion that sent a concussive wave out in all directions. The man was blown nearly fifteen feet and landed against a tree. His back was broken and it didn't take long for his lungs to stop pumping air. He had no apparent injuries but he was hurt bad none the less. His breaths grew weaker and weaker as the nerves that controlled his lung movement ceased to do their job. At the very last he even tried to gulp air like a fish, it must have been a painful death.

Trevor walked over and knelt beside the man. "You got any last words you want written down?"

"The man teared up as he struggled to breathe. "I didn't mean for any of this to happen. I'm sorry for the things I've done," He said as he struggled for air. Shortly after that he closed his eyes and went still.

Trevor looked up from the man and squarely at Furman. The big bully was the only one unhurt. Trevor jumped to his feet and kicked the big man squarely between the legs. Furman bent double and immediately began throwing up his breakfast.

"You son of a bitch. It was you that caused these three men to suffer from your stupidity. Two now dead and another over there with probably a cracked skull. Why it wouldn't take me much to put a bullet in your head right now." With that Trevor cocked the Colt he had taken from Furman and held it to the big man's head. Furman started crying, it probably saved his life.

Just then one of the big doors opened just enough to allow a man in, it was Billy. He looked over the scene in the hallway and then looked at the two teamsters. "I came over to help with the harness work on the hitch. Looks like I missed the excitement."

"You did at that. This damn fool tried to come in here and take two of our mules," Mathew said.

Billy looked at Furman and noticed he was tied and bound. He noticed the two men lying on the ground and could tell they were dead. The one in the corner was about to come to, he was moaning and starting to struggle against his restraints.

The Trail

"By the looks of things I'd say you two handled things pretty well," Billy said.

"Naw, wasn't neither of us at all, it was Satan over there. He killed them two and knocked that one over there out cold. All me and Mathew had to do was tie up the ones that weren't dead," Trevor said. He then added, "That's twice that big long eared beast has saved our bacon, Mathew. I think me and you should pull the wagon and let Satan be the boss."

"Not a bad idea, Trevor. Me and you join the ones on the hitch and let Satan give the orders," Mathew said. Satan didn't know what Trevor and Mathew were talking about but he did wonder why he was the one pulling the wagon. It seemed he was always needing to get the two out of trouble.

The door opened again and Hartman came in. He was there to see about having a couple of his men hitch up his wagon and haul the two dead bodies from the stall. He saw the two might now have some company.

"Looks like trouble seems to follow that freight wagon around. What happened?" Hartman asked.

Trevor told the story as Furman looked on. The big bully wondered what was going to happen to him now. Somehow he figured he might have some liability for what had transpired this morning.

"You might want to add to that letter you're sending to the sheriff in Clear Creek. Looks like me and Satan might both be in need of an alibi," Billy said.

"Did Satan really do all this?" Hartman asked.

"He did at that," Mathew said as he poured a half scoop of grain in the big mule's trough. "There you go old buddy, you get a reward for what you did here this morning." Satan was going to enjoy his reward.

Hartman looked at Furman. "These two got any family that would claim the bodies?"

"Not that I know of. They been helping with the claim for the better part of six months now. Neither mentioned any family, so I suppose not."

"You want to take the bodies with you when you pull out this morning?" Hartman asked.

Furman wasn't expecting this. "You mean I'm free to go?"

"You intend on letting that big troublemaker go. He needs to be in a jail cell somewhere," Trevor said.

The lawyer in Mathew was starting to show. "Ain't got anything to lock him up for Trevor. Sure he's a loud mouth. Sure he's a bully. Sure he tried to take two of our mules but he didn't succeed and got two of his men killed in the process. Got nothing to hold him for, at least not this far from civilization." After some thought Mathew added, "A warrant for his arrest could read that he's a stupid bastard in need of a bath and damn good beating."

Hartman had it figured about the same way. "Furman, you are free to go but under one condition."

Furman was glad to see that he could leave. He figured he would be held and sent to a town that had a jail and a judge. "What's the condition?"

"Me and you never cross paths again. You stay out of the bunkhouse and away from the diner and trading post. If I ever lay eyes on you again then I reserve the right to have you arrested. I assume those four horses tied in front of the diner belong to you and these three other men."

"They do."

"You can help that one over there rubbing his head to his feet and then he can help you tie your two friends to the backs of their horses and then you can leave."

"What about our guns?" Furman asked.

"I'm sending them to Clear Creek on that freight wagon along with a letter explaining what happened here this morning. You can pick up your guns at the Sheriff's Office. Now gather your two dead friends and get the hell off my property. I ever see you around here again I might just kill you," Hartman said. It seemed the longer he talked the more agitated he was getting.

The look on Furman's face indicated that he didn't want anything to do with a sheriff. It was doubtful the four guns would ever be claimed. "I'd rather not be bothered with the bodies. Hell, they ain't no family of mine and I really didn't consider them friends."

This suited Hartman just fine. He would just include the two with the two he already had. He would dispose of the bodies and if anybody came around asking he would just say he had no information to share about the matter.

"In that case just leave their horses and saddles here," Hartman said.

"I'll be taking the two horses with me. Them two dead men would have wanted me to take possession of their mounts and saddles." Furman now decided to show a little backbone. He was going to sell the two men's saddles and horses and pocket the money. He might just make a little profit on this trip after all.

"I can't allow you to take the horses. They don't belong to you," Hartman said. "I'll be glad to have them sent to the sheriff in Clear Creek and let him decide. As it is I just can't let you take them."

Furman knew he was whipped. He wanted nothing to do with a sheriff. "Hell, just keep the damn horses. I'll be heading back to the claim now." Furman helped the other man to the door. Five minutes later the sound of horses heading away from the trading post could be heard.

"I'll bet that bastard don't have a silver claim. I think that was just a big story to get enough supplies so they could ride out the winter. He's been bragging about that claim for the better part of six months now," Hartman said.

After a moment's thought Hartman added, "I also ain't going to be bothered with them four guns. As far as I'm concerned the three of you are welcome to the guns and the two horses."

"What about the two horses that belong to them two Billy shot yesterday?" Mathew asked.

"Not just them two, don't forget about the five we led in here last evening. We got horses and guns starting to pile up everywhere," Trevor added.

Hartman wanted nothing to do with any of it. The last thing he wanted was to try and explain a horse or gun that someone recognized. "Take the whole lot with you. None of it pertains to my operation here. I'll see to a proper burial for the four men and after that I don't know anything if I'm asked." He knew a proper burial in this kind of freezing weather meant to dump the four in a ravine and then chip away a little dirt from the top to cover them up.

"Alright then, let's get the hitch mounted up and hit the trail. We'll tie the spare horses to the back of the wagon. We get to Clear Creek then it's the sheriff's problem. Them extra guns though are a different story. I say we sell them to the man that runs that general store in town. We'll take what we get and split it three ways. Mathew, Billy and me each take a third," Trevor said.

"You men work that out anyway you like. As I said, I'm not involved. You three take care of yourselves and stop in next chance you get," Hartman said as he headed for the door. He was intent on getting two of his men to take the four bodies and dispose of them as fast as he could. It wasn't that he had participated in anything wrong. He just wanted to be rid of the whole mess. He had a trading post and a diner to run.

Forty-five minutes later and the big wagon was hitched. There were nine spare horses total which meant Mathew would be using the one he liked best as his mount. He picked one that had belonged to the first three men that had come into camp two nights before with the intent of killing both teamsters and stealing the freight wagon. He gave the horse the name of Lady. It was a name he though suited the big horse.

Trevor decided to take another horse for himself, not that he would be riding, he always walked beside the lead mule. He picked another of the original three and decided he would name her Bessie. "Well, Bessie, I hope you like walking behind this old freight wagon. I figure you can stay in Clear Creek and wait for me while I'm gone to get another load. No need for you to walk that trip if you don't want to." Trevor waited for a reply, the big horse only snorted. This was good enough for Trevor.

It was just like the old teamster to talk to the horse like she understood. Both Trevor and Mathew took good care of their animals and they had just added two horses to go along with the eight mules that pulled the wagon.

"That leaves seven horses to tag along behind the wagon. What do you figure we do with them after we get to Clear Creek? I doubt the sheriff will want to stable that many horses at the town's expense," Billy asked.

"We'll keep the lot and sell them for whatever they bring. I figure you get a third of the money we make Billy. We get to town I say we let old Buster Adams at the livery take them off our hands. If anybody knows how to sell a horse then it would be Buster. We'll let him sell the tack as well. Some of those saddles are in poor shape but between the seven it ought to bring us a little cash. I for one could use a little extra. The old woman has been complaining about the shape the old house is getting in. I'll use any extra I get to try and make that pretty little thing happy," Trevor said with a smile.

"I believe a little extra sprucing up around the place might make my little woman a bit more friendly too. That's a real good idea, Trevor. I think I'll do that, same as you," Mathew said.

Going by the looks of the two old teamsters Billy wondered what the two men's wives really looked like. But then again most men have different degrees of judgement when it comes to a wife. Some men hate a pretty woman and others love an ugly one. Billy was glad he hadn't gone down the aisle yet. He was putting that task off for a few more years.

"Better check them two spare wagon wheels Trevor. I noticed one was wobbling a bit as we was coming into the station." The two men always carried two extra wagon wheels, just in case. It would have been easier to just keep one spare but the front and back wheels were of a different size.

The Trail

"I'll do that, wouldn't want one to get away from us and then beat us to Clear Creek. The way Satan was pulling yesterday I'm surprised everything on the wagon didn't shake loose and fall off."

Just after eight in the morning the big wagon pulled out with Trevor walking alongside Satan. Mathew rode Lady and was quite proud of his choice in horseflesh. It felt good to be on a horse rather than riding atop that rough old freight wagon. Not only did he now have a good horse but he also wore one of the better belts and holsters he had taken from one of the bushwhackers. In it was the best of the Colts in the bunch. He had filled every belt loop with the appropriate ammunition.

Trevor didn't like wearing a gun and hadn't since his days in the war. Both Billy and Mathew had convinced him that until they made it to Clear Creek he should be armed. Reluctantly he had done the same as Mathew. He picked out the Colt he wanted and then put it in one of the better belts and holsters. He had also filled every loop of the belt with ammunition. After so many close calls in the last two days he was edgy and felt Billy and Mathew were right.

Hartman came out as the men closed the doors to the barn. "Here's that letter for the sheriff in Clear Creek. It explains some of the trouble we've had in the last twenty four hours. I wish the three of you a safe journey."

"Thanks, Mister Hartman. Sorry to bring them fellers in here last evening," Trevor said.

"Well, I'm sorry about all that business with Furman a little while ago. You boys take care."

A little over two hours later and the three men turned toward Clear Creek. The fork in the road indicated where their wagon had come by the day before and also the tracks of the four men that chased them down. Billy stopped his horse and reached the reins to Mathew.

"You see something you don't like in them tracks young feller," Mathew asked.

Billy stooped and looked over the tracks. He walked back a ways and again stooped to inspect the trail. "Looks like Anderson came back through here after getting run out of the station last night. He turned toward Clear Creek at a trot. He wasn't running his horse hard."

"You think he's planning another ambush, Billy?" Trevor asked.

"Couldn't say for sure. I do know that he's mighty interested in that wagon of yours, or at least something it's carrying."

"Them three we tangled with night before last said something about the mail bags. We might have mentioned it to you earlier," Trevor said.

Billy looked at the wagon. "You think it's something as simple as a piece of mail?"

"Could be. I doubt the freight we're hauling has anything to do with it. It's just stuff for the general store and the blacksmith. Even the town barber gets his supplies from the general store. Everything we haul to Clear Creek goes to one spot and I doubt we got anything worth the number of lives lost so far," Mathew said.

"I'd feel better with a long gun; you got anything like that in the side box?" Billy asked.

Trevor nodded at the box, "Have a look, might be something in there that will work."

When Billy walked over and raised the lid he let out a whistle. "Why you got four or five Winchesters, two Sharps and

212

a couple of shotguns." Billy looked up at the two men. "You two going to war or something?"

"Sonny, we been at war for the last two days. Them are some of the guns we picked off the bodies of the men that's tried to kill us. You take what you want. Ammunition is in the front of the box," Trevor said with a grin.

Billy picked out one of the Winchesters and a box of ammunition. As he headed for his horse Mathew said, "Better reach me one of them Greeners and ten or twelve shells. I'm pretty damn good with a Colt but a shotgun has a bit more of an intimidation factor."

Once the two had the long guns they wanted Billy mounted up and the three headed toward Clear Creek. All three figured they were in for more trouble. Trevor and Mathew knew they had been lucky so far, real lucky. You might say they had Satan looking over them.

"You two have traveled this road now for years. If you were going to stage an ambush where would it be?" Billy asked.

"You know that is a real good question. Mathew, if it was you, where would you waylay somebody between here and Clear Creek?"

The two teamsters were silent for a while as they considered Billy's question. Both thought long and hard and finally it was Mathew that spoke. "Trevor, you know that spot about a mile or so from where we make camp when we go through here? It's got some slide rock that the trail goes through. Rocks large enough to hide a man, maybe even several men."

"I know the spot, I was thinking about that myself. There's also a couple of high benches on the slope where a man with a sharp eye and a good rifle could pick us off no trouble at all.

Even if we made it past the slide rock then all they would have to do is shoot us in the back. I reckon if I was going to do a waylay job then that would be the place."

Billy knew the two old men had thought hard on the question. For some reason he trusted the two, both had experience in such things, they had each fought in the war.

"Any place between here and there where we could be ambushed?" Billy asked. "Before we even make it to the slide rock?"

Again the two old teamsters were silent as they both thought hard on the subject. They knew a mistake could cost each of them their lives.

"Not really. There's that one spot where we pull through a dry creek bed. Puts us in a spot where we can't maneuver. It also give anyone wanting to cause mischief the high ground," Trevor said.

"I wouldn't worry about that spot, Trevor. We can get a good view of the area as we approach. Naw, the best place is the one with the slide rock. That's where I'd do my killing if I was of the outlaw type," Mathew said.

Trevor gave the man a sideways look. "You are of the outlaw type, you fought for the South."

Mathew never gave that insult a second thought. He had been listening to that same brand of talk for years now and had finally learned to ignore it.

"About what time today would we be getting to that spot with the slide rock?" Billy asked.

"Oh, I figure it's about ten now. This time of year it gets dark around five-thirty. Best I can remember it should be around five this evening. You think that's about right, Mathew?"

The Trail

Mathew looked at the sky, he agreed that it was close to ten, give or take a few minutes in either direction. The only pocket watch the two teamsters ever carried was the one that intercepted the bullet meant for Trevor's hide two nights back.

"I believe that's about right. Say, Trevor, you plan on making the purchase of another pocket watch to replace that one with the bullet in it?"

"Maybe, that's another reason to keep them bushwhacker's guns and horses," Trevor said with a twinge of anger in his voice.

Billy had already heard that story but intended to have a look at the watch some time anyway.

During the day Billy stayed in front of the slow moving wagon. The slow speed of the freight wagon allowed him time to dismount from time to time and check the trail. He also rode on either side of the trail to see if a campsite from the previous night could be found. He would range ahead a half mile or so and then make his way back.

Mathew stayed behind the wagon keeping a sharp eye on their back trail. The last thing they needed was to be keeping a close eye out front and then get caught from behind.

As it worked out they were a mile or so from the slide rock a good hour ahead of time. Satan had the hitch pulling hard and had no intention of slowing. The big mule had done enough damage in the last two days. All he wanted was to get to Clear Creek and the sooner the better.

Trevor, who had walked alongside Satan the entire day slowed the hitch for a hundred feet or so and then stopped. "This is about as far as I want to go with the wagon. If we got trouble up ahead then we'll leave the wagon and mules here while we go have us a look."

Mathew caught up with the wagon and climbed down. He tied Lady to the back of the wagon beside Bessie. Both horses looked bothered by the slow pace.

"We got a plan, Trevor?" Mathew asked.

"We wait here until Billy gets back. He went a little farther ahead to see if he could spot anything."

The two men waited beside the front of the hitch. Satan wasn't one to wait idly by if there was a juicy hat within reach, so he decided to sample Trevor's. Before the old teamster could move Satan had it by the brim and was chomping away. Trevor yanked it free, "Just because you saved our lives at least twice in the last two days don't mean you can eat my hat." As he tried to straighten the brim back out he reached over and patted the big mule on the forehead. Satan considered all was even.

"Sounds like Billy," Mathew said.

Around the next bend in the road a horse could be heard and a second later there was Billy riding hard toward them. He pulled up to the wagon.

"You were right. I could see the slide way before I got there. I made the last half mile on foot. They're there alright. I count maybe four men. Could be more but no way to tell."

"Well now, what do you want to do?" Mathew asked.

Trevor had an idea but didn't have all the particulars yet. "Say, Billy, you reckon anyone up ahead would recognize that horse of yours?"

Billy looked at his horse, it was a big lean brute but had no particular markings that would identify her. "I doubt it. Anderson saw this horse a few times but she looks about like any other horse of this color I reckon."

The Trail

"Well here's what I'm thinking. The two horses me and Mathew have come off them first three that attacked us two nights ago. I doubt them varmints up ahead have ever laid eyes on them. I say the three of us go through there just like nothing's wrong and just keep on going. If it is an ambush then they wouldn't be looking for three riders. They want two old teamsters and one big ass wagon pulled by eight mules," Trevor said with a grin.

"Now that just might work. The only problem is that Anderson has seen all three of us. What if he recognizes us?" Mathew asked.

"You're right, that just might work. It's damn cold out here so all we got to do is turn our collars up high and pull our hats down low. From where I saw them they were back off the trail about fifty feet or so. There were two men on a couple of rises with rifles. None of the ones I saw were trying too hard to hide. I think they must believe it's at least an hour before they expect that wagon," Billy said.

"But what if they start shooting at us? We would be right out in the open," Mathew said.

Billy had already thought of this. "They won't. We'll just look like three travelers heading toward Clear Creek. They won't shoot because the noise would alert the two old men driving the wagon. They'll let us pass."

Trevor looked at Billy, "Now where around here do you see two old men?"

"The three of us better all have long guns. I think a Greener will suit me just fine. I for one am going to turn my coat inside out. That Anderson might recognize it if I don't. Might not hurt either of you to do the same. That will change the looks of the three of us pretty good," Mathew said.

After the three managed to turn their coats they also switched hats. Billy was afraid Anderson might still recognize him but with a different hat maybe he could be fooled.

Billy looked at the two, "You ready?" Both nodded they were.

"Good, now here's the plan. We ride along not taking any precautions at all. If we look to be leery then it might tip them off to us. We just trot these horses up the trail like we ain't got a worry in the world. Once past the ambush site we'll come back on foot and deal with the bastards."

"What if they come out and stop us? Any of that bunch gets close then we'll be recognized," Mathew asked.

"They try to stop us then we start shooting. We can't take the chance of a conversation," Billy said as both Trevor and Mathew nodded in agreement.

Five minutes later and all three were heading toward a known ambush with the hopes that their deception would work.

Anderson had been leaning against a tree trying to nap but had finally just given up. His ride the night before had taken a lot out of the man. He hadn't had anything to eat, or any coffee, since earlier that morning. He knew from experience that the smell of wood smoke or coffee could, in the right conditions, travel for miles. For this reason he and the rest of his men were irritable and quick tempered. They all wanted to get this job finished and get back to town for a quick paycheck. Each was thinking of stove warmed air and the inside of a saloon.

"Got riders coming up the trail," Anderson said. A man by the name of Josh May had used a hand signal to signal the others. May was the man on high lookout. There were actually two but May knew for a fact that the other one was sound asleep. He'd bring that little fact up once they killed the two teamsters and took possession of the wagon. He hoped Anderson would see fit to cut sleepy out of his share and increase that of the others.

Anderson had seen the hand signal immediately and notified the other two men with him by the road. With the loss of three men the day before he now had five men, including himself, to take care of the job. It shouldn't be a problem.

"Get ready now. Make sure you don't hit any of the mules. We'll need all eight to move the wagon," Anderson whispered.

Keeping the wagon wasn't part of the deal Anderson had with his employer, a mysterious man from back east whom he would never meet. Anderson was to acquire the mail sacks and take them to Clear Creek where a man would be waiting to find one particular parcel and then discard the rest. In order to save time the wagon was to be burned after the mules were set free. The two old teamsters were to be burned with the wagon to hide any evidence. Hopefully it would be assumed the wagon was struck by lightning, something that was a possibility in the high country.

Anderson stayed low waiting for the first glimpse of the heavy freight wagon. The odd thing was the lack of freight wagon noises. No creaking of wooden wheels or the clanging of chain against hook. This sounded like horses, not mules pulling a wagon.

The first glimpse Anderson got was of three men riding three horses without even a pack horse. They wore their hats pulled low and their coat collars pulled up high. In this kind of weather it was no wonder. Anderson held up a clinched fist to indicate no one was to make a move on the three riders. All he needed now was for one of the other four men to fire a shot, a shot that could carry for at least two miles. Best to stay quiet and let these three pass.

As the three passed where they knew the bushwhackers were they each nearly held their breath. All were tense as could be. They suspected there were multiple long guns pointed their way. After about a hundred feet they noticed a felled tree blocking the road. There was no missing the fact that a man with an axe had done the deed.

"Just ease around and keep going," Billy whispered to the other two. The three horses had no trouble walking around the base of the fallen tree.

Two minutes later and all three were a couple hundred feet past the ambush site. They eased into the timber and found a safe spot where their horses could be tied without fear of one catching a bullet that was sure to come.

"Alright now, I'll take care of the two lookouts. I got a glimpse of both out of the corner of my eye as we rode by. Can the two of you handle the other three?" Billy asked.

Trevor looked at Mathew, "This is just like the old days. I'll be considering them three Johnnie Rebs and you can consider them Yanks."

"Alright, it might be five against three but we got the advantage of surprise. Don't wait for them to fire, if you get a shot then take it even if it's in the back. I figure that's what they had in store for you two," Billy said.

The Trail

"You read my mind Billy. Don't you worry about me and old Mathew here, we might have done a little bushwhacking back in the war so we know what to do."

"It'll take me the longest to get in position so as soon as I'm ready I'll assume both of you are too. When you hear me shoot then do away with them three," Billy said.

All three men headed off toward Anderson's unsuspecting men. It took Billy nearly ten minutes to get to a spot where he could outflank both lookouts. He looked the situation over and decided which he would shoot first. He decided to take the hardest of the shots immediately and then deal with the second lookout. The second man, even if he tried to return fire or find cover would be dealt with in short order after the first had fallen.

Billy waited another full minute hoping Trevor and Mathew were in place. He lined up his shot and exhaled. As still as a mouse he squeezed the trigger. The big gun bucked and Billy was rewarded with the sight of his target being knocked to the side by the force of the blast. He immediately lined up on the second man who apparently thought the shot was from his friend and aimed at the wagon, but where was the wagon. His hesitation cost him his life. Billy squeezed the trigger and the second man fell to the ground.

There hadn't been any other shots and this worried Billy. He wanted to race down the hill to check on the two teamsters but he couldn't leave his two targets. One might have only been winged and could still be a danger from his vantage point.

Just when he was ready to head down and help his friends he heard a shot quickly followed by others. Now satisfied that both his shots had killed their intended targets Billy rose and raced down the hill all the while trying to use the trees for cover. As fast as he was moving he doubted anyone could hit him anyway unless it was an extremely lucky shot.

In the time it took him to make it to the bottom he counted no less than ten shots. His fear was that he would find the two teamsters dead. Before he made it to the trail he heard the sound of a horse racing away hard.

When he stepped onto the road he saw both Trevor and Mathew standing over two bodies. Billy had only known the two for less than a day but he was extremely glad to see that both had made it.

Trevor looked at Billy as he came out of the tree line. "We heard you fire two shots, you get both of 'em?"

"I did, how about the three down here?"

"We didn't do that good. Only got two," Mathew said.

"I heard a horse heading down the road. Which one got away?"

"It was Anderson. I swear that man's like a cat, nine lives and all," Mathew said.

"It's gonna be dark soon. You think we outta stay here or try to make to that regular campsite the two of you usually use?"

"By the time we get that tree chopped out of the way and go back and get the wagon it will be good and dark. Maybe we'll stay here, this ain't such a bad campsite, other than the bodies everywhere," Mathew said. There were deadfalls for firewood and running water nearby for the mules and horses. It was all Trevor and Mathew ever looked for in a campsite.

"This spot will do just fine, hell I'm getting used to sleeping with dead men all over the place. We'll leave that fallen tree right where it is. I'll take Satan and one other mule and drag it out of the way at first light," Trevor said.

The Trail

"Tell you what, let's get our horses and while you two go after the wagon I'll track Anderson. As long as I got light I want to see how far he got. I sure wouldn't want that bastard to come back during the night and return the favor," Billy said.

By the time Billy made it back it was a good thirty minutes after dark. Trevor and Mathew had the wagon pulled up and the mules unhitched. Mathew was building a fire to start their supper while Trevor tended to feeding the mules.

"I think Satan is sorry he missed all the action earlier. If there's a killing I believe that long eared beast feels he needs to take part," Trevor said to Mathew just as Billy trotted in.

"Did you find Anderson?" Trevor asked.

Billy tied his horse near the other two. "I found evidence of him. One of you must have winged him. There was a blood trail, not much, but enough. I figure if that wound don't kill him then at least we won't need to worry about him backtracking and coming back here tonight. You two find the other horses?"

"Not yet. We figured it best to stay with the wagon until you made it back. I don't like my chances anymore and figure I ain't about to go traipsing about in the woods looking for them dead men's horses," Mathew said.

Just then Trevor had a thought, "Say now, besides Lady and Bessie, we got seven other horses tied out over there with the mules. It looks like we might have just increased that number by four more and maybe even five if they had a pack horse."

Mathew's eyes lit up. "Don't forget about their shooting irons. Let's get the other horses brought in and we'll worry about the guns in the morning. By the time we sell all that and split it three ways me and you should be able to slow down a bit."

Billy listened as he took the saddle off his horse. He knew the two old men had worked hard all their lives. If they profited off the men that were trying to kill them then he was glad for the two. "I say we cook first if that suits the two of you. If my memory is correct neither of us has had a bite since about six this morning. I can tell it's starting to affect my stomach in the worst way."

"Skillet bread and beans suit you, Billy?" Mathew asked.

Walker left the livery and headed in the direction of the sheriff's office. Night was now full on with the last rays of a weak sun being long gone. If Walker thought the trip back from the site where Dr. Ramey's patient had been attacked had been cold, he now thought better, this was worse. The wind seemed to be coming straight from the north and it cut to the bone.

Before he made it to the warmth of the big potbellied stove in the jail he decided to make a stop at Joe Ramey's to see how things were going. Maybe the patient might be a bit more talkative now, that is if the good doctor even allowed Walker in the door.

Walker stepped up on the front porch of Ramey's place. He figured the doctor was still up because there was the warm glow of lamplight coming from the front parlor.

After knocking once he stepped back from the door. This late in the evening, and with all the strange events taking place in town, he figured Ramey would answer the door with a gun, he was right.

No sooner had the front door cracked open than Walker saw the end of a shotgun peeking out. "State your business," was all Ramey said.

The Trail

"It's me, Doc. I just came by to check on things," Walker said.

Ramey recognized the voice. "Is that you Stank?"

Walker figured as much. "Yeah it's me. Can I come in?"

The door swung wide as Ramey stepped back. "Come on in. Sorry, Walker, it's going to take me a while to get used to your new name. Sorry about the gun too, I doubt I'll feel safe again until the sheriff figures out who these men are that won't give their names. And then there's you, you got an old name and a new name."

"Walker ain't a new name; I've been a Walker all my life. Stank was the new name I used for a while."

"I guess that makes sense. You want some coffee? You look damn near froze to death. Why are you outside on a night such as this anyway?"

Walker took off his hat and coat; he hung both on a fancy carved wooden coat tree. "Coffee would be nice as long as it's good and hot."

"It is, come on in the kitchen. I got a pot of green beans on the stove, you hungry?"

Walker followed the doctor. He was actually following the smell coming from the kitchen. "I'm starved, Doc. How is it you got green beans this time of year?"

"They're dried green beans, shuck beans some folks call 'em. There's a lady and her husband that lives about a mile outside of town. They got a big farm out there, supplies most of the produce for the general store. I take care of the mules old man Parsons uses to work his fields. He and that woman of his grow some really nice vegetables, and they grow plenty. They pay me in produce. After you taste those beans I think you'll say I'm getting the better part of the bargain."

225

Walker looked the kitchen over. He had been in the house earlier that day when he and the sheriff had come by to question the wounded man in the back. He hadn't made it as far as the kitchen; it looked to be a well thought out affair, as was the entire house. Sitting on top of the stove was a lidded pot. The stove was a big wood burner that had a good sized cooktop and an oven to the side of the firebox.

Ramey took a pot holder from a hook near the stove and grabbed the lid. The room was suddenly filled with the delicious aroma of ham. "I smell something way better than just green beans in that pot."

"You do at that, the man that owns the butcher shop sent me a big ham bone late yesterday. It wasn't just a ham bone but had what looked like a whole ham still attached. I decided to put it in with the beans. I put a few big potatoes in there too. The potatoes came from the Parsons' garden, same as the beans. I thought I was gonna need a bigger pot, but finally got everything in there. It ought to be a good meal."

Walker figured the man at the butcher shop probably paid for the doc's services with cuts of beef and pork. It seemed all small towns used a barter system rather than money and in Clear Creek it appeared to work out well.

"You come over about daylight in the morning and I'll have fresh eggs and biscuits, that is if you like such as that. I been doctoring in this town for better than twenty years now, don't make much money but I sure do eat good. Me and my wife came through here all them years ago; she liked it so we stayed. She's been gone now going on three years, I sure do miss her," Ramey said, his voice suddenly sad.

The Trail

"Sorry to hear that, Doc. Sounds like you and your wife made a wise decision, Clear Creek is a good place to put down roots. It would be perfect if only the winters weren't so cold."

Ramey snapped out of his memories as he said, "Cold is one thing Clear Creek has plenty of this time of year. Folks around here are good at putting back during the summer and fall to last through the winter and spring months. That's one reason I like most folks around here. They believe in hard work and fair play. I take nearly all my pay in barter and I've never felt short-changed."

As the doc was talking he was also setting the table with plates and utensils. It seemed he was glad to have someone to talk to and share his stories with. Walker wondered what his own life would be like when, and if, he reached the age of Ramey. He wondered if he would be alone hoping for a visitor to share a meal with, same as the doc?

As Ramey finished setting the table there was a knock at the door. "Tell you what, Walker, how about you getting that. I don't like answering the door holding a gun. It just goes against everything I was trained to do in life."

"Be glad to, what should I tell them?"

"Well, if you see they mean no harm then invite them in. I got plenty of beans and ham. It makes my evening go better if I don't have to eat alone."

Walker went to the front parlor but decided he wouldn't be holding a gun when he opened the door. "Well howdy Sheriff. Ramey said if whoever was out here looked tame I was to let them in." After a short pause Walker asked with a grin, "Are you tame?"

"I'm tame, Walker, I'm also frozen now step aside so I can come in."

Walker closed the door after the sheriff was inside. He had flakes of snow on his hat and shoulders. "It's starting to come down out there. What are you doing here, Walker; I figured you would have been back at the jail by now?"

"I was on my way there, Sheriff but decided to come by here and check on things first. Glad I did, I've been invited to supper."

Bevins was putting his hat and coat on the same coat tree Walker had used. "Everyone still alive?"

"I suppose, doc hasn't mentioned any deaths. We have been in the kitchen ever since I got here twenty minutes ago."

Bevins could smell something and it was a really good smell. He had dropped in at this time on purpose. He knew when the doc liked to eat and that time was right about now. The sheriff had taken more than one meal at the doc's table and it had always been good. As good as the food always was he still only stopped by if he needed to check on someone the doc was tending to. He didn't want to wear out his welcome.

Bevins and Walker headed toward the kitchen; both were drawn by the smell. Doc had already put another place setting on the table. He looked up to see Bevins walk in followed by Walker.

"Evening, Sheriff. You're just in time for a little supper if you haven't already eaten?"

"Howdy, Doc, naw I ain't ate yet. Just stopped by to check on the patients you got in the back."

"All three are doing fine. Amos is awake and cussing up a storm. I guess getting shot will make a man lose his religion. That other feller, the one with no name, has been awake too. Funny thing though, he don't use the same foul language he did earlier. I got a theory about that," Doc said. "The third one back there, the one that shot Amos, can be taken to the jail as soon as you two eat. I don't feel comfortable with him here."

Walker looked at the sheriff. If the doc had a theory then they both wanted to hear it.

"What would that theory be, Doc?" Bevins asked.

"Well I think it was all a big put on. I think that man's running, or hiding, from something. He seems scared, always looking at the door real scared like. Even when I go in the room it startles him. Kind of like he's expecting a visitor that wants to do him in rather than wish him a quick recovery."

"Sounds like a possibility, Doc. He ever say who he is or where he's from?" Bevins asked.

"Not a word about that. Say, Sheriff, I went ahead and set another plate if you would be interested in joining me and Walker for a little supper. You did say you haven't ate yet. My specialty of the day is ham and green beans. I also got a pitcher of fresh milk, just brought over by Miss Tompkins." Doc looked at Walker, "She's the same lady that brings over the eggs every three or four days."

Bevins wanted nothing more than to share a meal at the doc's table. "It would be my pleasure, Doc. Me and Walker, along with Buster Adams from over at the livery, been outside of town a few miles trying to get some information on what happened to that man back there. We got some clues but damn near froze to death in the process."

Just then Amos came through the door. He was walking slow but looked a sight better than he did the night before. "Well howdy, Sheriff. I thought I heard you and Stank out here talking to doc." Amos used Walker's alias on purpose. He still didn't know how he felt about the ruse the big Tennessean had pulled on the town.

"Doc, is he well enough to be out here aggravating us while we have super?" Bevins said with a grin.

Ramey turned from the stove. "Ain't you a little dizzy Amos? You lost some blood last night. It might be better if you rested another day or two before you go traipsing around here and pull loose one of those sutures I used to put you back together with last night."

"You know, Doc, I feel pretty good so if any of these two called the undertaker then send him back. I done rallied," Amos said as he gave a mean look to the sheriff and Walker.

"What smells so good in here? I feel like I could eat a bushel and drink a barrel."

"Beans and ham but you ain't getting any," Doc said.

Amos acted like he didn't hear what the doc said as he pulled out one of the chairs meant for either the sheriff or Walker.

Ramey rolled his eyes as he turned back to the stove. "I'll give you a bowl of warm broth Amos. It might be a day or two before you get back on solid food."

Amos thought that sounded harsh. "I get shot at the diner and now the doc is trying to starve me to death, Sheriff. I would think that should go against his profession."

"Amos, I expect you to do as the doc says. He says no solid food then you'll take the broth and like it. How long before he can come back to work, Doc?"

Ramey looked at the sheriff. "As hard headed as he is I reckon he can amble back over there tomorrow. But keep that bunk room he uses good and warm. He don't need to be catching a chill while he sleeps. He'll still need to come back and see me every day so I can change the bandages and make sure no infection is setting up."

The Trail

Ramey took a bowl from the stack beside the sink and filled it half way full with broth. He sat it, along with a big spoon, beside Amos. "There you go, Deputy. If you want out of here in the morning then eat that. Any more belly aching out of you and I promise to get me a horse needle and give you a shot of something where it hurts."

Amos didn't pay any attention to the doc, he was too hungry. He took a spoon full and said, "This is real good, Doc, you know what would make it better? Something in it to chew on, you cheapskate."

Ramey looked at Bevins and Walker as he took up his plate. "This ain't no restaurant, boys; if you want food then it's on the stove. Grab a plate and come over here and take up what you want."

After all three had their plates filled Ramey took out four glasses. He had a big icebox in his kitchen and in it was the pitcher of milk he had mentioned earlier. "Sheriff, how about you doing the honors. Milk for the three of us, ice water for Amos."

"Ice water sounds fine, Doc, but beer sounds better. I saw some bottles in that icebox when you opened the door," Amos said.

"I think ice water will do it for now Amos. As soon as you're finished I want you to go straight back there and lay down. Doctor's orders."

No sooner had Amos finished his bowl of broth than he began to feel tired again, getting shot will do that to a man. "I believe I've had enough. Thanks, Doc, for the meal, and for taking care of me. I think I'll go lay down now." With that Amos stood and headed toward the back.

Sheriff Bevins watched him go. "He gonna be alright Doc?"

"He's going to be fine. It might take a few days for him to get his strength back but he'll be alright. I got something else in the oven but didn't want to get it out until Amos left."

Ramey opened the oven door and, using the same potholder as earlier, he removed a big skillet of cornbread. "I knew if Amos saw this then he would want a slice. I hate to keep it from him but did it just the same." He sat the skillet on the stove and then sliced the pone in eight equal pieces, reaching one each to the two men at the table.

"You mentioned earlier that the other patient in the back is afraid of someone. Is that all you figured out since he's been here?" Walker asked.

Ramey was buttering one end of his cornbread as he said, "Not all I figured out. That man ain't worked a hard day in his life."

"You think he's just a drifter going from town to town?" Bevins asked.

"Not at all, I think he works. Just not hard work. If he did hard work then his hands would show it. As it is I'd say he does some sort of clerical work. Maybe a bookkeeper or banker or something. Might even be a school teacher or reporter, someone that works ten hours a day but has no lasting physical signs of it."

"Maybe I'll mention that to him when I go talk to him. That is if you allow it, Doc," the sheriff said.

"Oh I'll allow it. You can talk to him all you want now. He's out of danger and could probably use some of this broth. Once he's able to walk around are you planning to put him over in the jail, Sheriff?"

"Not sure yet. I've got a hunch that man we got over at the jail knows about the knife victim. Me and Walker figure he's the one that did it. I want to put him in the jail just to see the reaction on the face of our mysterious prisoner. That will tell me if the two have ever crossed paths before. How long before we can take him over, Doc?"

"In the morning I reckon. I got him sewn back together and bandaged tight. I'll need to check on him every day, same as Amos. How you going to keep him in jail though. He's committed no crime that we know of," Ramey asked the sheriff.

"Same as the other one I got locked up now. If I can't check out his name then he gets locked up. Same as anyone on the street. If a man don't want to tell me who he is then he's got something to hide. Is there any way you can keep that third feller back there, Doc, the one that shot Amos. If he's no threat then I'll see that he gets to the jail in the morning."

Ramey thought for a second and then answered, "I suppose that would be okay. The real reason I wanted him out of here is to keep Amos from going in there and killing him. Amos has a temper you know."

The three finished their meals and Walker and Bevins were saddled with the dishes while Ramey went back to check on his three patients. Both were glad to comply, it was the least they could do for such a meal.

As they wiped their hands Ramey came back in. "Amos is sound asleep. You come over in the morning around ten and fetch him. Bring another coat and a couple of blankets to wrap him up in. That coat he was wearing when he got shot is going to need a good cleaning, if it can even be cleaned at all. Blood has a way of wanting to stay on clothes, real hard to wash out.

"You can either go back there and talk to that other feller, the one with the knife wound, or we can help him out here. He needs to get up and walk a little anyway. He can also try out some of this broth," Ramey said.

"Let's bring him out here. Maybe a little food will loosen his tongue a bit. I'll break it to him that tomorrow morning he'll be moved to the jail. He don't know who we got over there and I don't want him to know. I need to see the look on both their faces when they first meet. I think that will tell a lot."

"Sounds like what I'd do if I was looking for answers. One thing though, Sheriff. Put the two in different cells and put at least one empty cell between them. If that varmint you got over there did this you don't want to give him the opportunity to finish the job," Ramey said.

This wasn't the first time the doc had tried to tell Bevins how to do his job. The sheriff let it pass. He wasn't about to snap at the man after the meal he had just been served.

Before the men had a chance to bring the patient with the knife wound out for a little broth and a little conversation they heard the sound of a horse walking down the street. The iron shoes on frozen ground made a noise that carried and this was the sound that got their attention.

Bevins looked at Walker. "Now who would be out on such a night? I better check and see. Anyone traveling this late must have a good reason."

"I'll go with you Sheriff. I need to stretch my legs a bit after such a big meal," Walker said.

The two stepped onto the front porch of Ramey's house, neither took the time to put on their coats. They figured it was just someone looking for the hotel that needed directions and they could come right back in. Neither could leave anyway because they both wanted to talk to the man in the back.

The Trail

What Bevins and Walker saw through the blowing snow was a horse with a stooped over man in the saddle. It was unusual, but not unknown, for a drunk to ride a horse that way, bent over half passed out.

"You looking for the hotel, Mister?" Bevins shouted to the man.

There was no reply as the horse continued to amble down main street.

"We better go over and see if he's drunk. I'd hate for that man to freeze to death during the night. We'll take him to the jail and put him in a cell till he sobers up. In the morning I'll make the coffee really strong and give it to him nice and hot," Bevins said.

Bevins and Walker stepped from the porch and headed for the horse and rider. "He better be drunk for making me come and get him without my coat," the sheriff said.

As the two approached the horse stopped and looked at them. She was glad to be in a town and glad two men were on their way over to check on the load she carried. The same load she had carried for over a day.

"Mister, I reckon you got a good reason to be out this late in this kind of weather. I for one would like to know that reason if you got the time," Bevins said with a hint of sarcasm in his voice. Again the man didn't answer.

Bevins pulled his gun from its holster. He suspected something was wrong and didn't want to be shot by a drunk that was about to be woken up.

He held the Colt at the ready as he grabbed the sleeve of the man's coat. "You hear what I asked you, mister?" The man fell to the other side of the horse, the grip the sheriff had wasn't good enough to keep him in the saddle.

"Help me get him to his feet, Walker, before he freezes to death. We'll walk him over to the jail so he can sober up. I'll tell Buster to come and get his horse," Bevins said. The two got the man to his feet but he immediately collapsed back to the ground.

"Help me throw him across his saddle. We'll just use his horse to carry him over to the jail," Bevins said.

With no small amount of effort the sheriff and Walker finally got the man over his saddle. Walker walked along to make sure the man didn't fall off again as Bevins led the horse. Ten minutes later and they had him in the front office. In the light they now noticed both had blood on their hands. They also noticed the blood on the man's coat and pants.

"You want to get him over to Ramey's or have the Doc hurry over here?" Walker asked.

"This man is nearly dead. Better see if the Doc can come here?"

Walker hurried out and within ten minutes he and Ramey came through the front door. The doctor was holding a small leather bag he used to carry the basics. Not knowing what he might find was always a challenge.

"Clear off your desk, Sheriff, so I can get a look at him," Ramey said.

Once sprawled on top of the desk the three men took the man's coat off so the doctor could see what had happened. It only took a minute to determine the man had been shot.

"We better get him over to my place. He needs more than I got in this little bag if he's going to survive."

"Help me get his coat back on, Walker," Bevins said.

"Forget the coat; the cold is probably what saved his life. Just take him by the shoulders and get him to my place. I need to see where that bullet is and get him warmed up. I'll just take the bullet out and let the cold be his anesthetic," Ramey said.

Both Bevins and Walker got the man off the desk and each took an arm and hoisted him up. His toes drug the ground as the two men raced to the Doc's place as fast as their load would allow.

"Put him back there in my exam room. After that, Walker, how about you boiling some water and get me some clean towels from my supply room. Sheriff, this place is starting to fill up, why don't you hang around until I get this feller seen to. Help yourself to some cornbread and butter from the icebox. If everything goes alright I should be done in an hour or so," Ramey said.

True to his word the doctor came out of his examination, slash operating room, a little over an hour later. He was wiping his hands on a stained towel as he headed toward the coffee pot. He looked at the sheriff with a look that said if the pot wasn't full and hot then the sheriff would have some explaining to do.

"How is he, Doc," Bevins asked.

"Doing okay I guess. His body temperature was less than ninety three degrees, a little more and he wouldn't have made it. As it is I think the cold weather saved his life. Slowed down the bleeding. If it had been warm he would have surely bleed to death."

"He give his name, Doc? If he did then he'll be the first in a while," Bevins said.

"Not voluntarily. He came to while I was digging that bullet out and I had to give him a big dose of Laudanum, it knocked him right out. I had to wait a few minutes for the stuff to take effect so I tried to talk to him. I asked his name and he told me right off, James Anderson. That name mean anything to you Sheriff?"

Bevins had to think a minute before it came to him. "It does at that. If I ain't mistaken, I believe I got a dodger on him over at the jail. Can't remember off hand what he's wanted for but I'm sure that's the name. He say anything else?"

"He did but I figured it was probably the Laudanum talking. He'll be coming around in a couple of hours after that stuff wears off. Normally I wouldn't want anyone bothering a man in that kind of shape but I think you ought to be here when he comes to, can you do that?"

"I'll make sure I am. While he's getting over that stuff you gave him I think I'll go over to the jail and look for that dodger. I need to check on the prisoner I got over there anyway, you know the other bastard that won't tell me his name. I might have time to make my rounds before coming back. Wouldn't want some drunk to pass out and freeze to death. Normally that would be Amos doing the rounds tonight but I doubt you will let him do that," Bevins said as he grinned at Ramey.

Ramey never caught the joke. "You head on out Sheriff. Be back here in two hours. If he ain't come to by then I got something that will wake him up, smelling salts."

Bevins had heard of smelling salts, "Sounds like the thing to do. I'll be back. Walker is snoozing in the front parlor. I'll tell him to hang around in case you need him."

Ramey was glad to know the big Tennessean would be staying. With so much mischief he felt he needed a full time deputy sleeping on the chase in the front parlor.

Once at the jail Bevins found the dodger he was looking for. It read, *"James Anderson, Wanted for the charge of Assault, Robbery, Impersonating a Doctor and numerous other charges. Subject is to be considered dangerous. A reward of five-hundred dollars is offered.* At the bottom in all capital letters were the words, ***DEAD OR ALIVE.***

The sheriff continued to look at the paper. There was a line drawing that, with a little imagination, looked like the man over at Ramey's place.

Bevins stood and went to the coffee pot, what was left was at least eight hours old and scalding hot. What the hell, he thought. Strong and hot might help keep him awake. It was looking to be a long night.

He stepped into the cell room. The man with no name was sound asleep. It was surprising because as far as he knew the man hadn't had his supper yet. No one was around to let the man from the diner in to bring any food. Upon second thought the man had been fed. It had arrived before they went looking for the site of the attack on the man over at Ramey's. All these people with no names was starting to wear on the sheriff.

Bevins relocked the door to the jail and then made his rounds. No passed out drunks were found. As he walked the town he made sure to tell Buster Adams about the horse tied up in front of the sheriff's office. He told him the animal might need a little extra attention, un-telling how long she had been out and most likely needed fresh water and grain. At the two hour mark Bevins was back at Ramey's ready to see if anything could be found out about the latest mystery that had shown up in town.

"The patient come around yet Doc?"

Ramey was in the kitchen fixing another pot of coffee. "Not yet, let me finish another cup and then I'll break out the smelling salts. I haven't had an opportunity to try them on anybody yet. You might say I'm anxious to use it."

Bevins noticed the good doctor seemed to be excited to use his new medicine. His tone wasn't that much different than an excited child on Christmas morning.

Just then Walker came in and stretched. "You got any more of that coffee Doc?"

"Got plenty. You enjoy your little nap?"

"I did. That chase of yours in the front parlor makes a fine bed. It could have been a little wider, and a little longer, but I slept just fine. How about you, Sheriff, you take a little snooze over at the jail?"

Bevins was in line to get some of the Doc's coffee. Ramey always kept a better brand than the jail could afford. It was called Arbuckle or something like that. "Walker, I'll have you know I'm the High Sheriff. I got everyone in town believing I never sleep."

Walker picked up his cup from the dinner table. "Pardon me Sheriff. What in the world was I thinking?"

"Doc here is about to go and give his new patient a little something to bring him out of his coma. I for one want to be there when he wakes up to see if he says anything useful."

Walker looked suspiciously at the sheriff. "The way you talk I take it you found some information on the man over at the jail."

"I did, as a matter of fact what I found is no less than a warrant for his arrest. And get this, it's dead or alive," the sheriff whispered.

Ramey sat down his cup. "Well in that case let's go wake him up. I was starting to feel a bit guilty for wanting to use them salts on that stranger but if he is who you say he is then I could care less. As a matter of fact I got him patched up good enough that you can haul his ass to the jail and put him up at taxpayers' expense. I'm getting tired of patching up wounded men and then having to board the outlaws at my expense."

Walker and Bevins were surprised at the sudden outburst. Walker wondered if it had anything to do with the fact that the man had nothing to barter. As the three went down the hall Bevins was stopped by the stranger with the knife wound. He spoke as he saw Bevins go by.

"Sheriff, you got a minute," the man asked.

Bevins stopped and looked in the room. "You need something?"

"Maybe, but can you step inside, I don't want to talk too loud."

Bevins entered the room but was agitated the man was keeping him from seeing the effects of the smelling salts. "What is it?"

"That man you got in the next room, not the deputy you call Amos. The other one that just got brought in tonight."

"What about him," Bevins asked.

"If he comes to is there any way you can keep the fact that I'm here to yourself?"

"Do you know that man? If so I would like to know how. You couldn't have seen him when we brought him in, he was unconscious and the doc had him covered to try to thaw him out."

"You're right, Sheriff, I didn't see the man and I don't know who he is but all the same, I'd like to remain anonymous if that's possible. As a matter of fact I'd like for you not to mention that I'm here at all."

"Anonymous seems to be the way everyone wants to be known around here these days. I need you to tell me who you are and what in hell is going on if you want me to protect you.

All this cloak and dagger stuff is starting to make me nervous. It's also starting to make me mad."

"I figure that's fair, Sheriff. You keep quiet about me and I promise to tell you everything. I promise I haven't broken any laws but I will also tell you that I'm in grave danger If certain men knew I was here they would spare no expense to have me killed. Also, anyone that knows about me might also be in danger. You don't know me or know anything about me but I promise what I've just said is true."

Bevins suspected the man was telling the truth. "You stay here and don't make a sound. I'll close the door to this room when I leave so anyone that comes, or goes, down the hallway will think this room is empty. Doc only keeps occupied rooms open to let the warm air circulate. In a little while I'll be back and then you are going to tell me everything, I mean it!"

Bevins left, making sure to close the door as he went. When he made it to the room where Walker and Ramey were, he was surprised to see that they were waiting. He was afraid they might have already roused the patient.

"About time, Sheriff, I was just about to continue without you," Ramey said.

"Listen you two. The man in the next room doesn't want this man to know he's here. He might know something about this feller but wants to make sure this man doesn't know about him. We keep things quiet for the time being. He also says we might be in danger if the wrong people know he's here," Bevins said. Both Ramey and Walker looked toward the other room.

"Let's get this over with, Doc. Things are starting to get a little confusing around here. The faster we get some answers the safer we all will be," Bevins added.

The Trail

Ramey reached into a pocket and pulled out a small white item that almost looked like a hand rolled cigarette, but shorter. "Now when I break this open you two try not to breath any of the vapors. It's made to irritate the nasal passages to the point that a man, even a man that's unconscious, will react violently to the smell. I need each of you to hold an arm and when I put this under his nose you hold him tight. The effect is only momentary and after that he will just have watery eyes, but he'll be wide awake."

Ramey looked at the two men, "You ready?"

"Go ahead, Doc," Bevins said.

Ramey quickly broke the smelling salt in two and held it under the man's nose. His next breath brought an immediate response. He jerked his eyes open and started trying to raise his arms.

"Hold him tight, I don't want him to tear his stitches loose," Ramey said.

"What the hell did you do to me?" the man shouted.

"Just calm down, I only gave you something to wake you up. You've been shot. If you keep struggling then you'll bleed to death," Ramey said, more to scare the man than anything else.

The threat had the wanted affect; the man grew still as he looked the room over. He also looked at Walker and Bevins and the two badges pinned to their chests.

"What am I doing here and who are you men?"

My name's Doctor Ramey, you are under my care. You came in here a few hours ago with a bullet wound in the chest. I managed to get the bullet out and clean the wound enough that you should be alright. Anytime we got a gunshot wound then the sheriff here needs to know how you happened to come about it. All of us would also like to know your name," Ramey said.

"How bad was it, Doc?"

"Not as bad as I first thought. The bullet went in between two ribs and stopped there. I managed to get it out without much trouble. That bullet must have hit something else before it hit you because if it hadn't it would have blown a hole clean through you. I'd say that's pretty lucky."

Anderson looked at Bevins, the badge on his chest clearly said Sheriff. "I ain't done nothing Sheriff. You got no investigating to do here. The doc said I ain't hurt that bad and I expect to leave here as soon as someone reaches me my boots and coat."

"I didn't say you did anything wrong but I would like to know who shot you. And like the doc said, I need to know who you are?"

Anderson thought a second, undoubtedly trying to figure out what to say to the sheriff.

"I guess you troubled yourself for nothing Sheriff. I was cleaning my gun a night or so back and managed to let the damn thing go off. I didn't think it was that bad at first. How did I get here anyway?"

"Your horse brought you. You say you shot yourself while cleaning your gun? Where is your gun so we can verify the caliber? Doc saved the bullet so all I got to do is match it up," Bevins said.

The man suspected he had just been caught lying. What he needed was time to formulate a more believable story. "I don't know where my gun is. My head is a bit fuzzy and I can't think straight. Can I rest a while and then I'll be glad to answer your questions. At least the ones I know the answer to. I seem to be a bit forgetful; I guess shooting myself affected my memory a little."

"You can rest as soon as you tell me your name," Bevins said.

The man thought a second and then said, "Willie Carter. That's it, Sheriff, it's Willy Carter."

The name James Anderson just used was the name of a man he had robbed back in the summer. Now he had not only robbed the man of his belongings but also his name.

Bevins looked at the doc. He suspected the name was another lie, which would make two in the last five minutes. "What do you say, Doc. Is he ready to head on over to the jail? I got a nice cold place for men that give me a name I suspect ain't true."

"Well, I suppose you could head him on over there. First thing in the morning would be better though. I need to make sure those sutures hold. I wouldn't want him to bleed to death in that jail overnight. But like you say, it's so cold over there he'd probably freeze to death before he ever had the chance to bleed to death," Doc said. He wanted to scare the man a little.

"You rest easy, Mister Carter. When you feel a bit better we need to have us a little talk," Bevins said as he left the room.

Walker and Ramey met the sheriff back at the coffee pot. "That man is lying out both sides of his mouth, Sheriff. The only reason I didn't let you take him out of here tonight is he might still break open if he moves the wrong way. I'll know in the morning how things are and I'm pretty sure you can take him then," Ramey said.

"You say that other man back there wants to talk, Sheriff," Walker asked.

"He does, but I don't want to take the chance that Anderson, or Carter, whoever in hell he is, might hear what he says. We'll take Anderson to the jail first thing in the morning and then I'll come back and talk to him. In the meantime though, one of us needs to be here at all times. Doc, go in and tell that man in the next room to keep as quite as possible tonight. Keep the door locked too, just in case."

"You want me to stay here tonight, Sheriff? I've grown quite fond of that chase in there. Doc keeps it nice and warm in here and the coffee is better," Walker said.

"That okay with you, Doc? I need to get back to the livery and see that Adams got that horse put away. I also want to see what the man was carrying in his saddlebags. Starting to think I need to look in every saddlebag that comes into town."

"That sounds good, Sheriff. I don't think anybody here could cause me much trouble but with Walker here I'll sleep better. You just come on back anytime in the morning and I'm pretty sure you can take that lying bastard that says he shot himself over to the jail. I'll feel better when he's gone."

"So you don't think he shot himself either, do you Doc?" Bevins asked.

"Not a chance. There's no powder burns on him, or his clothes. You shoot yourself there's gonna be some evidence that it was self-inflected. I saw a man a few years back that shot himself, accidentally of course, but I really think it was his wife. Anyway, his jacket caught fire from the powder burns. Now you think of that. I told him he deserved gittin shot for giving his wife a gun in the first place. I knew she done it and he knew that I knew. I wonder sometimes if that man's still alive," Ramey said as more of a question to himself.

The Trail

Bevins grabbed his coat and hat from the parlor and headed out the door. As he headed for the livery he promised himself he was going to save up and buy a warmer coat. He laughed to himself because he had been making that promise for years.

One of the big doors to the livery was unlocked so Bevins pushed his way in making sure to close it behind him. "You in here, Adams?"

"Is that you, Sheriff?"

"It's me. Did you get that horse off the street?"

"I did, come on back here."

Bevins headed to a stall toward the back, a stall that was lit by a lantern. "You strip that man's gear off his horse yet?"

"I did, it's laying on the other side of the hall there. Come in here and look at this, Sheriff," Adams said.

Adams had the horse tied close and it's legs hobbled. Bevins looked at the horse and immediately saw what was happening. Adams was sewing up a wound on the horses left hip. "What happened to that animal? Is that what I think it is?"

"Looks like a bullet went through the fleshy part of the hip and passed clean through. I found the entrance and exit wound. I cleaned both and am trying to sew things shut. How about you rubbing her neck and ears, it might help keep her calm. I'll be done in a few minutes. This is one lucky horse. Another inch and the bullet would have hit bone."

Bevins held the bridle and began talking to the horse as he stroked her neck. He felt sorry for the animal. She had been shot and traveled who knows how far with Anderson hanging on for dear life. He almost wished the man had fallen off so the horse could have made it to town sooner.

"All finished. That ought to heal up nicely. You know Sheriff, I almost went for the doc but knew he's got more patients over there than he can handle. I done me a little field doctoring back in the war and just decided to take care of it on my own. I think I done a pretty fair job of it if I do say so myself."

Bevins stepped out of the stall as Adams undid the hobble. As the liveryman was bringing in a bucket of water and a scoop of grain he said, "I thought you might want to go through that man's stuff. All I did was put it against the wall over there. And Sheriff, whatever he's got in those saddlebags is pretty heavy," Adams said.

Just then one of the big doors creaked open. Bevins took the Colt from its holster as he looked at Adams. He whispered, "You expecting anybody?" Adams shook his head no. In the dim light of the big barn both Bevins and Adams could see the outlines of two men.

"Anybody in here? came a shout.

Bevins recognized the voice of James Arthur Pack. He assumed the man with him was Leroy Cobb.

"In the back," Bevins said.

The two Baldwin Felts men walked toward the voice.

"We just heard a rumor up at the saloon that another wounded man came into town not long ago. I stopped by the jail and the door was locked. Figured we would try the livery first and then the doctor's office," Pack said.

"You heard right. Got a man over at Ramey's with a gunshot wound. I just came over to see if I could find out anything from the horse he rode and the gear he carried."

As the men talked Adams went to the front of the barn and lit another lantern. He also put another log in the stove and filled the coffee pot. He figured it was going to take a little while for the sheriff to go through the saddlebags. He'd probably want everything written down as well.

Bevins grabbed the saddle bags as Cobb and Pack got the saddle and the long gun sleeve. The items were placed on the same table as before, the one where Adams took his meals.

"I sure hope nothing falls out of them bags like the stuff before. I still have trouble enjoying my food eating off that table, and I scrubbed it good," Adams said.

Pack looked at the sheriff for an explanation. "I'll tell you about that other stuff when we got some time. Right now I just want to see if these bags might have some answers. Grab your pencil and paper, Adams, if you don't mind. We need to make an inventory, same as before," the sheriff said.

Cobb and Pack watched as each item was taken out and placed on the table. Nothing out of the ordinary came out until halfway through the second bag. Bevins reached in and pulled out a felt sack with a leather drawstring. It was similar to the one they found previously that contained the gruesome teeth.

"On no, Sheriff, not again," Adams said.

"Only one way to find out," he said as he untied the leather drawstring and poured the contents onto the table.

Cobb spoke first, "Are them teeth?"

All told the bag held twenty one teeth, some with dried blood on them but all with gold. There were six pairs of expensive looking glasses. Four gold pocket watches, and an assortment of rings of both the diamond and gold variety.

"I believe you got yourself a highwayman, Sheriff. Looks like he not only robs folks of their valuables but he also extracts a few teeth to boot," Cobb said.

"Do you think the people these teeth belong to are dead? I'm sure no one would hold still while someone pried their teeth out," Pack asked.

We got another man in jail, been there for three or four days now. We found a pouch of the same stuff in his saddlebags. I got it all locked up over at the bank," Bevins said.

"Probably a good idea, Sheriff. By the looks of this pile you might need to store it at the bank too. There must be better than two thousand dollars lying there in cash and gold coins, and that ain't even counting the jewelry. What kind of man travels with that kind of money anyway?" Pack asked.

"Where you gonna keep this stuff until the bank opens in the morning, Sheriff?" Adams asked.

"Same as before. I'll set it in the middle of an empty jail cell and lock the door. Works every time. Pack, would you and Cobb mind helping me back to the jail. The way things are going around here I believe there's someone around every corner ready to do mischief."

The sheriff and the two Baldwin men left the livery and headed for the jail. The three were nearly frozen by the time Bevins got the front door unlocked and they all got inside.

"You going home tonight, Sheriff, or you staying here?" Pack asked.

"This is my home about half the time. I got a room off the side over there where I sleep some nights. We got a bunkroom too but it ain't used much. I figure that's where Amos will be staying when the doc says he's ready. He's got him a place just outside of town but like me he spends about half his nights here at the jail."

"When were you expecting that freight wagon Sheriff," Pack asked.

Bevins thought a second before answering. "Should have been here day before yesterday. If they stopped to work on a section of the road that should have put them in here yesterday."

"I believe me and Cobb here are going to head out first thing in the morning. We're gonna backtrack the trail and see if we can meet up with that freight wagon. You said they should have pulled in here already. I got a feeling them two teamsters have met up with some trouble. We find them alright then we'll escort the wagon into Clear Creek. If there's been trouble then we'll see what we can find out and report back here to you."

Bevins was looking in the coffee pot as Pack talked. "I hope there's not been any trouble. Old Trevor and Mathew are two likable old cusses. You'll see when you meet them. I do have one stipulation though."

"What's that Sheriff?" Pack asked.

"When you find the wagon I don't want either of you looking in those mail bags. That's post office property and until it gets here they stay shut."

"That's acceptable. Me and Cobb wouldn't want to open any of those bags until you or a deputy is around to witness it anyway," Pack said.

As the sheriff filled the pot with water and sat it back on the stove he thought of something else. "Is there any way the two of you could help move two wounded men from the doctor's place over to the jail first thing in the morning before you go. I'm shorthanded in good times and these ain't good times."

"Be glad to help, Sheriff. Me and Cobb will be here at first light. After that we plan to see what we can see of that missing freight wagon. Hopefully we'll meet them on the trail heading this way within a day or two. If not then we might just ride the entire trail until we find out what's going on."

The next morning, as soon as the first light of a cold day arrived, both Pack and Cobb stepped on the board walk in front of the jail. Bevins heard them and unlocked the door. He was just about to make coffee when he heard the two outside.

"Step on in here out of the cold. Coffee will be ready shortly. Glad both of you are here, I got another favor to ask," Bevins said as he put the pot on the stove.

"What kind of favor, Sheriff? We already said we would be glad to help bring them wounded men over from doc's place," Pack said.

"It's besides that. I want you two to take that man I got locked up in the back to the livery. I want him to look at the horses down there and see if he recognizes any of them. I got a feeling he's associated in some way with the men that rode in here on those horses.

"He'll probably deny he's seen any of them before except maybe the one he told us about being abandoned out there and tied to a tree. The one I need to find out about is the one that brought that gunshot victim in here last night. Keep your eye on him, even if denies knowing you should be able to tell if he's telling the truth or not by the look on his face.

"Another reason to get him out of here is so I can give them three cells a quick sweeping. While you're gone me and Walker will bring the two men over from doc's place," Bevins told the two.

"Be glad to help out, Sheriff. How long do you want us to keep him down there? I got a feeling you don't want him here when the two wounded men are brought over."

The Trail

"Give me a good hour. I'll have the two new prisoners back here by then and locked up safe and sound. Better put a set of wrist irons on the one you're taking, I doubt he'd be any trouble for the two of you but I don't want to take any chances," Bevins said.

Ten minutes later and the three were on their way to the livery and the three cells had received a good sweeping. Bevins hurried over to Ramey's to fetch his first prisoner. As cold as it was, hurrying just seemed to come natural.

After the first prisoner was situated in the far right cell then the Sheriff went back to get Anderson. He doubted the man would be any trouble and if he was he'd just give him a second gunshot wound to go along with the one he already had.

An hour later the front door pushed open and Pack and Cobb walked in pushing the prisoner in front of them. They had let him look at the horse in question at the livery.

"Sheriff, do I have your permission to beat the living hell out of this bastard?" Cobb asked.

"I'd like nothing more but we better wait until the judge gets here in a few days. His circuit brings him through here once a month. He usually tries to be here when the freight wagon shows up. He likes his mail too. Let's put this one in the left hand cell. I got the sickest of the two we brought over in the right and the other one in the center. I was told to give the one man with the knife wound plenty of blankets. Doc said he's pretty weak and needs to be kept nice and warm."

Bevins looked at the prisoner Pack and Cobb had just brought in. "I'm a little short on blankets so I gave him yours."

"You go to hell, Sheriff," the man said.

Bevins laughed as he opened the door to the cell room. The man lying in the right hand cell was breathing weakly and shivering even with the extra blankets. He was covered from head to toe and still seemed cold. The other one, the one in the center cell, was standing at the bars. Even with a gunshot wound he seemed angry to have been brought to the jail.

The last man was being headed toward the left hand cell next to the man with the gunshot wound. Bevins, Pack, and Cobb all watched the two men's faces when they saw each other. They knew each other, Bevins and the two Baldwin men were sure of it.

As Bevins pushed the prisoner into the empty cell he said, "I would introduce you but seems nobody around here will give me their name. Now I want the two of you to behave yourselves. That one on the right probably won't make it, Doc says he's developed an infection and is running a fever. That's one reason he sent him over here, so he wouldn't die in the doctor's office. I hear any ruckus out of you then I'll be back. I hear either of you tormenting that man over there then I'll also be back, and I won't be happy."

Bevins looked at the man standing in the center cell. "And as far as me letting you go, Mister Willie Carter, I need time to think about that story you told last night about shooting yourself while cleaning that gun of yours, the gun we can't find. I might let you out of here in a few hours after I have me a cup of coffee. I reckon I can't hold you long just because I don't like you."

Bevins left the cell room, followed by Pack and Cobb. He shut the heavy door and headed to the coffee pot. "Did that other man say anything about them horses when you got him to the livery?"

"Not a word, Sheriff. He wouldn't even turn his eyes toward them horses. He acted like he didn't even know what a horse was. And the language, more than once I was tempted to crack his skull," Cobb said.

"That is one bad man, Sheriff. I wouldn't want to turn my back on him. I also think he and that man in the middle cell know each other. My guess is they are in cahoots. I doubt either will say a word that'll help you find out who they really are," Pack said.

The two prisoners waited for the sheriff and the two Baldwin men to leave the cell room before they talked. "What in hell are you doing here, Lem? I thought you would have found that lying newspaperman by now and finished the job," Anderson said.

"Keep your voice down. The last thing we need is for them lawmen out front to hear who we are or what we were sent here to do. And as far as your question, I did finish the job. I caught up with Dinsmore about a mile or so outside of town. I knifed that bastard. Last I saw of him was his body falling off a cliff, had to be a five-hundred foot drop."

"You better hope he was dead when he hit the bottom. Wilbur Westbrook expects all the loose ends to be tied up nice and tight," Anderson said.

"How about you? You catch up with that freight wagon?" Lem asked.

"I did, as a matter of fact I caught up with it twice. I wasn't able to get the mailbags though. I had a traitor in my ranks and he killed a few of my men. He also shot up an ambush we had set. I reckon I'm the only one that made it out alive," Anderson said.

"That's bad. Last I heard Westbrook has thrown in with William Butler. If me and you don't get that package then they will most likely put a price on our heads. I knew I shouldn't have signed on with them men from Chicago. They are dangerous on a good day and this ain't no good day," Lem said.

"What's the chance we can get out of here by the time that freight wagon arrives? If we can get out of here then we'll kill the sheriff and take possession of the mail when that wagon shows up. We need to kill them two Baldwin men too," Anderson said.

"Next time one of them comes in here you act like you're getting sick from that wound of yours. As soon as he unlocks the door you need to shove him against the bars here and I'll reach through and strangle the bastard. We'll take his gun and then deal with the rest of 'em. You strong enough to do that?" Lem asked.

"If it's the difference between living and dying then I'm strong enough. You just be ready when he unlocks the door to my cell," Anderson said.

"That sounds like a pretty good plan boys," came a voice from the next cell.

Lem and Anderson both looked at the right hand cell. The man who spoke was still covered from head to toe. Suddenly he flung the covers off and got to his feet, it was Walker.

"Sheriff, you can come back in now," Walker shouted.

Both Lem and Anderson were speechless. They had just given up their names as well as their plans. "Why you conniving bastard," Lem said.

The Trail

The door opened and Bevins walked in. He unlocked the door to Walkers cell as he smiled at the two prisoners. "You find anything out, Walker?" he asked.

"I did, I'll tell you all about it after I get me some coffee." As he walked by the cells he put the back of his hand to his forehead. "I believe my fever has broke," Walker said as he smiled at the two stone faced prisoners. Once they were back out front Bevins got to hear what was said.

"That's Anderson, Sheriff, just as you suspected. The other man is Lem Gravitt. Gravitt attacked the man still over at Doc Ramey's. Lem thinks he killed him, said his name is Dinsmore. They were just now planning on how to kill one of you and take your gun. They were going on a killing spree, or at least they were putting the plan together," Walker said as he stirred a spoonful of sugar into his cup.

"They say anything about the freight wagon or the mail it carried?" Pack asked.

"They did. From what I gather they are working for a couple of men back east. One is a Westbrook and the other goes by the name of Butler. Both are from the city of Chicago. Some pretty bad men from the way they talked. They said if they failed to do the job they were contracted to do then there would, most likely, be a price put on their heads."

Bevins stood and put his coffee cup on his desk. "I better get over to Ramey's and see if this Dinsmore is ready to talk. His tongue might have loosened up a bit once he knows I got Gravitt and Anderson locked up tight. Walker, could I get you to stay here and make sure them two don't try anything? I suppose Pack and Cobb might want to come with me to hear what Dinsmore has to say."

"I'll be glad to stay here. I plan on emptying this pot of coffee and if them two back there don't let me enjoy it in peace then I might not share any of it with them."

"That's harsh, Walker," Bevins said as he headed out the door.

Dinsmore was happy to know the two outlaws were in jail. But he was still worried. He was worried that they might find out he was still alive and try to finish what they started.

Bevins and the others left Dinsmore and stepped back out to the front parlor where they could talk in private. "I wonder if we might be able to convince the two I got locked up that we found Dinsmore's body at the foot of the cliff. If they think he's dead then maybe that will be the end of it? At least the end of them wanting to kill him," Bevins said.

"Won't work. If we convince the two that Dinsmore's dead then you are going to have to charge Gravitt with murder, but no murder's been committed. Can't do one without the other," Pack said.

"And if they think he's still alive then he won't last long when those folks back east find out. The judge will be here in a day or two. What if we convince him to charge Gravitt with murder but give the sentence according to the guidelines for attempted murder? He'll think Dinsmore is dead and also think he was sentenced for murder. He won't know the difference in the two sentences," Bevins said.

Pack and Cobb thought it over. "That might work. If it ever comes up that Dinsmore is found alive then the court paperwork can indicate that Gravitt was charged for attempted murder rather than murder. But Gravitt won't know the difference unless he has a good lawyer," Pack said.

The Trail

"Judge Wicker will know what to do. He might be here a full month before he finally gets all this straightened out. Do you and Cobb still plan on chasing down that wagon this morning," Bevins asked.

"I believe so. If we meet them on the trail then we ain't lost anything but our time. If something has happened then we can either lend a hand or investigate. Either way we'll be back here and let you know what we find out. I would also like to hear what that judge you mentioned intends to do. Clear Creek has a wagon load of problems and the wagon ain't even here yet," Pack said.

Pack and Cobb stood and headed for the door. "We left our saddlebags and supplies at the livery this morning before coming to the jail. If you don't need us for anything else I believe we'll head on out," Pack said.

The two Baldwin men pulled out of Clear Creek a little before eleven that morning. Both hated to leave the comforts of a town with a saloon and a hotel but they didn't get paid for dodging cold weather. Both made good time as the trail was easy to follow and the ground was frozen solid. The horses didn't mind the weather, or the pace the two Baldwin men set.

Trevor and Mathew both rode horses as they worked the big wagon down the trail. Satan was glad for a day where there wasn't any gunfire, or dead bodies for that matter.

"Sounds like a horse coming hard, Trevor," Mathew said. Of the two Mathew always had better hearing than Trevor. At the beginning of the war Trevor had been attached to a cannon detail. He only worked that job for two months before being transferred. The two months was still enough to do permanent damage to his hearing.

Trevor tapped the lead mule on the shoulder with his pole and said, "Whoa there, Satan." Satan heard the fast approaching horse and was more than willing to wait this one out.

"Let's me and you spread out a bit, Mathew. Better get that Greener ready just in case," Trevor said.

As the two men waited the sound grew louder until finally Billy rode around the bend. He was greeted by the two teamsters, both holding shotguns.

"Billy, you scared the devil out of me," Trevor said.

"Got two riders coming down the road. Be here in five minutes or so," Billy said as both he and his horse tried to catch their breath.

"Trevor, how about easing that wagon to the side a little. Then I think we should go forward and meet whoever it is on our terms. I don't want any of the mules in the way if bullets start flying," Mathew said. Once the wagon was safely beside the road and the wheel brake set the three men rode ahead in order to meet the two riders.

"Got three riders up ahead, Cobb. We don't mention the freight wagon, they could be some of Anderson's men. Better pull back the hammers on that scattergun just in case," Pack said.

When the two groups of riders were within fifty feet of each other all five men stopped.

Trevor decided to speak first. "Morning, which way you two heading?"

The Trail

Pack pointed a finger at the three and said, "That way, what about you?"

Trevor pointed a finger at the two riders and said, "That way."

Cobb wasn't a man to beat around the bush. "Well I reckon we've exchanged our pleasantries. Now if you don't mind me and my friend here will be on our way."

Trevor raised his shotgun. "Mind if I ask you a question first?"

Cobb raised his shotgun and said, "Go right ahead."

Billy and Mathew expected both shotguns to go off any second.

Trevor looked at Pack and Cobb. "Where would you two be going so well armed on such a cold day?"

Pack noticed the two older men fit the description of the two teamsters that Sheriff Bevins told him about. He decided to take a chance, "We are here on behalf of Sheriff Bevins from Clear Creek. We are looking for a freight wagon that's a couple of days late. Bevins gave us his blessing to try and find that wagon and lend assistance if it's needed."

Trevor didn't believe the two men. He thought this was just another attempt to steal the wagon. "Any way you can prove you are really here on behalf of the sheriff?"

Now Pack and Cobb had a problem. They had nothing in writing that backed up what they said. Finally Pack said, "We pulled out of Clear Creek around eleven this morning. I can tell you that there has been a fair amount of trouble there. Doctor Ramey has had as many as four men at his place with anything from gunshot to stab wounds. I also know it's damn cold out here and if you three are with the freight wagon then go get the damn thing and let's all head into town so the sheriff can verify what we say. By the looks of the three of you I'd say the saloon could use some of your business."

Mathew looked at Trevor and Billy. "He just might be telling the truth. How we going to trust them long enough to make it to town though?"

Billy looked at Pack and Cobb. "Tell you what. You two can ride along with us but you'll do it from in front. I doubt the three of us want to turn our backs to you."

Pack thought that would work. He was now certain Trevor and Mathew were the two teamsters they were looking for. He didn't know this young feller though. "One question first. Who's the kid?"

Trevor looked at Billy and then said, "He saved our bacon a few days back. He shot two of Anderson's gang. After that I told him to ride along with me and Mathew so we could protect him. To be honest with you I think he's afraid of the dark." Billy just shook his head.

"Anderson is locked up in the Clear Creek jail so he won't be giving anyone any trouble for some time. You say you won't turn your backs to us and I respect that. But I don't think me or Cobb here want to turn our backs on you either until we see a freight wagon. After that I reckon we will be convinced."

"Sounds like the thing I would do if I was you. How about the four of us sit here facing each other while Trevor goes for the wagon?" Mathew said.

Ten minutes later the big freight wagon came around the bend in the road being led by Satan and Trevor. "There you go mister. Now if you don't mind I would like to get everyone pointed toward Clear Creek. The way I got it figured we won't get there until a good two hours past dark."

The Trail

Pack and Cobb put away their guns and turned their horses. Mathew had it figured about right because a little over two hours past dark the dim lamp lights of town could be seen. Traveling after dark didn't bother Satan in the least. He had worked the trail so long he knew they were close and close meant a stable and rest.

"We're going to pull into the livery. I don't want the wagon left outside overnight and I sure don't feel like unloading it as cold as it is," Trevor said.

Thirty minutes later the wagon was tucked away in the big hallway of the livery. Buster Adams and the two teamsters quickly undid the hitch and put all eight mules in stalls. Satan as well as the other mules knew exactly where they were and also knew they would get a few days to rest.

Sheriff Bevins got word that the freight wagon had made it and came straight to the livery. "Trevor, you and Mathew are sure a sight for sore eyes. I was just about to give up on you two."

"Say, Sheriff, you know these two men. They met us on the trail a few hours back and told some big story about knowing you," Trevor said with an evil grin. "They was lying about knowing you, right, Sheriff?"

Bevins looked at the two Baldwin men and smiled. "Well, Pack, you said you was going to go look for that wagon, I believe you found it."

"We did at that, Sheriff. Cobb and that one named Trevor had to sit in the middle of the road for a while before we headed back. Both sat their horses pointing Greeners at each other. I think the standoff did the two good though," Pack said.

Just then Adams came from the back of the barn. "I had to put two mules to a stall, which included Satan. This barn ain't been this full since last summer. I got horses and mules everywhere. Trevor, I put your horse in with the judge's."

Pack looked at Bevins. "Is that the judge you mentioned this morning, Sheriff?"

"It is. He pulled in here about an hour after you left. I filled him in on some of the particulars of the situation in town. He went to his room at the hotel to rest for a couple of hours. Said he was going to think on things."

"Which direction did he come from, Sheriff? We didn't meet any riders on the trail until we found these three and the wagon," Pack said as he pointed at the two teamsters and Billy.

"Found us you say? I didn't know we was lost," Trevor said.

The sheriff waved Trevor off. "He meant nothing by it. Why don't you go and get your rooms at the hotel."

After Billy and the teamsters left, Bevins answered the question. "The judge comes through the pass. The route he takes is only three days between towns. There are a couple of families the judge stays with on the trail so he doesn't have to bed down out of doors in weather like this. The freight wagon has to take the long way around. Anyway, the judge said to meet him at the restaurant at sunup in the morning. I plan to do just that."

"I think we'll be there too, Sheriff. What about the wagon?" Pack asked.

"Got that taken care of. Adams will lock this place up tight after we leave. He also has a double-barreled shotgun and a Colt if the occasion calls for it," Bevins said.

The next morning over breakfast Judge Fred Wicker was told of the events that had transpired over the last several days. He was also presented with the problem of how to keep Dinsmore alive after he tried and sentenced Gravitt and Anderson.

Wicker was a well-seasoned judge with more than thirty years riding the circuit. He had come across some tough cases in his day and this one ranked right up there with the others.

"Sheriff, I have two main concerns. One is to keep this Dinsmore alive after he gives me his deposition. The other concerns this man Anderson," Wicker said.

"What about Gravitt," Bevins asked.

"Gravitt is small potatoes. He tried to kill a man and failed, so what. I plan to use his guilt in the attempted murder to get him to testify against Anderson. Anderson is bad, I signed that warrant on him, it reads dead or alive for a reason," Wicker said as he attacked his scrambled eggs.

"I don't understand, Judge," Bevins said.

"I've been after Anderson for the better part of two years now. He's done some bad things and it's my job to make sure he either hangs for it or lives out the rest of his days in the territorial prison up north. This man Gravitt has worked side by side with Anderson from time to time. Gravitt isn't the brains behind the operation, he's more or less just an accomplice. But being an accomplice will go a long way in convincing a jury. Anderson hired on with Westbrook for this job out west and that job is going to finally be his downfall.

"I can't prove that Anderson's killed anyone but I can't prove he hasn't either. He's been masquerading as a doctor for years now. He pulls into out of the way towns and advertises that he can cure almost anything from a cavity to a cancer. Folks come to him for cures he's incapable of furnishing. He sends most away but keeps the ones with means. By the time folks come to their senses they have had their personal belongings pilfered. He's even been known to extract teeth with gold fillings.

"He sells an elixir that he says will cure whatever the patient is suffering from. An elixir with a tremendous price attached for the folks that have the cash to pay for it. The reason it is critical to stop him is that more than one has died shortly after Anderson pulled out of town. We don't know if the elixir he sold them did them in or if they succumbed from their illness. I plan for a jury of our fine citizens to end this man's crimes once and for all."

"So where does Gravitt come into all this?" Bevins asked.

"He's the only witness. No, patients we'll call them, in any of the towns Anderson has worked have survived. Again I can't say they died because of anything Anderson has done but he is the common denominator. If Gravitt will testify against Anderson I'm willing to give him a year in jail. If not then he'll be an old man before he ever experiences freedom again," Wicker said.

"So now what do we do, Judge," Bevins asked.

"Simple, we bring Gravitt from his cell and offer him a deal. If he agrees to testify against Anderson in exchange for a guilty plea and a year in the territorial prison then we move him to another town immediately. We can't let Anderson know we have a witness," Wicker said.

"How do we do that, Judge. I only have Walker here as it is. My full time deputy is laid up at Doc Ramey's," Bevins said.

"I intend to let Pack and Cobb transport him. I know both and consider them good men. Would the two of you agree to that."

The Trail

"We were sent here to intercept a parcel of mail that's sitting in a mailbag over at the livery Judge. I doubt our bosses will allow us to detour without that parcel," Pack said.

Wicker started laughing. He reached into his inside coat pocket and pulled out an envelope, a thick envelope. "Is this what you're looking for," he said as he tossed it on the table. No one else at the table moved. Could this really be the parcel that had cost so many men their lives?

"Go ahead, open it," Wicker said.

Pack took the envelope, it wasn't sealed. He opened the flap and pulled out a folded newspaper article. It was the front page of the Chicago Post-Dispatch. The headline read, **Organized Crime in the Greater Chicago Area.** Pack quickly read the first paragraph and then put the paper clipping back in the envelope.

"So all this was a front in order to get Dinsmore safely out of Chicago?" Pack asked.

"It was. I was contacted three months ago by another judge back east. He and several of the higher ups were after two men by the name of Wilbur Westbrook and William Butler. They knew Dinsmore, the newspaper man, had completed his story. They also knew he wouldn't live a week unless a plan was put in place to get him out of the city.

"Dinsmore was given two thousand dollars, what amounted to a reward for information that would put Westbrook and Butler behind bars. The money was paid in advance of a conviction in order to allow Dinsmore time to escape. They had the article and Dinsmore's sworn statement to use at trial so they bid the reporter farewell and wished him safe passage.

"Somehow Westbrook found out where Dinsmore was heading and we knew he would have men waiting. The plan was to let the criminals chase a parcel which they thought contained the story and all the research material. It was hoped this diversion would protect the reporter as the culprits went after the parcel rather than Dinsmore.

"It seems though that Westbrook wanted the parcel and also Dinsmore in order to silence him in some gruesome way. Other reporters would think twice before investigating crime in Chicago after they heard how Dinsmore was dealt with.

"I am glad to know that everything has worked out after all. Dinsmore, for all intents and purposes, was killed by Gravitt. If the knife didn't do the job then the fall from the cliff surely did. His body was never found, probably consumed by any number of fearsome predators that live in the Colorado high country," Judge Wicker said.

"So now what happens, Judge?" Bevins asked.

"Dinsmore can rest up here for a few weeks and as soon as he can travel give him a horse and head him west. California or even Alaska might be a safe place for him to end up. He'll need to use a new name from here on out. I think he'll be just fine as long as he never goes back to Chicago. His newspaper career is over but at least he still has his life.

"Gravitt will take the deal I'll make him, I just know it. Mister Pack and Mister Cobb can transport him away from here and put him in a safe jail where he can wait out his time until his year is up. Once I have his deposition he will be ready to go.

"I think Anderson needs to stay here in Clear Creek. I trust the Sheriff and Clarence Walker here can handle things," Wicker said.

The Trail

Bevins looked at the judge, he had just used Walker's first name. "You know Walker?"

"I do, why do you think he ended up here in the first place. I sent him here two months ago. He was told to blend in and wait. We didn't know exactly what to wait for but we did know where, Clear Creek."

Bevins looked at Walker and said, "Why you secretive son-of-a-bitch."

The End

Made in the USA
Las Vegas, NV
20 March 2023